THE STRANGE BREW

M. N. Cox

Published by The Long Hot Spell.

www.thelonghotspell.com

Copyright © 2022 M. N. Cox.

Written by M. N. Cox

Book Cover Design by ebooklaunch.com

Editing and proofreading by Plume Services.

Epub ISBN: 978-0-6454922-0-0
Paperback ISBN: 978-0-6454922-1-7
Hardcover - ISBN:978-0-6454922-2-4

For Nanna Cox ♡

CHAPTER ONE

The doorbell tinkled. Before I could look up, I smelled the patchouli. There was a flourish of red hair and arms reaching for me.

'How are things, Dor?' she asked me quietly. It was my best friend, Jules. Tall, with curls twisting and framing her face, she always looked like she had just left the salon, even though she never bothered with styling.

'Never better,' I said, as Jules and I settled in for a catch-up behind the counter.

Within moments, Mrs Sloper, my ex's mother, rammed open the café's red door and made a beeline straight for me, bringing with her a cloud of oppressive heat from the street.

Sayed and I hadn't seen the Mother Sloper in the café for a while. However, she had dropped in regularly years before when her son, Troy, was on trial for attempting to murder me. First, she came to castigate me. Then—after I threatened to take action against her—to silently fume. Once she'd settled down, I would serve and then ignore her as she sat with her mouth puckered like she was eating grapefruit. Then, two months after Troy's sentencing, Mrs Sloper stopped altogether. I assumed she'd had herself a reality check; he did the crime, and he'd be gone a long while.

As Mrs Sloper arrived at the counter that day, I noticed something more than heat came with her—a peculiar feeling. But I had no time to gather my thoughts.

'Lying whore!' she screamed. 'You've taken everything from me. Bitch!'

1

'Oh-kay,' I whispered slowly, hyper-aware of my patrons. I saw Margie nearly spit out a mouthful of carrot cake—and it took a lot to ruffle her as a single mum of six boys. I'd made a conscious decision to be strong and stand up for myself in those past years, but I also had no wish to make the situation worse than it was. Instead, I bundled out a script I'd used many times with difficult people—including Mrs Sloper herself—which gave them a chance to turn their behaviour around.

'What can I get you today?' I asked calmly.

A snicker could be heard in the background. Jules always found it funny when I ignored outrageous behaviour and continued like it wasn't bothering me an iota. Of course, I'd done that with Troy many times in the past, too. It was a matter of self-preservation back then. Jules would have given back as good as she got.

Mrs Sloper glanced at Jules' grinning face for a second before her unhinged eyes returned to me. Just then, my husband, Sayed, rushed in from the kitchen at the rear of the café and took up a firm stance between us.

'You need to leave immediately,' he told her.

'Why should I? I have a right to be here,' Mrs Sloper asserted.

'How in hell do you figure that?' Jules said, fully entering the conflict. 'After what your son did? I don't think so. I mean, how frickin' dare you?'

'How dare I? How dare she!'

It didn't sit well with me that her pointing finger almost touched my nose.

With the Slopers, it seemed I would never be free. As if for them, all roads led straight back to me. Who knew I was so special, right?

Inexplicably, I did sympathise with a small part of Mrs Sloper's plight, though doing so didn't make a lick of sense. Mothers love their children, and this mother was now by herself since her only child was in prison because of his treatment of me. Okay, maybe 'sympathise' wasn't the correct word. Perhaps 'understand' was a better fit.

I set about defusing the situation while remaining firm. 'I get that you're upset. Really, I do. But you can't come in acting like ... this.' I had been going to say 'like a fruitcake' but thought better of it. 'Not when it disturbs the other customers,' I said, ignoring the bleeding obvious—that it was unfair to me.

'You shouldn't be in The Brew at all,' Sayed said. 'You're not welcome.'

The Brew, one of Deepwell's three cafés, was our business. Sayed and I owned it, and the last thing we needed was insane drama. Besides, I'd had enough of the Slopers over the years, and so had Sayed. His remarkable composure had helped our relationship get off the ground when we met, not long after Troy's attack. I was still so fragile then. Sayed gave me stability and security in abundance. But that day, with Mrs Sloper returning to unload on me after a long period of calm, Sayed bordered on losing his shit. The rigid way he stood gave him away.

The Brew was everything to us. It was our livelihood. We owned the whole property—mortgaged it, anyway—including another shop tacked on the end of the building that we rented out to a hairdresser, Leanne Cusimano. It was also our home since we lived in an apartment upstairs. I certainly didn't appreciate anyone messing with our living. Luckily, late afternoon wasn't the café's busiest time. But I assumed our customers wouldn't be too impressed with the fracas. In Deepwell, this kind of news could spread like wildfire on a dry and windy day.

I scanned the room. There were only about a dozen people dotted around the tables. Still, every eye was on us, even Leanne's as she stopped in for a pick-me-up. That was our town. Deepwell was like a soft pillow that you could relax into for some, and a carpet snake that would squeeze the life right out of you for others. The stereotype of a close-knit community in small towns was a reality. One reality, anyway. Each resident had their story, of course, but the marrow of the town's relationships was often found in guarded secrets that were downright difficult to extricate. Deepwell contained all the contradictions that any village of four thousand might, and it wrapped them up in the lush greenery of the Noosa hinterland.

I had a secret, too. Something only my nearest and dearest knew about me, and it was not about Troy. What happened with him was already a matter of public record, whether I wanted it to be or not. No, my secret was that I could see and feel the dead. It was like a sensitivity, I suppose. I often saw the recently deceased who, for whatever reason, remained close by. Actually, that happened a lot more than people imagined. Many people weren't happy about becoming life-challenged, it seemed, and it caused them to get stuck while they adjusted.

There were times that I also smelled things. That sounds gross, but I don't mean dead bodies. Ugh, wouldn't that be awful? It's just that sometimes I recognised odours associated with a specific deceased person, like a couple of years back when a sweet teen, Jessica Crawford, died out on Vantage Road. Her car hit a tree late at night and, for two months, every time I drove by to visit Jules, I caught the fragrance of summer blossoms. Turned out that Jessica loved frangipani, and she even had a sticker on her car—the classic variety with the yellow centre and waxy white petals. I noticed it the morning after the accident while the tow truck was removing the wreck.

My whole, weird affliction came about after Troy's assault, but I never knew why, or how, that was even possible. Believe me, I thought long and hard about it.

Initially, I couldn't understand what was happening to me. I spent weeks recuperating in hospital after the attack and, naturally, a large hospital gets damn busy with the energy of those who, you know … don't make it out. It was incredibly confusing because, on top of all that, I had developed Post Traumatic Stress

Disorder. Eventually, I suspected something unusual was occurring—something dead strange, no pun intended. I wondered who the patients were that wandered the halls looking odd, quiet, and lost. Once, I attempted to speak to an older gent wearing striped flannel pyjamas and a smart camel fedora. I'd noticed him shuffling up and down my ward for two days, though I didn't recognise him.

'Are you lost?' I ventured. 'Do you need some help?' He looked at me with the greatest surprise, then responded. But I couldn't hear one word he said. Not one.

Of course, I didn't accept that I could see dead people right off the bat. It seemed ridiculous. You tell yourself you're mistaken. You worry that you've completely lost it. But by the time they discharged me from the hospital, I knew. I felt it in every bone of my body, though it remained impossible to explain. Fortunately, my work meant I rarely encountered the life-challenged. Spirits weren't likely to pop on down to the café for an espresso. I was glad about that because sometimes I had trouble distinguishing them from everyone else. When they appeared, they looked so … well, *alive*. What a pickle.

That afternoon in The Brew, Mrs Sloper wouldn't be distracted from hating on me. Nostrils flared, she taunted me. 'That bitch knows what she's done. She took everything from me.'

My eyes rolled, having heard it all before—and worse. But I was careful not to let Mrs Sloper see that. It would have been fanning the flames. Besides, what was she even talking about?

'Yeah, a deadbeat abuser,' Jules answered bluntly, undoing any good I'd managed.

I stifled a smile because Jules wasn't exactly wrong. Troy was that. But Jules' comment was too much for Mrs Sloper to bear. The old woman's face quivered, and her arm made a horizontal sweeping motion that knocked several cups and saucers off the counter. The crockery smashed to the floor as she screeched, 'You'll get what's coming!'

That was the final straw for me. I had stayed strong through the verbals, but at that point, I stepped backwards and leaned against the wall. The world closed in on me. A dark, well-worn bubble enveloped me. It separated me from Mrs Sloper's offensive words, yet I had the odd feeling that I was being pummelled by something. What was that incessant energy that had arrived with her? And what was that odour? The Brew seemed airless and stale.

Within moments I found odd comfort in the familiarity of psychological retreat. However, I could still hear the vague clamouring of those outside my imaginary bubble. Then there was a rush of air beside me. Sparks flew from above, accompanied by a God-almighty noise.

The old railway clock on the wall behind the counter had fallen to the floor. Sparks came from the wiring and, being solid metal with a thick glass cover, the clock fell hard. Fortunately, it missed me by inches.

Jules, by my side, pulled me further away from danger. My soles crunched with each step I took and, looking down, I noticed the glass pieces strewn across the tiles and wondered what the shiny redness was. Had a strip of the Christmas tinsel I'd recently put up fallen on my foot? I had taken to decorating The Brew diligently in early December after being shamed in my initial year of ownership by other shopkeepers, and customers alike. Australia was hardly big on religion, but many of our citizens still took Christmas in the summer heat very seriously indeed.

'Oh my God,' Jules shrieked as she saw what I was gazing at. 'Sayed! Sayed!'

'Oops,' I said grimly. There was a piece of glass wedged in the top of my foot. At first, I didn't notice because it wasn't so much gushing as oozing a thin line of blood. 'I should have worn better shoes,' I maundered, my voice lost amongst the commotion. Then wooziness overtook me.

'We have to get it out,' Jules said evenly—unnaturally evenly.

That's all I remembered for a few minutes, aside from some vague kerfuffle involving Mrs Sloper, who was obviously still upset.

My wounding was far from fatal, but I never had a great stomach for injuries. The colour drained from my face and, quite the sook, I lay down on the tiles and started to slip in and out of consciousness.

'Oh, gosh, I can't look,' I repeated several times until Jules got sick of it and shushed me with a, 'Good. Don't look then, but at least shut up!'

There was some chatter.

'Get her something soft for her head. She looks so pale,' Leanne said.

Customers voices followed. 'Crikey, you don't see that every day,' and, 'Well, bound to happen. What with Sloper and all,' and finally, 'What a fuckin' palaver, mate.'

Sayed asked, more to himself than anything, 'What in God's name?' as he sifted through the debris.

'If I were you, I'd focus on getting it cleaned up before someone else gets hurt. Deal with how it happened later,' Jules advised him.

'I'm a bit better. I'll give you a hand, hey?' I said, hoisting myself up from the floor.

'No,' Jules and Sayed snapped in unison.

'Fine,' I said, miffed.

'Well, you're still pale,' Jules told me.

Sayed felt the need to add, 'And honestly, Dora, look at your foot.'

Unfortunately, I listened to him, looked down, and began to feel light-headed again.

'Oh, Dor,' said Sayed, kneeling to cuddle me and stroke my arm.

'I'll be fine. Jules is right. You clean up first. She can deal with me.' I was resigned. 'Also, open the front door please. It smells nasty in here,' I said, as quietly as I could.

'Does it?' he asked. Obviously, he hadn't noticed the smell. Leanne went to pin back the front door for us, while Sayed grabbed a broom and started to sweep glass towards the rear of the café. I could tell he was stewing over what had caused the clock to tumble as he swept because he kept glancing up at the dark patch of paint where the clock had been hanging. The Brew badly needed repainting and other maintenance work, but that clock had been fixed securely to the wall. We'd made sure of it because it was so weighty.

At some point, there was no more Mrs Sloper, and I heard customers getting involved again, giving Sayed their two cents' worth. Tom, a pineapple farmer from the south, was in town to pick up supplies. He did mental gymnastics and insisted that the cups' vibrations hitting the floor must have knocked the clock right off its screws. Ridiculous, I thought, and most patrons that afternoon seemed to agree.

'Nope. It just fell outta nowhere, mate,' said Margie. No-nonsense Margie Baxter wasn't afraid of giving her opinion, that's for sure. I supposed that came from raising all those boys on her own.

'There was no cup, I'm telling you, Mum,' insisted her son, who should have been at school that day. 'I dunno what happened,' he continued, 'but it was weird as.'

As Jules helped me up, I saw Mrs Sloper out the front talking to the police on the footpath. When we turned towards the back door, I felt that we'd left the energy still looming in the café. That's when I realised for sure that it was someone's spirit, and a chill moved through me.

'Are you all right?' blurted Jules.

'Fine. It's just … there's a ghost here somewhere.'

'Here in The Brew? Who is it?'

'I don't know. I only felt it. But I am damn well going to find out. As soon as I'm back on my feet.'

CHAPTER TWO

The Saturday morning before the clock fell, had started like any other. At around seven-thirty, Sayed and I enjoyed coffee on our verandah, the one that ran along the front of our apartment above The Brew. It overlooked the main road into Deepwell. The temperature was balmy. By eight it would be hot and by late morning, scorched with a side of humid.

That morning, Sayed had expressed his concern that if we didn't repair the verandah railing soon, we would lose it. It was hard to ignore our mounting maintenance issues, yet we had no choice. Built in the late 1800s, the double-storey timber building, which used to be a pub, always needed work. There was delicate wrought iron fretwork lining the front and back verandahs and, rusty though it was, it was a feature we would hate to lose.

The problem was that our financial situation was precarious. The Brew had never done as well as we'd hoped, and our mortgage repayments were a tad too high for our current earnings. Keeping up with payments was one thing. But there was never money left for maintenance or improvements that might better our position.

As Sayed and I threw ourselves into making it all work, I carried some guilt for my insistence on settling in Deepwell. I had plenty of gripes about small-town life but, in the end, I was born here, my family still lived here, and I didn't *want* to leave. Sayed agreed, and so we stayed, but several years on we remained on the back foot. Some residents saw me as the crazy, tainted woman who put Troy Sloper away—like it was my fault he did what he did. Meanwhile, Sayed remained an eternal foreigner to some people, considering he was born in Algeria and only arrived in Australia aged ten. They say the eyes are windows to the soul and some of Deepwell's citizens revealed their provincial minds through theirs.

'The wrought iron's on the list,' I replied. It was just another thing we couldn't afford. But Sayed knew that. I didn't need to say it out loud.

Afterwards, Sayed and I had breakfast, got dressed, and went downstairs to set up and start serving our customers. No odd happenings, no revelations, no bombshells.

See? A normal start. But believe me, I've had stranger days than how that one turned out. On the day my ex-boyfriend, Troy, tried to murder me years before, we'd begun with scrambled eggs and a thorough dust and vacuum. Midday saw us discussing current affairs. The Chilean miners, trapped underground, had just sent a note to the surface reading 'We are fine in the shelter, the 33 of us'. Troy had seemed obsessed with the miners' stoicism. Prone to hubris, I'm pretty sure he hoped to be forced into a similar situation one day so that he could prove to the world his deep awesomeness. It certainly *would not* be that day. By the evening, as Troy and I sat down together to watch The Block teams battle it out, it morphed into something else. Something terrifying.

But that was a long time ago. I'd moved past it. I recovered from the physical injuries. I got married and now I had a business to run. My life was full. I did much more than just survive.

It was around three-thirty, on the afternoon of the falling clock, when I saw Leanne approach The Brew. Though silhouetted against the sunlight that streamed through the front glass windows, I knew it was her from the outline of her soccer-mum hair and stout figure. I had been flicking absently through the newspaper: a shooting in Brisbane's west, another tourist caught in a rip on the Gold Coast, a prisoner's life support turned off. It was hardly a quality rag, and nothing grabbed my eye beyond some local news on Stonebridge Reserve's development. Stonebridge was a longstanding wildlife haven in Deepwell, but the fight was on to save it from becoming another medium density housing estate. Typical. Greed threatening more of Deepwell's treasures. It made me so cranky. I had already signed a petition against the change, but I certainly did not trust the council to make the correct decision. I gave a heavy sigh.

'Hi, Leanne. How're you doing?' I asked, pushing the paper aside gruffly as she arrived at the counter.

'Oh, you know, Eudora. Getting there.'

Leanne was pretty much the only person who called me by my full name. Everyone else shortened it to Dora or Dor.

'What can I get you?' I said, stuffing my pen and notebook into my apron pocket. The PTSD hadn't done my short-term memory any favours so I made a habit of writing things down. But Leanne ordered several times a day, so I knew what she wanted. Asking her was a formality, nothing more.

'A cappuccino, sweetie. That's all. How are your Christmas plans shaping up?'

'Good, good,' I said. 'We'll spend the day at Dad's.'

'Won't Sayed's family want … oh, I forget they don't celebrate.'

'They celebrate well enough, just not Christmas,' I said pointedly. As Muslims, the Bousaids had their own traditions which included a gold-accented gift-giving and feasting extravaganza called Eid that followed the fasting and spiritual renewal of Ramadan. That meant Sayed and I celebrated with his family at a different time of the year. Not having to stretch ourselves between Deepwell and his family's home in Brisbane reduced our December stress levels considerably. I thought it all worked out pretty darn well.

'It just seems such a shame not to celebrate Christmas, you know?' Leanne continued.

'Not really. The Bousaids probably think it's a shame you don't celebrate Eid,' I said, holding back a roll of my eyes.

'Pff!' she said with a gentle wave of her hand, then moved forward with, 'Have you seen that sibling of yours recently?'

'No. Why?'

I can't say if I was more perturbed because Leanne was such a gossip, or the fear of what my sister, Wren, might have done. Like the drugs, and the accompanying unsavoury lifestyle, wasn't enough. We kept hoping she would grow out of her addiction. We have to let people grow and change and improve themselves, of course. But it was hard to stop the niggling concerns in the back of your mind. Would my gorgeous sister die before she managed to get clean? Still, Wren was always a good person. Sure, she made some poor decisions—and people are quick to judge—but I loved her before, and I still loved her.

I took the bait. 'Go on then, Leanne. What's she been up to?' I adjusted my apron and leaned over the counter so she wouldn't have to speak so loudly.

'No sugar for me,' she reminded me, unnecessarily, before continuing. 'You really are out of touch, aren't you?'

Leanne loved it. Never had someone personified the expression 'the cat that ate the canary' more than Leanne did at that moment.

'Not Wren. Lionel,' she corrected me, eyes twinkling.

I stopped in my tracks and looked at her wide-eyed. My brother, Lionel, might have been a cheeky wag as a child, but he'd grown up to be more of a straight shooter. Well, sort of. He joined the police force, at any rate, and was a cop stationed right here in Deepwell. What gossip could there be about Lionel? Tales from a drunken night, perhaps?

'Okay … I admit this is getting interesting. What have you got?' Hey, I was only human. I felt guilty about wanting to hear Leanne's gossip if that makes it any better.

'Well, Lionel is seeing that new girl. You know, the one who dresses all bohemian and does the psychic readings at the markets every Sunday. Real pretty. What's her name again?' You could tell Leanne was straining her brain. 'Storm, I think. No, wait, Cloud. That's it. Sounds like it's getting serious, too.'

Well, blow me down. I hadn't seen that coming. Don't get me wrong, we Hermansens grew up with long hair, whole foods and astrology. It's just that Lionel never paid much attention to the metaphysical worlds ... until I told him I saw ghosts, anyway. That was hard to ignore. He took a while to accept it, but eventually he did. As did Jules, my sister, then Dad, and finally, Sayed.

Seeing the dead was a difficult subject to broach with a fiancé, I can tell you. 'Yes, I want to marry you, but there's this one little thing you need to understand about me first ...' It was not like admitting you were an obsessive scrapbooker, or that you watched *The bold and the beautiful* every afternoon. In the end, Sayed took it much better than I expected. Turns out his Nanna used to talk about spirits a lot. In Islamic folklore, there were ghosts called djinn that lived parallel to humans, and while djinn could watch us, the living couldn't even see the djinn. Well, that sounded about right to me. Except that I *did* see ghosts!

The nearest and dearest who I shared my little problem with—and, to be clear, I considered it a problem—were the ones I could count on to still accept me ... and to zip their lips. If ever I wanted to make it public, though, I'd probably just tell Leanne. She couldn't keep a secret if her life depended on it.

'Guess you can't wring the hippy out of a Hermansen that easy, huh?' I grinned at Leanne and she chuckled, knowing our family's background.

'Cloud's Mum is some kind of psychic too, so I hear. I don't know if I believe in all that, mind.'

'I'm not sure if I do either, Leanne, but it's good to keep an open mind.'

When you had a secret as big as being able to see dead people, you had to be a colossal liar sometimes. Still, I didn't want to encourage Leanne, either, since she was a little closed-minded.

After that, Leanne sat at a window table instead of returning to work. She often did that when she needed a break, which I could understand as a business owner myself. Anyway, most of Leanne's customers knew to find her in The Brew if the 'back in a minute' sign was on the salon door.

Immediately, I grabbed my phone to text Lionel. During Troy's trial, my relationship with Lionel had become strained. Frankly, I hadn't wanted to see my brother for a long time after that. I always sensed judgement. *I'm a police officer. Why couldn't you come to me?* And worse, *Why didn't you just leave him?* My brother wasn't the only one. You'd be surprised how many people still didn't understand the complexity of abusive relationships. Lionel and I had some time apart after that, but eventually we grew close again. We were siblings, after all. I guess lately we'd just been busy. *Lionel's been real busy, it sounded like.*

Turning my mind back to messaging, I decided not to mention Cloud directly: *Hey. What's up? I'd love to see you soon. D x*

I took Leanne's coffee to her table so she wouldn't have to get up. Then, as I was reading Lionel's reply—*Gidday Dor. all good. talk soon*—Jules arrived, with a fuming Mrs Sloper following close behind.

The afternoon's altercation raised so many questions. What the heck was Mrs Sloper doing firing up again after all these years? It made no sense. Who belonged to the energy I'd sensed with her? And how on earth did the clock fall?

CHAPTER THREE

When Jules drove me back from Noosa Hospital that afternoon, we pulled off the main road to park next to the courtyard at the back of The Brew. The paved area was the extent of our backyard, and it was all Sayed and I wanted. Gratitude had been trending in positive psychology, and I sure was grateful not to have to mow any grass on top of working the café.

The Brew perched on the perimeter of Deepwell proper. To the south sprawled acres of sugarcane. To the west, farmers ran cattle. North and east offered up large swathes of forest. Deepwell Lake could be found to the north, and driving east, past the forest, were the coastal holiday and retirement towns of Noosa and Tewantin.

Sayed came out of the now-closed café to check on us. 'Poor baby,' he said to me, his eyes all puppy dog caring. 'Unbelievable.'

'It's nothing. A few stitches, that's all. I'm great, actually,' I told him.

I was, too. I was feeling good as Sayed gave me a hand out of the car.

'She's high as a fucking kite on painkillers right now,' Jules said. 'Within fifteen minutes of the drugs kicking in, Dora was joking with the hospital staff as they stitched her up. Here's the proof of how strong those drugs are.' Jules' hands fluttered around me like she was a model on a game show. The ridiculous prize, with drooping eyelids and dilated pupils, was me.

Sayed and Jules laughed. Were they laughing with me? Or at me? It didn't seem to matter. I giggled too, and it was a much-needed release from the tension of the afternoon.

Then, turning to more serious matters, I said, 'I'm so sorry about all this. I can't believe Sloper's carrying on again. Was everything okay?' My talking skills were lacking from the painkillers, but I got my message across.

Sayed was still smiling gently at me when he said, 'Don't worry about a thing, Dor.' He was trying to divert my mind from anything stressful, but I was insistent.

'I'll do better knowing,' I said.

Sayed drew in a breath. 'The incident frightened some customers. Not good.' He grimaced.

Sayed would be concerned as he hated making people feel awkward. It was surprising that he'd stood up to Mrs Sloper so publicly earlier that day as he hated confrontation. Not that he was weak. Sayed had a quiet strength; he aimed for politeness, considered his actions, and cared about our business. A good man. That summed up my husband.

'I reckon your customers enjoyed it,' posited Jules. 'It'd be the most excitement they've seen all year.'

'Right, and it's December,' I guffawed as I stumbled.

Sayed caught me and continued, 'Anyway, I made sure they were okay. I didn't charge anyone, and I offered them the same order on another day for free, to make up for it.'

'Smort,' I praised him.

I contemplated sharing the ghost-in-the-café information with Sayed right then, but decided it was unnecessary. My husband had enough on his plate, cleaning up my mess, and it wasn't like the spirit was an immediate danger to him.

'And Mrs Sloper?' I continued. 'What the hell *was* that? She's been good for a long time.'

Sayed and Jules stole a quick glance at each other, then turned back to me.

'My guess is that Mrs Sloper won't be a problem again,' Sayed said. 'Your brother spoke to her, even took her down to the station to do it. They don't intend to charge her this time. But only as long as she doesn't return to The Brew.' He sounded so sure that I let it go. I was tired.

Sayed went to the finish up at The Brew. Meanwhile, since I wouldn't be much help in the café, Jules helped me towards the back stairs to our apartment.

'Eudora!' yelled Leanne. 'Oh my gosh. Are you okay? I was so worried about you, sweetie. You looked so pale earlier. Poor thing.'

'Just fine,' I said, turning toward her. 'A few stitches, that's all.' I eased myself down onto the steps—any conversation with Leanne usually took a while. I thanked Jules for looking after me and suggested she could head home if she wanted. An exchange with Leanne was something Jules would rather avoid, given her limited tolerance for small talk.

'The way she spoke to you was terrible, Eudora. You shouldn't have to put up with that,' Leanne continued as soon as Jules started her car.

'Thanks, Leanne. I know I shouldn't, and I'm sorry you had to witness it.'

'Well, it was expect—' she stopped, then promptly began again. 'Oh, you know, it's nothing. I mean, I'm fine of course and the other customers will get over it. She's just a nasty old bag, always bloody was.'

I smiled at her. Leanne was a gossip, but she sure could be a loyal friend, too.

'She had to be removed by the cops, you know? She refused to leave. Can you imagine? Lionel had to escort her out. Very handsome he looks in his uniform, doesn't he? Your Dad must be pleased as punch. What a shame your Mum isn't here to see it all.' Then she quickly added, 'I mean, not Mrs Sloper acting all crazy. Just Lionel. She'd be so proud.'

Lynette, my mother, had passed away a decade before from an aggressive form of cancer. She was greatly missed, not least by my father, Peter. I often wonder whether I would have seen and sensed Mum after her death if she had died five years later. I couldn't know for sure, but I remembered her as organised and practical, so I guessed she would have accepted her death once she knew it was coming.

'And what a day, with ol' Becker, too,' Leanne continued.

'Wha?' I still couldn't speak clearly. I sounded drunk.

'You haven't heard? Oh, well. It's terrible. Just dreadful. So sudden. Becker had a heart attack earlier today. He's gone.'

'Oh,' I said, my eyes widening to match Leanne's. It *was* a shock. Not that I was close to him. It was just so left of field.

Ol' Becker was Bruce Becker, CEO of the Deepwell Water Treatment Plant for several decades. The plant had run successfully under his leadership. He was a wheeler-dealer through and through, with his finger in several private business pies. Becker hadn't been that likeable, mind you, with his inflated sense of self-importance—and inflated sense of the importance of the rest of the Becker family as well, for what my opinion was worth. They were always one of those families that believed they owned the joint by virtue of their history in the town. It was incredibly irritating.

Worse than Becker himself was his eldest daughter. I recalled an incident in The Brew the week before. Jules and I were chatting when Annika's voice rang out. Annika Cotter, née Becker, and her long-suffering sister Candy had sashayed towards the counter. If Annika's dark hair had been any straighter, it would have stabbed her, and if she'd pulled it back any harder into that ponytail, it might've ripped her face off. It was like a crime waiting to happen.

'Aww fuck, look who it is,' I'd heard Jules say under her breath. I hoped Annika hadn't heard her, and I gave Jules a half-hearted dirty look.

'My, oh my, it's Jules,' Annika had sing-songed. 'To what do we owe this pleasure? I thought we'd lost you to the country, girl!'

The truth was that Jules was more comfortable on the out-skirts. She ventured into town as little as possible. She had waved to Annika in reply from her perch behind the counter, but it was one of those waves that cut people off, like you're trying to wave them away.

Annika had married a few years before, and it was rumoured that her husband, Tristan Cotter, would take over Bruce's job after his retirement, which was predicted to be within a few years. Tristan had already shot into senior management at the plant a little too quickly, and I wasn't the only person in town to have thought it. It was a classic case of keeping it in the family.

'Anyhoo. What can I get you?' I had asked Annika, distract-ing her from torturing Jules.

'Lattes for both of us,' Annika said. 'You need more staff in here, Dora. Where's that husband of yours? Don't tell me he's leaving you to do all the work.'

No one could stir the pot like Annika. We had just the right amount of staff; Annika was trying to make something out of nothing.

Jules was fuming. In primary school, Jules had grown to hate Annika. Pretty much since the day that Annika, the leader of the popular girls, had ordered someone to put chewing gum in Jules' fiery-red curls at the sports carnival.

'I allow him time off sometimes,' I'd quipped. 'Would you like to make a formal complaint?'

'Pah!' she'd spat. 'You're so funny, Dora. You always were.'

That's how it was with Annika. You survived the conversa-tion; you never really enjoyed it.

On the other hand, Leanne may have been a first-class gos-sip with a bit of a small mind, but she cared for the individuals she knew—more than anyone I'd met. You could tell she did. I looked up at her as she stood by me on the stairs that evening and smiled. I was warm and fuzzy inside.

'Are you alright, Dora?'

'Yes. Sorry,' I said, realising I'd been staring up at Leanne like a first-class idiot. 'Candy and Annika must be pretty upset right now.' I turned my face to a frown.

'Especially Annika. She was there. Only one at home when it happened.'

'So, he wasn't at work? Becker seemed like the type who would die at his desk. Sorry, but I always thought that. You know? He was so …' I searched for a more pleasant term for greedy. 'Driven,' I said, pleased my groggy mind had grasped it.

I suddenly recalled the energy I'd sensed in The Brew when Mrs Sloper swept in with her fury. Urgently I asked, 'What time did he pass?'

'Sometime after lunch, I think.'

'Okay …' So Becker was dead at the time Mrs Sloper had caused the scene. That explained the who, but why on earth would Becker's spirit even be near Mrs Sloper? Or The Brew? Or me?

'What is it?' Leanne said. I had been gazing like an idiot again.

'Must be the medication they put me on at the hospital.' I pulled a silly face. 'Big opportunity for Tristan,' I added, sounding bitchy but feeling the need to say something.

'You're terrible, Eudora. Though I see your point. I reckon he's even more ambitious than Becker.'

'Guess I'd better dig out the funeral clothes, then.'

'They've set it for Monday.'

'You're kidding me.'

'That's what I heard.'

'Holy rushed internment, Batman.'

Even before I met Sayed, I knew Muslims held their funerals very quickly after their loved ones passed. It was a striking cultural difference, yet one of many that I had grown used to. But it struck me as an odd choice for the Beckers. They weren't Muslim.

'They're not wasting any time,' Leanne agreed.

'Weird.'

'What a tragedy for those girls, hey? With their mother already gone, and now Becker too.' Leanne looked forlorn. She really did feel deeply for others, despite her foibles.

Candy and Annika's mother, Robyn, had also died from cancer, four years earlier. I saw Robyn at the hospital afterwards. Her spirit didn't hang around long, though. She had battled breast cancer for months and had said her goodbyes.

Suddenly I felt tired. 'Leanne, could you come up the stairs with me? Just in case I'm wobbly.'

'No problem. Do you want me to put on some dinner for you? Or do any chores?'

'No, nothing. But thank you. You're a good friend, Leanne.' I really meant it, too, and gave her arm a slight squeeze.

As I reached the back verandah, I let our rescue dog, Doggie Brasco, out for a minute while Leanne and I stood taking in the view. We enjoyed the last light of a day that had been stifling in more ways than one. But a breeze was picking up, and the humidity was lifting. The scent of jasmine wafted gently from a pot at the top of the stairs.

Looking out beyond the small courtyard below, I could see the forest all the way to where the trees ended, which was where the Plant was located. It employed many locals, including Leanne's husband, my Dad before he retired, and, at one time, my ex, Troy.

Leanne picked absently at some peeling paint. When we bought the property, Sayed and I spent weeks cleaning it, but a full repaint was beyond our budget. We had washed away a lot of deep, red mud from the back doorstep. The red stains prevailed, though. Scrubbing couldn't fix everything. Still, the building's original grandeur remained apparent through any dis-colouration, peeling varnish, or rust.

'Sayed and I want to repaint. Soon as we can, Leanne. Your salon included.'

'I didn't mean—'

Dog tired, I said to Leanne, 'It's okay. You don't have to come inside. I've got this now. And honestly, I just want to hole up for a bit.'

'Right,' she said, 'but if you need anything, absolutely any-thing, you call me. The boys have soccer tonight, but I can send Don with them easy as pie.'

'Thank you. You got it,' I replied. It was a sweet offer be-cause the only person I knew who liked soccer as much as her two boys did was Leanne herself. But I just wanted to be alone for a while. I had an awful lot to consider.

CHAPTER FOUR

It didn't matter whether it was a tiny shack or a sprawling Queenslander, home was my castle, where *I* controlled things.

'I am the queen of these lands,' I proclaimed in a whisper as I let the door slam shut behind me—not so hard that Leanne would notice as she left, but just enough to be symbolic.

As I hobbled up the long hall, Doggie Brasco sniffed at my bandaged foot with each step. The smells from the hospital were fascinating to him. Doggie was the pet that the newly married brought home to cement their relationship and trial the idea of becoming parents. Early on, Sayed and I concluded that Cleo the cat, now fourteen, and Doggie, would be plenty for us.

Dumping my bag on the side table, I set about turning on fans and opening windows. It was a routine when coming back home in the Queensland summer. Next, I pinned back the two sets of French doors from the lounge and the bedroom. They opened to the front verandah and overlooked the main street. It was as busy as it ever got in Deepwell, with people returning home from the coast for the night.

When Sayed and I purchased the building four years earlier, the apartment was already set up. The publican, Marty Johns, had raised a family there. I can only imagine what it was like for his two kids, growing up listening to drunken conversations yelled from the bar below, and doing jobs after school a decade before the legal drinking age. Eventually, the pub's red door closed for good, leaving the newer, more upmarket hotel right in the centre of town to service Deepwell and its rural surrounds. Nearly ten years later, a real estate agent showed Sayed and I around the property. With its hundred-year-plus history and rambling atmosphere at a shockingly reasonable price, we had been sold. Instantly.

It was sundress weather now I'd left the hospital's air-conditioning behind, so I switched out of my work clothes. Besides, it was hard to spend time in a hospital and not worry about the number of bacteria you'd picked up.

Throwing on a loose voile mini-dress, I felt much better. In the long mirror attached to our bedroom door, I saw myself as I fastened a tie around my waist. That'll do, I thought, smoothing the fabric over my curves. Perhaps a little pale and milky. I didn't get much chance to spend time outdoors, I had to admit. I didn't bother putting on thongs; for the most part, Sayed and I ran a barefoot home.

Doggie's whining could be heard over the whoosh of the fans. I assumed he was ordering me to feed him—pushy dog. I was heading back to the kitchen with Doggie in tow when my mobile rang.

'Lionel!'

'Are you okay?'

'Yeah, fine. How was Mrs Sloper?'

'Still refusing to accept reality. But I don't think she'll be back to hassle you again. Alright?'

'That's what Sayed said, too. We'll see. You must have given her a talking to,' I said lightly, flopping down on the couch and patting Cleo.

'Sure did. Sorry I didn't get to talk to you this arvo. There was too much going on. Hey, you hear about Becker?'

'Mm. Leanne told me.'

'She would.'

'Shush up, Lionel.'

'Yeah, yeah. It's terrible, huh?'

'Very. Weird how the funeral will be so soon. Monday. I mean, is that normal?'

'Monday?'

'You didn't know?'

'No. That *is* early. Weird family though. But he clearly died of a heart attack, so I suppose the Beckers are free to inter him Monday if they want to.'

Doggie jumped up and began whining, looking towards the kitchen. I put my finger to my mouth. 'Shh, Doggie.' I shifted my focus back to Lionel as Doggie quietened down. 'I guess. I need to find our clothes for the funeral tonight, so I can hang them in the bathroom and avoid the ironing.'

'You and ironing, Dora. Great wife you are.'

'Really, Lionel? Like Sayed married me for housekeeping. You sound like a dick sometimes.' Lionel wasn't perfect, but he wasn't half that sexist.

'So, the foot?' Lionel asked, ignoring my complaint.

'Doctor said the glass narrowly missed the tendons. Yay,' I celebrated sombrely. 'I have to keep it clean for a couple of weeks. I'll be good as new, then. Hey, when you spoke to her, did Mrs Sloper explain why? I mean, that's the million-dollar question.'

Doggie's whining started up again and Lionel gave me a man grunt that I assumed was negative. 'So, she mentioned nothing specific to you?' he asked back at me.

'Yes. She said I was a devil bitch.'

'Right,' he said. 'Of course.' We laughed. 'That woman will always be pissed off,' said Lionel by way of encouragement, adding in a solemn tone, 'I mean, she's always been angry as fuck. Did you feel anything?'

'Not at first, but then it hurt like hell.'

'Not your foot, Dor.'

'Oh. Becker?'

'Yeah, sure. Yes,' said Lionel, though he sounded decidedly unsure to me. 'Yeah, Becker, since he's the one that died.'

'Well, when Mrs Sloper arrived, I did feel something. Seems odd, though. I don't think Becker and Mrs Sloper had any connec—'

There was a thump from the kitchen. I turned to look as swiftly as I could manage, given I was still recovering from the painkillers.

'Right,' Lionel replied awkwardly.

There was nothing to see in the kitchen. Just Doggie, standing with his paws on the side of the sink, sniffing.

'Down,' I called out.

Lionel continued, ignoring the incident with Doggie completely. 'Just the normal feelings that you have? Nothing out of the ordinary?'

'Lionel, I sense dead people. That's pretty bloody extraordinary.' I wondered why talking about this would be so awkward for him. He'd known about my sense for years. We'd discussed it many times. Besides, word on the street was he was seeing a psychic tarot reader, for heaven's sake! I noted that he still hadn't told me about her, although the rest of the town obviously knew already.

'The spirit felt a tad aggressive, you know?' I continued. 'But Becker wasn't the sweetest of guys, so it kind of makes sense.'

'Yeah. Look, I've got to go. Talk to you soon, okay? Keep off the foot. Take care. Love you.'

I struggled to get myself up off the couch, but I steadied myself with the coffee table and pushed past the pain that was once again creeping into my foot. As I hobbled to the kitchen, I found nothing that could have caused Doggie's little tantrum, so I assumed he merely wanted his dinner; he got his way, as did Cleo.

I pondered dinner for Sayed and I. Though I knew my husband wouldn't want me on my feet, I didn't want to leave him to cook on top of clearing up the mess in The Brew. Especially as I saw that debacle as being my problem that had been forced upon him once again.

I selected vegetables from the fridge, ready for a cauliflower and chickpea tajine. I had become vegetarian after Troy's attack for my own reasons. At the same time, Sayed was happy to eat mostly meat-free fare. He worried about the environment more than I did. His family had griped considerably about his near vegetarianism. But then again, so had mine.

Grabbing for the cauliflower, I found it wasn't there on the bench. *Didn't I get it out just a moment ago?* I was sure I did, yet when I opened the fridge door, I saw the cauliflower sitting there in the crisper. The pain meds were making me a moron, I decided.

I took out the cauliflower—for sure that time—and cut it in two, then I washed the veggies and cut them into pieces, taking more care with the knife than I ever had before. The last thing I needed was to lose a finger.

I placed plenty of spices in the pot with the vegetables and added a tin of chickpeas. Then I returned to the couch to rest. Cleo waddled over after finishing her dinner and rolled over next to me for a belly rub.

Lionel had said nothing personal. Perhaps I should have asked him plainly about this Cloud person. Then again, Lionel was one of those men who kept the important stuff close. The Hermansens didn't really find out about his first serious girlfriend, Jennifer, until they'd been seeing each other for nearly a year. I mean, we knew, but Lionel wasn't the one informing us.

My mind turned towards the strange connection—or lack thereof—between Mrs Sloper and Bruce Becker. It made no sense. It was rare that I wished for *more* skill in connecting with the dead rather than less. Imagine being able to glean factual information from those who had passed over, rather than a gossamer sense grasped during the effort to avoid them. That would open my life up to a world of trouble though ...I shuddered slightly at the idea.

At that moment I noticed that Doggie hadn't finished the food in his bowl. He usually inhaled the entire meal in fifteen seconds, then tried to trick us into feeding him extra. 'What are you doing sitting there, Doggie?' He was directly outside the kitchen door, staring in at his food. He took a second to turn to me and whine, then shifted his focus back. There was no movement in the kitchen.

My thoughts swung to the clock in The Brew. How the hell did Mrs Sloper manage that? I had a mind to make her pay for the damages. It was a beautiful clock. It looked good in the café too and, being wired, it had always kept perfect time. Not anymore. I felt edgy, and I glanced to recheck the Doggie situation. Nothing had changed, but on top of the scent of cinnamon wafting from the tajine, there was something more: a metallic smell.

I got up as briskly as I could and checked the stovetop, but everything looked just fine. A little steam was escaping the rim of the pot, bringing with it delicious spices. Nothing that would cause a metal odour.

The afternoon's incident, Becker's spirit, the stifling air in The Brew, the clock, this strange smell … an uneasy feeling spread through my body. Something wasn't right, but I couldn't say precisely what.

I glanced around, but still, there was nothing to see, so I grabbed my paperback copy of *Eleanor Oliphant is completely fine* from the kitchen bench where I'd left it that morning. I fanned the surrounding air using the novel. As soon as I heal my foot, I'm doing some late spring cleaning, I decided with conviction. A practical thought, even though I knew cleaning wasn't the issue. Something much more serious was underway.

CHAPTER FIVE

'I'm going to work. You can count on that,' I'd near-threatened Sayed. It wasn't that I wanted to cause trouble; it's just I didn't want to avoid the scene of Saturday's dispute. It was Monday and I needed to face it all head-on. In the end, Sayed didn't argue because he understood where I was coming from. Ruminations—about everything and nothing—had formed strong neural pathways during my struggle with PTSD. No way was I sitting around in the apartment, further strengthening synapses I didn't care for.

'I'll try not to be a bother,' I told Sayed as I left home and limped down the back stairs to open up The Brew. I felt the humidity building already as I unlocked the back door. It was going to be stifling.

Jeans and a short-sleeved white shirt were my preference for work. Jeans were comfortable and manageable because we almost always had the air-conditioning running in the café anyway. Teamed with a half apron, my jeans and button-up looked smart enough, and I never had to agonise over what to wear. That morning I'd gone to a little extra trouble with my hair and makeup —part pick-me-up, part public statement. I was telling the good folk of Deepwell, 'I'm okay. There's nothing to see here. Move along now'.

Limping through the back room and the kitchen into the café itself, I saw a clear sky through the front windows. The sunshine and heat would most likely last until mid to late afternoon. Then we'd have a storm, which would bring fleeting relief.

Standing inside, I could hear Sayed overhead in the final throes of preparing for work, his trajectory tread on the timber floor above me. Then Doggie Brasco's sharp bark rang out. I guessed that Doggie would be waiting at the door and barking to hurry Sayed up. That dog thought he ruled the show. When Sayed and I got engaged and became dog parents, we'd never imagined ending up with such a recalcitrant child. It made us pretty glad we had decided against kids. Imagine. It seemed like neither of us could impart any steady or practical discipline over those in our care. Still, Doggie had brought us closer together.

I half expected the café to look different after the disturbance on Saturday. But Sayed had done an expert job of cleaning up. Aside from the outline of faded paint where the clock had hung, everything looked the same as always. Yet something *felt* off. The café remained a little stuffy. Was that a yucky undertone I smelled? Worry gnawed at me but, determined to keep an open mind to less supernatural causes, I took to wondering if our cleaner, Mark, had missed something. He invariably came in on Sundays when The Brew was closed. He did an exemplary job, too, so it didn't seem right to cast aspersions on his workmanship.

I unlocked the front door and scanned up and down both sides of the street as Mrs Sloper had rattled me. I didn't feel too safe. But I saw nothing beyond a couple of still-closed stores on the opposite side of the road, and the houses lining the route out of town. I pinned back the café's door, and the problem seemed to evaporate in the fresh air.

Pleased, I began the routine that Sayed and I had been performing every morning, six days a week, since we got married. Barring my early sick days, of course. The coffee machine needed firing up, the till had to be set, and salads prepped in sandwich-making readiness. It was the same-old, same-old, and that was a good thing sometimes.

I heard Sayed arrive at the back door and felt Doggie rush past me.

'What you doing, boy? Careful!' I called, raising my voice a little.

Doggie was taking exactly no notice of me. Instead, he placed his bum to the floor near the front door and looked up at the ceiling.

He growled a low rumble and followed up with two sharp barks.

'What's Doggie's problem?'

'You tell me,' said Sayed. 'He was acting the fool upstairs, too.'

The moment broke with John, the pastry chef, knocking at the open front door, causing Doggie to turn and bark again, only this time at John.

'Shush, shush, Dog. It's John. Sorry, Johnno,' I said. Doggie stopped quickly and wagged his tail. He knew John well enough because not only was John our pastry chef, he was also Sayed's best mate. 'So, how're things?'

While edging the plastic baker's tray through the front door, he replied, 'All good, Dor.' Seeing Sayed approach, he added, 'Hey, man.' They did one of those high-five handshakes and looked well-pleased to see each other.

Doggie followed John, without getting under his feet but staying close enough to catch anything that might fall from a tray. That had happened just the once—with Doggie enjoying himself a lamington—yet Doggie acted as though it was a regular occurrence.

Once the tray was laid near our refrigerated display case, John addressed me. 'I heard about Saturday. Sorry, Dor. You 'right?'

As tiresome as it was having people worrying about me, I had to remind myself that they were asking out of care. If no one enquired, I reckoned it would feel bad.

'Yes, fine. It's the same old crap, John, y'know?'

'I know, mate.'

I displayed my foot with a little twist of my leg in front of him. 'The foot'll be fine, but The Brew … the business is what I worry about. And Sayed. It's not fair on him.'

Sayed seemed ready to interject, to tell me that he didn't mind and I shouldn't fret, when a thud from upstairs caused us all to look up.

'What the hell?' I asked.

'Hope you don't have mice,' said John, ever helpful.

'Oh, come on, John,' I chastised, feeling a deep annoyance at him for even joking about pests in The Brew.

'Sorry, love,' he grimaced while I scowled at him. Meanwhile, my suspicions were aroused again. Mice would be easier to fix than my actual fear—that it was something supernatural.

Sayed was taking down our mismatched chairs from the tables. We'd decided on a shabby cool with a slight fifties edge for décor; it was all we could afford.

'We should at least look into it,' I called to Sayed. Then, addressing John, I said, 'It won't be an issue, because we take all the precautions we need. Just so you know.' I didn't want word getting out that we had a pest problem. On top of Saturday's fiasco, that was all we needed.

'It was a joke,' John said with a hint of exasperation.

'Anyway, it wouldn't be mice, Dora,' added Sayed. I didn't think so either.

'I'll zip upstairs, see if it was Cleo.' Though she was an old lady at fourteen, few benches remained safe if she really put her mind to it. Perhaps she'd knocked something over. That was our best hope.

'More likely a rhino issue. Or a poltergeist,' John quipped on his way out. Oh, yeah, John's hilarious, all right. I rolled my eyes in his wake.

There was nothing to see upstairs, and Cleo was curled up asleep on the coffee table. On my return to The Brew, I found the air had freshened nicely, so I shut the front door.

I turned my mind to the other problem. 'Did you burn something in the café yesterday?' I asked Sayed.

'Like what?'

'I don't know. Food?'

'Me? That sounds more like your thing.' He grinned.

***

A few hours later our waitress, Laura, swayed orders to a table as Cold Chisel's 'Breakfast at Sweethearts' played over the café stereo. Her small beehive bobbed as she moved and I could just about make out her silent crooning of the lyrics. When it came to style, Laura worshipped Amy Winehouse.

Most of our tables were taken. It was always busy mid-morning, and I was glad to see that The Brew wasn't suffering after Saturday's events. Everyone still needed their coffee.

'Right! Off that foot, Dora,' called Jules authoritatively on her way inside.

'Thank you,' exclaimed Sayed, irritated with me. 'She wouldn't listen to me.'

I was pretty sure I saw Sayed's eyes roll that time, and I was ashamed to say he was correct. There was never a chance in hell that I would have taken his advice and rested up. Sunday's rest was plenty for me. I wanted to keep moving, stay occupied.

Jules had arrived to attend the funeral with Sayed and I, while Laura kept The Brew open on her own.

Most of Deepwell had known each other for a long time. Jules and I had first met in kindy, although we weren't tight friends back then. Not until we turned up in a support group for domestic violence survivors in Nambour, half an hour's drive away. There was no such group in Deepwell, the population being too small to sustain it. Besides that, neither of us would have wanted to attend a group so close to home. It was bad enough that the residents of Deepwell knew as much as they did already.

From that moment, Jules and I became firm friends. Jules was a woman you could count on. Her ex-husband had since moved away, and Jules had retreated to a soothing life on the outskirts of Deepwell, surrounded by forest. There she spent her days painting and making friends with the birds around her shack.

Jules wrapped her arms around me, and I leaned closer, kissing her on the cheek.

'What a shit-show Saturday was,' she said. 'How's the foot?'

'Fine.' I paused. 'Well, sore. But I take my tablets from the hospital when I need to. Can't believe they're legal.'

'Yeah, well, don't get carried away with them,' she replied dryly.

I lowered my voice to confide in her. 'I know it's awful, but the last thing I want to do is go to this funeral.'

'I'm hardly going to judge you. Don't you think I'd get out of it if I could? I hoped you'd ask me to work The Brew instead.'

'Oh. Sorry.'

'What's your issue, then? Is it the energy situation?' Jules asked, making little quote signs with her fingers, but not sarcastically.

'Exactly that. It's draining. The feeling is so intense. I don't usually have anything to complain about. I mean, it'd be difficult to work at a funeral parlour … but here? It's not like spirits turn up for coffee and a hedgehog. Well, until Saturday.'

'Right. Have you worked out what's going on?' Jules suddenly looked as though she was gritting her teeth. Was it possible she wasn't as comfortable with my ability as I'd thought?

'No, but it seems to have gotten worse. Odd things have happened since then. Smells and …' I thought about the cauliflower the night before and the noise that morning, but decided I was spiralling. I sighed. 'It must have been Becker.'

'I guess so,' Jules replied, looking unsure. 'Have you mentioned all this to Sayed?'

'No, and please don't say anything yet. I want to be sure. But who else would it be?'

'Yeah, who the hell else would it be?' Jules replied absently.

I checked my watch and realised I had no time to delve further. Sayed and I went upstairs to get changed for Becker's funeral. Inside, the apartment was musty with a metallic edge again. A coincidence? I didn't think so. It was clear I needed to investigate, but it would have to wait until after I'd done my civic duty.

CHAPTER SIX

Turns out a quick-as-lightening funeral wasn't enough to prevent a massive crowd from paying their respects to a man like Bruce Becker. It was confounding given what I considered the essential unpleasantness framing his character, but there you go. Parking was a nightmare, with cars lining the main and side streets. In the end, Sayed, Jules, and I had nearly a kilometre to walk in the sun—and dressed almost entirely in black.

Walking in silence, I spent the time thinking. My, admittedly minimal, experience with the dead told me that those who lingered only did so for a short time. A few hours, or a few days, was my guess—time they used to adjust to the new order of things after the big shock of death. When a spirit remained on this plane, I assumed that there was a more serious reason behind it. For example, I considered that Jessica Crawford was experiencing more suffering than average because she'd died in such a violent car crash. Perhaps she had trouble accepting that her life could be taken from her so young. It was not uncommon for teens to feel invincible, after all. I reasoned that the shock of losing her life caused her to linger on Vantage Road for several weeks after the accident.

In that case, Becker should be gone by now.

Sayed caught me sighing and asked, 'Are you okay?'

'Fine,' I said and smiled. We kept walking.

Approaching the White Light Chapel, I saw that it had burst its gates. Chairs were being set up outside, and two large speakers would help the latecomers to hear the service. The energy hit me immediately: bloody Becker. It was like running into a brick wall. Even in death, he seemed determined not to be overlooked.

As Sayed and I entered the funeral home and edged around strangers and Deepwell residents alike, I had a concern. Would I be capable of finding out why Becker remained behind? For the first time, I pondered whether my ability could be improved upon; I had never before wanted to do anything other than dampen it. On top of the PTSD, it felt like seeing the dead was just another shit-show that I had to live through. As we signed the attendees' book in the vestibule of the chapel, I asked myself whether I had been wrong to view it like that.

Had Becker remained on this plane to ensure his importance, then I felt confident that he would soon be able to leave. Seats were at a premium, and mourners would be left sitting outside. Fortunately, Dad had arrived earlier and saved seats for the three of us. We squeezed in just as the service began. The officiant and others gave eulogies, focussing on how much Becker had been loved by his family and the great things he had achieved in the Deepwell community. I felt a dramatic sigh building but cut it off.

The service was followed by a procession to the closed coffin to place flowers on top and say final goodbyes. Sayed and I lined up for our turn next to Leanne and Don Cusimano, while Jules dawdled with my Dad. The coffin's dark timber glistened, with perfect lacquer and silver fixtures, from a platform at the end of the aisle. By the time it was our turn, the roses had started to overflow, with a couple of blooms tumbling to the floor.

Then I recognised him behind the coffin: Becker himself. 'Oh, good grief,' I said under my breath. He was easy to spot, wearing shorts and a t-shirt with the local mechanic's logo printed on the front. He looked so out of place amongst the well-garbed mourners who were mostly in dark colours. Also, I wasn't used to seeing him dressed in anything other than slacks and a business shirt, the required formality for a CEO in little old Deepwell. Only once, a decade ago, had I seen Becker's pasty legs. They had been poking out of his boardies as the Hermansens passed the Beckers on a Noosa National Park hike.

Looking away quickly, I wondered what to do. The last thing I needed was for Becker to realise—here, among hundreds of people—that I had seen his ethereal form. Experience told me that those with a bone to pick about dying can go a little over the top once they realise you can see them. I understand it. It must be very confusing and frightening to be stuck in limbo without the ability to affect the world around you in the way in which you're accustomed.

Still, I didn't want to give someone like Becker any opening in a public place. I imagined he might start making a fuss and trying to make me hear him. No, if I was going to attempt to help him, it wasn't going to be here in front of the entire funeral hall.

I held back a grimace as I looked away.

'What was that? That look?' whispered Sayed.

'What?' I sought to put him off the scent. 'Oh, just, you know ...'

'The energy?'

'Yes,' I said, feeling relieved to finally admit it. 'Also, my foot's a little sore,' I added, not wanting Sayed to worry too much.

'We'll be out soon,' he said sympathetically and squeezed my hand.

As we stood by the coffin, I focussed on the flowers. I was so close to Becker that I felt his energy pressing towards me, even though he probably wasn't aware of sending it out. I wondered if Becker was leaving any olfactory trail. Stale air, perhaps? Like I'd smelled in The Brew? But above the hundred (and counting) roses, I detected nothing.

Head down, I placed a white bud with the others. Then Sayed and I turned and got in line to make our exit. Halfway down, Dad and Jules entered the throng near us. Jules had that same look Mum used to get when she was exasperated with Dad. Mum had always worn it at funerals, and for a good reason. There had not been a funeral at which Dad didn't drag out, 'You know what they say. Nothing's certain except death and taxes.' Or worse.

I caught Jules' eyes and said, 'Like that, is it?' She said nothing but sucked in some air through clenched teeth.

Once, spurred on by a polite audience, Dad had followed up with, 'And the death rate's one per person, you know.' Mum had managed to shut him down after that. I rubbed Jules' shoulder a couple of times to transfer some strength.

But Dad wasn't the loudest, or the most awkward, at Becker's funeral that day. A woman close to the casket was squawking about the importance of funerals for closure. That was fine. But then she said something about how sometimes the spirit needs closure too, and a funeral isn't always the right way to achieve that. Personally, I would agree … but talk about not reading the temperature of the room. I craned my neck, trying to establish who it was. All I managed was that she had red hair. I wondered what Becker thought of it all.

On the way out, Becker's spirit continued to create a desperate atmosphere. Of course, he had no idea that he was affecting anyone—and there was certainly no one else who appeared to notice anything out of the ordinary. Even so, I didn't think he would care that much about his impact on others. Difficult and persistent, Becker's energy was pushy. When I thought about it, that was him in life, too. To Becker, feelings were something to be minimised, and the strong would be the victors. Yet he seemed to be feeling something now. I sensed a vulnerability, a neediness. My, how things change.

Finally, outside, we found Lionel standing in the shade of a jacaranda tree. As we approached, he swung someone around in front of him and presented her to us. The girlfriend! She was a well-dressed blonde in fitted black pants and a crisp shirt. No hippy clothes to be seen. But my eyes widened at the spectacle of Lionel spinning her—a tall thirty-year-old—about as though she was a small child.

'This is Cloud. Cloud Cowles,' he beamed. Wow. He was really pleased with this one. Good, I thought. Lionel deserved it.

'Hi, Cloud. I'm Dora, Lionel's sister. This is my husband, Sayed.'

We shook hands as Cloud told us how delighted she was to meet us. 'I've wanted to for weeks now. Hoped I would run into you serendipitously and, well, here we are.'

'I'm glad. I mean, not pleased we're meeting at a funeral, of course,' I replied awkwardly. 'Oh, this is our Dad, and my friend, Jules.'

'Yes, hello again. Nice to see you.'

So, she'd met Dad. Suddenly I decided a get-together was in order and invited everyone.

'I'd really love it if you could come for dinner,' I said to Cloud. 'Tonight? Our place?'

'We'd like that,' answered Cloud.

'Is this for all of us?' Jules butted in.

'Oh, I suppose so.'

'Good, good. So tonight at—' said Lionel.

'About six-thirty?' Cloud butted in.

'Yes,' I said. Did Cloud just cut him off? Or was she just finishing his sentence for him?

'I'd better get going. My Mum's still back in the crowd inside. I'm going to collect her and drive her home.' She looked at her watch. 'What can we bring?'

'Salad would be great if it's not too much trouble.'

'No problem at all,' said Cloud. 'Until tonight.'

Lionel was nodding enthusiastically beside her like her personal bobblehead.

As they walked away, Jules touched my arm. 'You sure you're up to dinner?'

'Yeah. I'm fine.'

'Fine enough to make caramel slice kind of fine? You are the slice lady.'

I chuckled at the thought of being known as Slice Lady. It sounded like a female serial killer. 'I'll see, but I can't guarantee anything on such short notice, especially caramel.'

Jules drew me in for a hug and whispered, 'How did you manage energy-wise?'

'Oh, you have no idea! You should feel him. And worse, I could *see* him standing down the front behind the coffin. Becker is *not* a happy chappy, let me tell you. But I've got no notion of why.'

'Well, he is dead.'

'Yes, but …' I bit my lip gently. I mean, of course, Jules was right. It's just that I felt like there was something more; my gut feeling was that the story was deeper than that.

On the way out with Jules and Dad, Sayed and I passed Mrs Sloper with a posse of her friends. It never ceased to amaze me that she continued to have so many supporters. She didn't make eye contact with me, but a couple of her friends glanced and frowned on the way past. I understood Troy's mother holding what happened against me. Even though it was illogical, love and dysfunction would do that to a person. But the others? People could view the same event and judge it in entirely opposite ways. That, I had learned.

Sayed grabbed my hand and squeezed it as we walked. I squeezed back.

CHAPTER SEVEN

'Here she is,' Jules said, approaching the kitchen. Stepping towards me, a wine bottle in each hand, she added, 'I should never have asked you to bake, or even let you cook. I knew you had that sore foot, then I had to go and beg you to make a dessert, like an idiot. Too wrapped up in my own—'

'Desire for awesome caramel slice? No harm, no foul. It's in the fridge.'

'Oooh, you managed it? Well done, Dor.' Leaving a bottle of red on the bench, Jules placed the white in the fridge and viewed the slice, holding centre stage on the middle shelf, ardently.

'Don't get too excited, though. Ready-made caramel's all you're getting. Not exactly the real deal.'

'Poor thing. Here. Get off that foot,' she said, pulling out a chair for me from the kitchen table. She took the wooden spoon and began stirring the pasta sauce.

'Going straight back to work after Saturday's fiasco? Unbelievable. I would have stayed home with my feet up,' Jules continued. Doggie came rushing in. 'Hey, Doggie. Who's a good boy? You are. Yes, you are.' Her fingers ran through his thick fur.

'That's what you do anyway,' I said.

'Not with my feet up,' Jules said pointedly.

'That came out wrong. It was meant to sound breezier and not at all a dig about working from home. Anyway, I *was* sitting down at work … mostly.'

'I'll tell you what …' Jules' tone was low and serious. 'If that mad bitch comes in again, call Lionel on her. Straight up. I'm no fan of the cops, you know that. But no more chances. Seriously.'

'I know,' I said. 'I've just always wanted to keep the peace, you know? It's a small town.'

'That hasn't really worked for you, though. And, listen. If you and Sayed need someone in The Brew to help out …'

'We don't at the moment,' I said. 'But I'll keep you in mind.'

'It's probably hard for you to imagine me in customer service, I know. And I've got no one to blame but myself. I accept that.'

Jules was referring to her 'angry periods'. Jules had had a whole lot to be angry about, and it had consumed her for several years. But I'd watched her apply herself to painting and come out of that bitterness. People change, people heal, and Jules, fortunately, was no different.

'It's not that. It's because of Laura.'

While I'd lived the previous four years expecting something (else) awful to happen, Laura—The Brew's only permanent wait-ress—had been a calm, consistent influence. A cool breeze that came through for Sayed and me when it was most needed. She was fun to have around, too, with her love of music and signature style.

'Laura's not family, but she's been a godsend. I couldn't limit her shifts to make room for you. It wouldn't be right. But if you're serious, you'll be our first choice when we need some-one.'

'So you would actually consider me?'

'Absolutely,' I said, as though it would be ridiculous to think any other way. 'I know you'll hold your tongue when you need to … at least most of the time.'

Jules flicked me with the tea towel hanging over her shoulder. 'I would understand if you didn't trust me, though.'

'You know what? We all have bad times. We all have de-mons, even here in little old Deepwell. Perhaps more so here. Honestly? I admire you. You have been through so much. You got some help, but you still had to do most of the work on your own, and you managed that because you're strong and amazing. I believe in you, and that's the truth.'

Jules looked watery along her bottom lashes and, to be hon-est, I felt teary as well. I couldn't help but think of my sister, Wren, and whether I was doing enough to give her a hand up.

Jules smiled at me. 'I am pretty awesome, aren't I? But you are as well. Remember how far you've come.'

'I have, and I've been lucky too. Meeting Sayed.'

I thought back briefly to our courtship. It had taken me a long time to trust him—not through any fault of his, but after what had happened to me. Over time, I realised that his clear communication, lack of drama, and thoughtfulness were signs that I could trust the man. I don't know why it was that I had previously mistaken drama and control for love and care.

I landed my fist playfully on Jules' shoulder. 'If we need someone in the future, you're next in line. I hope it's soon, too, because business really needs to pick up for us to stay afloat.'

My gaze turned towards the lounge as Cloud and Lionel ar-rived. I saw a sudden flash of red. 'What the …? Who's that?' It was the flame-haired woman from the funeral.

Jules leaned around to see before returning her focus to the stovetop. 'Cloud's Mum, Leila Cowles. Another weirdo.' Jules could be judgemental, but on this I had to agree.

From a distance, I watched Sayed's introduction, then Dad's greeting. Dad and the woman looked to know each other well enough.

The woman's hairstyle was bouffant but not through curls like Jules'. Instead, it had a life of its own, and it was the colour of deep henna, more towards the maroon side than carrot. Her skin was so white.

'What a strange person,' I said.

'Yeah. I only met her once, a couple of weeks ago. She is unusual, but she's also just quiet, I think.'

'Quiet?' I felt confused. It couldn't be the same person from the funeral then, surely?

I hobbled into the lounge to meet her.

CHAPTER EIGHT

A cool breeze flowed through the open casement window as we eventually sat down to eat. Our solid timber dining table was piled with pasta, salad, bread, and wine—an Italian feast, made Aussie style.

'Do you live in Deepwell?' I asked Leila, while scooping sauce onto my plate. I'd been looking forward to finishing dinner preparations to get to know her a bit.

'Yes. Off Vantage Road.'

'Nice. Jules lives out that way, and it's very peaceful.'

'Outside town. There aren't many people living there.'

Thinking this was an introduction to some other point, I waited. But no other words came. Okay …

'How long have you lived here?' I pressed on.

'Five years.'

'Surprising that we haven't met before now, isn't it? Sayed and I run The Brew, downstairs.'

'Leila's a bit like Jules. She likes a quiet life, don't you, Leila?' said Lionel.

'I do.'

Lionel's point was well illustrated, given that Leila appeared to need a good deal of conversational help. Fair enough, I thought. I could relate. Socialising was enjoyable, yet there had been times, mainly when the PTSD was severe, that I needed to be alone.

Jules jumped in. 'The funeral was huge. As expected, I guess.' Her lips were vaguely pursed, giving away her true feelings on the Becker family.

'Actually, it amazed me that so many people were able to attend on such short notice,' I said.

'I guess. So typical of Annika.' Then, raising her voice in a bitchy way, Jules added 'Whatever Annika wants...'

'You sense them, too,' blurted Leila. Turning, I found Leila looking straight at me. She certainly appeared more animated than previously that evening.

'Annika and Candy?' I asked, genuinely confused. I glanced at Lionel, hoping he could interpret what the odd woman was trying to convey.

'She knows,' Lionel said quietly. I squinted at him. 'It's really not our fault. Well, we might have said something about you being "sensitive". But Leila worked it out from there.' He smiled at Leila. I frowned at him.

'We?' I mumbled, and Cloud scrunched her shoulders at me.

'That's an important skill you have,' Leila started again.

Sitting in silence for a second, I realised it wasn't possible to take back the whole seeing ghosts conversation. Turning back time wasn't an option. Even Cher didn't manage that in the end.

With no chance to moderate my reaction, I blurted, 'I disagree. It is more of a burden. A right pain in the arse.' There was something about the woman that rubbed me up the wrong way and, clearly, caused me to err on the side of impolite.

Then I remembered what Leanne had said: Cloud's mother was a psychic. Most likely, she had a more positive view of the supernatural world than I did.

'It is an adjustment, I suppose,' said Leila. Then, with no shadow of discomfort, let alone embarrassment, she added, 'Still, it's a useful skill. Personally, I communicate with the life-force, or souls if you like, that stay behind.'

'You actually speak to them?'

'Yes, and you probably can, too. When you're sensitive enough to interact using one sense, sometimes the others are available to you. They just need to be unlocked. One needs to know how.'

That's when it occurred to me: if I stopped being reactive, this woman might be able to help with Becker. Excitement rose. The kind you experience on realising that you're not entirely alone in the strange parallel world you've been living in. So, if I want to learn and improve on my skill, it's possible. This could be good for me. So why was I so harsh with her? Leila just made me so damn cranky.

I wondered, should I ask Leila about Becker outright? My interest had been piqued. I no longer saw her only as the odd, quiet lady who had arrived barely an hour before, or the noisy, inappropriate one I'd heard at the funeral earlier that day. But that moment wasn't the best time, I decided. Still, I couldn't entirely stamp out the curiosity inside me.

'Is it dangerous?' I pushed on, bravely.

'Can be. But there are ways to protect yourself. It's a skill I've built up with many years of practice. There are various methods of gaining information from these lost souls, but I've been channelling since I was a teen. It works for me.'

Leila sure got chatty enough when talking about ghosts. She was like a different person. And channelling? I'd heard of it before. 'Hold on. You let spirits inside you?'

Glancing around, I found Jules and Dad were shocked, too. They obviously weren't fully acquainted with Leila and her ways. Lionel and Cloud looked as if they'd already made peace with it.

'What if the ghosts aren't good? What if they're dead set evil?' In my heart of hearts, I didn't like the idea.

'Rest assured, I know what I'm doing,' said Leila with a hardness I hadn't noted previously.

Troy came to my mind. He had slowly taken over my life in the year we were together. Though I had not agreed to it, he had successfully taken over my body and my spirit in many respects. By the year's anniversary, he was calling most of the shots. So indeed, if a person offered an invite to ghosts to inhabit their body, weren't they asking for trouble?

I nodded in acceptance of the difference between us, but I didn't have to like it. I just hoped my brother wouldn't get mixed up in anything weird or dangerous.

As we scooped at further helpings, Leila seemed as though the disagreement had not bothered her. It appeared we were moving on—and I was glad for it—until Leila said, 'So, how does your ability work?'

Having accepted that everyone at the table was now part of my inner circle, I answered. 'I see the dead and sense them. Occasionally, I smell something that is related to their lives somehow. I try to stay away from places like hospitals and road accidents, for obvious reasons. And I hide the fact that I can see them. They tend to get over-exuberant if they know.'

'Avoidance of the souls that stay on?'

'Yes,' I agreed, though it didn't sound very gracious when Leila put it like that.

'You attended the funeral, though?'

'Yes, well, I had to go. It would have been rude not to attend. Plus, it would reflect poorly on Sayed and me as members of the community, and business owners no less, if we'd skipped Bruce Becker's funeral.'

'So, you went because you felt you should? See, I don't really worry about that stuff.'

My cheeks flushed. Leila was having a go at me with my entire family looking on. Like I hadn't already been through enough! What was her problem? Nit-picky, argumentative woman. However, I couldn't shake the sensation that my own words and behaviour had left me appearing shallow and selfish. I gave Lionel a flabbergasted look that screamed *why did you invite her here?*

'Water, anyone?' Once more, I hoped to elicit a topic change.

There was an awkward silence until Jules chimed in brightly. 'Dinner was great. Perhaps we'd better call it a night, though?' I was enormously relieved by that idea and impressed that Jules was being so helpful socially.

Before long we had the guests standing on the threshold for goodbyes. Leila pointed to the deep red mud stain on the ground at the door and asked, 'Was this you?'

'No,' Sayed said calmly. 'We think it's dirt from the farms. This was a pub until about a decade and a half ago, and part of the upstairs area contained rooms for rent. I reckon they hosted farmworkers who probably cleaned off their boots here before going inside. There was a ton of red mud lining the verandahs when we moved in.'

'More than that, I'd say. Looks like red brick dust,' Leila said. Cloud nodded in agreement while everyone else looked baffled. 'A basic form of protection magic used in hoodoo. Grind an old red brick and lay a line of the dust across the door well or window, wherever you want to stop negative influences crossing.'

'Hoodoo? Isn't that some practice from America? The American south, right?' I asked, exasperated. After everything that flame-haired woman had said that evening, this was the last straw.

Sayed's mouth hung open slightly. Dad was having a similar reaction.

'Well, yes, but witches will do whatever works and many hoodoo practices are good, strong magic. Anyway, you have a problem right here,' continued Leila, giving a sweep of her hand.

Cloud looked mortified. 'Mum, please …' She seemed genuine in her attempt to stop Leila, but it was too late.

'Who lived here before?' Leila pointed to the building.

'The publican and his family, but that was years ago. Plus, the hotel guests, like Sayed said. It sat empty for years before we bought—'

'When we arrived here tonight, Cloud immediately sensed the energy was really … busy. And not in a good way. Cloud tells me there's a very negative feel in your apartment. I feel it myself, but Cloud senses better than I do at times.'

Right. Now Leila's bagging my home and dragging her daughter into it as well. Like a runaway train, she continued down the track. 'It's not healthy to be around that. It can affect you psychologically and sap your physical energy, too. Have you been feeling okay lately?'

Well, now I had no choice but to spill the beans. 'Are you talking about the dead? Are you saying there are ghosts here? Actually, I've felt Becker lately. It's probably just that.' Sayed turned to me, shocked. 'I'm sorry. I didn't want to worry you,' I told him, but his face had lost its colour.

'Well, I only know what Cloud has told me, of course,' Leila continued.

'So, it's Becker. Surely,' I stated emphatically.

Sayed and Lionel turned to glare at Cloud. Cloud and I were glaring at Leila. Meanwhile, Jules and my father looked like deer caught in headlights. This was exactly the sort of situation Jules had no patience for.

Annoyed at the further blindside—and lambasting no less—I said, 'Look, I've sensed him lately, since his death on Saturday, and he's a difficult person. But I don't think that means there's some huge problem here. I don't really appreciate this intrusion. I'm not as comfortable with all this as you seem to be.'

'I'm sorry. I needed to say it, and I meant it for your benefit. But maybe I shouldn't have said anything. Sometimes I don't think before I speak. But if you ever need anything. If you want me to do a clearing or a blessing, please call me. I won't mind at all.'

'Sure. I'll keep it in mind,' I told Leila coolly, raising my hands to suggest she should stop talking. I glanced at Cloud. She was a goldfish mouthing, 'I'm … so … sorry.'

Sayed's brow was furrowed, and he and Lionel kept exchanging furtive glances.

'I really am sorry. I meant no harm. I just misjudged.' Leila seemed sheepish now, but it was too late.

51

'I'd best get some sleep, I think,' I said. I kissed my brother and Dad goodnight and bid farewell to our other guests. I'd had more than enough for one night—one year, even. If I never saw Leila again, it would be too soon.

CHAPTER NINE

As soon as the door closed, I turned to Sayed, incredulous.

'What the hell was that?' he mouthed, not wanting to be heard by our guests who were still trundling down the back stairs.

'I know, right? And Lionel said to give Leila a chance!'

'Seems like that might be hard. Still, you really went for her.'

'There's something about that woman. The tone she uses rubs me up the wrong way.'

'Plus, the rest. You've sensed Becker around, but you haven't told me? No need to hide events like that from me. I'm anxious about it, too, Dor.'

'I didn't want to upset you,' I repeated. That's what people always say when they have secrets. 'But, there's nothing to worry about. It's Becker. He was an arsehole, and he still is an arsehole. But he's not after me or anything.'

Aware of how lame I sounded, I tried to bring Sayed up to date as best I could, although even I couldn't fathom exactly what was going on. I laid out each odd incident, from my sense in The Brew the day Mrs Sloper crashed her way in, to the metallic smell, and seeing Becker at the funeral.

'Wow. There's been a lot happening. So, you're definitely sure it's Becker?' Sayed looked genuinely worried.

'Absolutely. I saw him. Can't get more certain than that.'

'Good point. I can see why you were on edge, and perhaps why you snapped at Leila. Still, she may be able to help you. Us, even. Have you thought of that?'

'Yes, and I hate the idea. Just shoot me now!' I said dramatically. 'Seemed like she was trying to spook me. That stuff about brick dust? Come on. There are plenty of farms with red dirt right here on the coast, and it's obvious that the old owners provided accommodation for itinerant workers. No surprise that some of that red dirt came home with them and was left on the verandah. The entrance needs a coat of paint, nothing more.' I spoke with conviction even though my stomach churned.

'True, but did you ever wonder how it got onto the front verandah? The front doesn't have stairs. The only access is through the house. A bit weird, isn't it?'

To be honest, the red stains at the front had passed through my consciousness.

Perhaps seeing my distress, Sayed said, 'Let's see how things pan out, huh? Don't let it get to you. But we need to be careful and look out for danger. And remember, you can share anything with me. We're in this together, Dor. You've got to know that by now.'

I choked back tears. Past trauma was a blot on the marriage, to say the least. Sayed was the one who had given me stability and security. From my side, I brought family dramas, gossip, the Slopers, and violent crime. What a contribution. The lack of balance in our relationship sapped my confidence at times. Yet Sayed had never wavered in the way he related to me. Never had he told me that I wasn't enough—nor that I was too much.

'Are we going to be okay?' I asked him.

Nodding, Sayed grabbed my waist and bent his knees to snuggle into my neck. I relaxed into him.

Twenty minutes later, I had washed up the last of the evening's pots and Sayed had taken out the garbage. I continued to mull over the awkward evening. Leila had made a terrible impression. Perhaps I *was* too sensitive, particularly when stressed, but still. The audacity! Did Cloud really say those things about the energy she identified in my home? There certainly had not been any denial when Leila started to mouth off. Was I right to stay the hell away from both of them? Or was Leila the only person who might be able to help me?

Noticing another dirty wine glass, I submerged it in the soapy water. A change of light to the rear caught my eye, the reflection flashing briefly in the kitchen window above the sink. Spinning around, I found nothing but my own abstraction on the stainless-steel fridge. My heart beat hard in my chest. Bloody nerves.

I remained in front of the fridge for a few moments, moving my arms up and down, watching the light and dark dance on the brushed stainless surface. It seemed there was nobody there except me.

Then there was a sudden pressure pushing through me. I stumbled backwards. Frightened, I caught myself clumsily on the edge of the kitchen counter and straightened as rapidly as I could. I backed up against the bench, bracing myself with my hands, my eyes darting quickly around for further danger.

Fricking Becker with his unhappy blustering! I had never liked him when he was alive, and I was not growing fonder of him now that he was dead. This was harassment.

'What do you want, Becker?' I asked firmly. 'Just state your trouble. Otherwise, I can't do anything for you.'

Despite the indigestion-creating dinner with Leila and Cloud, here I was trying something different: communication. Of course, if Becker did tell me his problem, I had no idea what the hell I would do then.

'Last chance. What's your issue?' I waited a few seconds before continuing. 'Fine. Work it out yourself, then. And do not touch me again.'

This fresh attempt at conversation, and fixing firm boundaries, was followed by a hot rush of embarrassment. This isn't a paranormal film, I reminded myself. Trying to be psychic ... I must have sounded like an idiot. Talking to the dead? Pah! I don't *communicate*, and I certainly don't *channel*.

I continued scanning the kitchen for anything out of the ordinary. Aside from Sayed's steps coming up the back stairs, all was quiet.

With continuing unease, I turned towards the sink. I noticed the window above it had fogged from the hot water below. I wrote 'piss off' in the steam with my finger—just in case Becker's reading skills were better than his listening.

I wanted to finish and get out of the kitchen, so I grabbed for the glass, the edge of which jutted from the bubbles. It was there, in my fingers. Then the glass was gone. I moved my palm gently under the water and felt something sharp. With a gasp, I pulled my hand away and examined it.

'You right in there?' yelled Sayed from the hall.

'A broken glass, that's all. No blood. I'm okay.'

Once again, I was giving partial information to my husband. Why was I continuing to do that?

It was clear that the glass had exploded, but the noise hadn't escaped the sink of hot water. It was a thin glass, I reasoned, and that certainly wasn't the first time I'd broken something in the kitchen. But this didn't feel like one of those times. Not straight off the back of being pushed around by a bully ghost. It seemed way too coincidental.

Pulling gently on the plug's ring, I collected each piece of glass as it appeared through the receding dishwater, then wrapped them in an old newspaper. Done. Then, instead of talking to Sayed about what had transpired—like I should have done—I made a decision to visit Becker's grave the next morning. I knew Sayed would never be comfortable with me going to the cemetery on my own, so I kept it to myself—the very thing he had just told me not to do. But, for right or wrong, I decided I would spill everything to him afterwards, when I had more to go on.

First, I had to find some answers.

CHAPTER TEN

On waking, hope surged. A new day, a new beginning. Thinking like that didn't always pan out, mind you, but it was a habit of mine to force my thoughts in a positive direction whenever I was able. Anyone who's had as many crappy days as me became well versed in little tricks like this. Besides, there was a simple truth to the idea that each morning was a fresh start.

I stretched out in bed, my eyes adjusting to the light and my toes touching the footboard momentarily. Sayed lay to my side, his back warm and reassuring. Dark hair brushed against my face as I turned and hugged him, feeling his chest firm against my palm. Sayed would soon be awake, too.

The clock read 6:47 AM as I shuffled down the hall to let Doggie Brasco and Cleo out for their morning ablutions—swift, with breakfast on their minds. When I returned, I filled their bowls with food, with Cleo brushing about my legs as if to make the process as difficult as possible. Fourteen years of living together hadn't taught her that she would always be fed in reasonable time. She continued to act as though I might simply forget her one day.

Doggie, on the other hand, sat watching, intently—his canine instincts entirely on display. Occasionally he stole a glance towards his empty bowl before turning back to me. This procedure was well known to me and was designed to focus my gaze towards his bowl. For, if I saw it, I would have that lightbulb moment, 'Ah, yes. Doggie needs breakfast.' The fact that I was already in the process of putting out food didn't register with him. I supposed it could never come quick enough for Doggie Brasco.

Sayed roused as I went to take a shower. 'Cleo and Doggie are up to their usual tricks,' I muttered in warning on the way to the bathroom. Just before I turned the tap on, I heard Sayed reach the kitchen and start singing 'Here comes the sun'. He was singing to Cleo and Doggie, something he often did in the morning. I occasionally caught a hint of an Algerian accent—almost lost—as he sang. I smiled as the warm water hit me.

In the bedroom after my shower, my attention was drawn to a metallic odour. Again. What was it? I certainly didn't notice anything before my shower.

Jumping into action, my nose followed the scent. But it didn't seem to come from anywhere specific. There it was, floating about in my personal space. I gave up on locating a source and opened the French doors that led to the front verandah from the bedroom. The exhaust fan continued to run in the bathroom, too, which I figured might help.

Standing in the centre of the room, I waited as the air freshened. Then I began to lay out my cards—in this case, suspicions—on the proverbial table. At that point, I was beyond wondering if something supernatural was occurring.

'It is,' I said, nodding lightly to myself.

The most immediate answer to 'who?' was Becker. Had to be. But there were two problems with the theory that Becker was haunting me. One, there seemed to be no reason for it. Becker and my philosophies on life were vastly different, yes, but we had barely had more than half a dozen exchanges with each other, despite living in Deepwell our entire lives.

'Why me?' was a fair question. I was pretty sure Becker didn't know about my ability. Knowing would, of course, give him a reason for ghost-him to hang around me like a bad smell.

The second thing was the metal scent. What did it mean?

Once I smelled cigars in an empty store. I mean, who smokes cigars outside of the movies? John Shillen, that's who. Robyn Becker—wife of Bruce Becker, and a local real estate agent—showed Sayed and I Shillens' property when we were in the market for bricks and mortar to open The Brew. Shillens' shop was over the other side of town, though, offering less benefit in position and, worse, the old man had passed away right in the shop. Robyn needed to tell us about his fatal heart attack, I guessed. Before Deepwell did.

That day, inspecting the property, I sensed Shillens among the shelving which had previously held car parts. I felt the usual energy and pressure, then on top of all that hung a spicy acid tang. Sayed said it was from the cigars that Shillens puffed on, even against regulations, inside the store. Sayed wondered if the smoke had attached and clung to the walls over the years, something that had happened in The Brew's building. But I knew that wasn't the full story. Mr Shillens was right there with us that day, and he'd brought the bold scent with him. What had he thought having us, little more than strangers, look over his store, and judge it for our purposes? Based on the energy he had put out, not very much.

Six months after my assault, I established that the smells had meaning; they weren't random. They were always linked in some way to the person who had passed. What link did metal have with Bruce Becker? It wasn't immediately apparent. My brain worked overtime until I remembered the Deepwell Water Treatment Plant. The plant itself was essentially a large metal structure so that made sense. Not that Becker worked the equipment himself. As the CEO, no doubt he worked in a plush office when he wasn't out attending meetings. But he would have visited the plant regularly, I thought. I felt I had solved the puzzle.

Then, as I stood there, happy to have gotten somewhere, the atmosphere changed and surrounded me. It was as though the very air around me thickened and started to push against me. The air was squeezing. I grabbed at my face to feel my skin starting to move out of place. Horrified, I rushed to turn the ceiling fan on. It was all I could think of to do. As the fan's blades picked up speed quickly, I did achieve some relief. A lessening of pressure. I must remember that trick, I told myself.

Still, I was rattled. I sat down on the edge of the bed and tried to catch my breath and organise my thoughts. The event was winding down. I scanned the room, and all looked normal, so I found Sayed. He was standing in the kitchen, a small mug in his hand. 'Coffee?'

'Yes, please.' I needed it.

He handed me a cup of medium roast poured directly from the coffee press. The mechanism got wonkier with each use. Small chunks of grounds turned up in our cups, which we tried to ignore.

'Did you smell anything?' I asked him.

'Like what?'

'Metal. Perhaps something more as well. I don't know.' I took a sip.

'Just coffee,' he offered weakly, tipping his cup gently to me. 'I guess it's a bit stuffy. I can open a window?'

'I did that already,' I said, staring at my feet and wondering how to proceed.

'Is this one of those times—' began Sayed.

'Yes,' I jumped in. 'I don't know what's going on. And I would hate for *her* to be right.'

'Leila.'

'Yes, Leila,' I frowned at Sayed. 'Or Cloud.'

'But?'

'Well, it's just …' I was wringing my hands gently. I had second thoughts about telling him everything.

Was there any way that the events of the last few days might not be what I thought? Given my PTSD, I felt the need to ask the question. So far, there had been the energy along with Mrs

Sloper, and a couple of instances of out-of-place odours. I had been pushed in my own kitchen, plus there had been Becker, shorts and all, at the funeral. Indeed, that was too much to imagine or misconstrue, I told myself.

No, it was real. There was something up with Becker. He wasn't settling down the way he should.

The most important question then was, did Sayed deserve to be dragged into further drama?

'You know what? It's just a weird odour, that's all. And I guess I'm still a bit nervy from everything that's happened. Cloud and Leila, and Mrs Sloper.'

'Okay, well, you let me know if there's anything else, or if there's something I can do.'

Sayed brushed past me to the hall. I followed him, and when we stepped through the bedroom door, both of us caught it.

'Oh my God, no. It wasn't like that a minute ago,' I exclaimed, my face scrunching up.

'What do you mean?'

'It smelled different. Not this.' My stomach lurched.

'This is rotten,' Sayed said, stating the bleeding obvious. He was covering his face to protect his nose and mouth. He moved swiftly through the bedroom, then the bathroom, checking to see if he could find any cause as he went.

'I already opened it up. The fans are on. What more can we do?' I yelled to him, almost choking.

'How about I call the plumber today?'

'You think a plumber can fix *this*?'

'Could be a problem in a pipe,' Sayed said with a shrug of his shoulders. 'Perhaps something died and got stuck in one. Let's get out of here. Leave the front doors open today.' If anyone was going to climb up to the verandah to break in, they'd be seen from The Brew's front windows. Besides, we weren't exactly stashing riches up there.

Sayed was right, I supposed a sewerage problem was possible. Better to check it off the list. That might account for the metal odour, too.

'You're right,' I said. 'Call. And let's get the hell out of here.'

We took Cleo and Doggie with us. No need to sacrifice either of them. By the time we reached the verandah, we were beginning to laugh. It was gross, but what else could we do?

'After we set up, I'm going to do a few things in town this morning, okay?' I asked Sayed.

'No probs. I'll organise the plumber.'

'Thanks, hon,' I said and started down the stairs to The Brew with Cleo and Doggie in tow.

CHAPTER ELEVEN

When I told Sayed I was going into town that morning, I left out the pertinent information: that by 'town' I meant the cemetery.

Unable to set off early with The Brew too busy, I took my only chance before the next rush began at lunch. The midday sun was already beating me down as I walked through Deepwell Cemetery to Becker's grave.

Set on three acres, the cemetery covered more area than seemed necessary but, like the funeral home and various other local businesses, it serviced surrounding areas as well. Besides, when the cemetery was initially planned, and the land plotted out, cremation's popularity wasn't foreseen.

Becker had only been interred twenty-four hours before, so the site remained a work in progress. Bouquets and wreaths of flowers decorated the grave. Their petal edges had started to decay, and the mound of soil was covered in astroturf. I imagined it would soon have a full-length marble cover with an engraved headstone. The Becker family would take no shortcuts in honouring Bruce and there would be no financial considerations to hold them back.

From where I stood, I overlooked the cemetery on a rise that looked down over town. These days such land would never be chosen for burial lands. Had Becker lived on, he might even have moved those graves in the name of progress. But now Becker himself rested in a prime position on the crest—well, it wasn't exactly rest, I reminded myself.

A visual sweep of the grounds told me I was the only visitor. Perfect. A light breeze rustled the trees lining the cemetery's perimeter. Magpies and butcher birds strode the mauve carpet from the jacarandas, hunting for insects and occasionally breaking into song. A kookaburra waited on the fence line. Sounds carried from town, two kilometres away, like the occasional hoon, a car horn, or a 'good morning' yelled to a neighbour from across the street. Beyond that, the only human noise came from the houses surrounding the cemetery: a child's cry, a dog barking, and some bloke in his yard fixing a lawnmower and wanting his girlfriend to throw him a hat.

Long before my sense kicked in, I remember asking Wren, 'Who would live next to a cemetery?' Yet, the Deepwell Cemetery was surrounded chock-a-block—on the two sides that weren't bushland—by homes. Suburbia with, I supposed, ordinary people who didn't see the dead. I may have been mildly squeamish about living near a graveyard before but, post-ability, the idea had taken on a mega-awkward air. I imagined never getting a good night's sleep again, and certainly wouldn't expect quiet during daylight hours either!

Standing over Becker's plot that morning, I put out feelers. While trying to connect to him, I felt sad. This should have been his final resting place. 'Rest in peace' is what we all say. But as far as I could tell, he wasn't getting any. He was turning and churning in his grave, grinding his teeth over a problem that I couldn't grasp.

'But why?' I asked aloud.

Nothing happened. Of course.

Taking another quick look around, I crouched down, a bit embarrassed at the thought of someone arriving at the cemetery and seeing me. I took solace that, from a distance at least, nobody would recognise me. I pulled my straw hat down over my face a little further.

On the astroturf, I let my left hand steady me with my fingers splayed, while I touched the earth at the edge with my right.

I picked up a small clump, and massaged it lightly, allowed the small fragments to fall through my open fingers. I was trying to connect to Becker in whatever way I could, yet I was hamstrung by lack of experience. How do you start picking up on the signals from the dead when you want to? I scooped up another handful of dirt, this time crushing the larger pieces as well, and letting it all tumble back to the ground.

Rosella Estate.

I remembered clearly the day Troy and I planted out the front garden of the home we shared. We'd moved in after a few months of courtship. With hindsight, way too fast. My shoulders drooped at the memory of how determined I was to make it a home. I planted lavender, rosemary, and pretty little flowers that changed colour from purple to white. The soil at Rosella Estate was similar to that at the cemetery.

It was no surprise that I had successfully avoided Rosella Estate since that time. Fortunately, it wasn't on the way to anything significant. Not for me, anyway.

The scent of lavender wafted past me as I crouched by Becker's grave. Quickly, I turned and scanned—no other humans. I sniffed the air. No lavender. The sky was bright to a fault. There was a light, almost gentle, energy. It had to be Becker. In a good mood, perhaps?

That's when I fell forward. There was a change in the surrounding atmosphere, like the intensity of it had suddenly increased. Putting my hands out swiftly to stop my face meeting the ground, I felt a sharp pain in my wrists as I caught myself.

Pushing my body up, I looked around again, heart beating hard against my chest. All appeared clear. I held my hands out in front of me and twisted my forearms around slowly to assess the damage. Nothing serious.

This was the second time in less than twenty-four hours that I had been physically pushed around by something I couldn't even see. I was hardly surprised at that point, just indignant. And scared that my bully was someone who didn't own a body or a heartbeat. That wasn't right.

Gently, I rotated my hands a couple more times. Jumping up, I grabbed my handbag from beside me and took several steps away from Becker's grave. I wanted to run but I had gone that day to find answers. The sound of my heart was loud and, although the sunshine continued to try and offer a false sense of security, a cold chill crept over my limbs. I wrapped my arms around myself, the way you might do subconsciously when talking to someone you don't particularly like.

Then came the compression. Energy pressing as my pulse quickened. I scanned the environment again, this time hoping that I would see someone—anyone—but I was still the only person there. The only living, breathing person. I no longer wished to be alone and anonymous. It was now apparent that I wasn't the only soul on the grounds, and I would have given anything to have back up.

Dread washed over me. I tried to take some deep breaths, but it was difficult. Shallow gasps were all I could manage. Becker was pushing against me, pressing into my flesh again. I saw indents on my forearms. 'Stop!' I yelled, my voice sounding shrill and unnerving. I took a deep breath, then exhaled a second warning, 'Stop it! Just leave me alone!'

Then I smelled it: a rank odour with caustic, acrimonious undertones. No more lavender.

Tapping into my senses was all new for me. I was trying to walk towards my ability, instead of trying to ignore it like I had spent years doing. I had always wanted to be separate from that world. But now it appeared there was no way out; as the pressure continued, I was trapped. What had I gotten myself into? If I had just a little more knowledge, a pinch more understanding of the processes, I might have been able to escape.

It was a big ask to expect my body to calm. But I tried, with several deep breaths, as my limbs and trunk continued to be hammered. Instead of relief came malice. It floated in the air around me, and it seemed like I was inhaling it. The feeling made me want to suspend breathing altogether—just stop right then and there.

'Why? Why are you doing this to me, Becker?' I called out again.

Though Becker was certainly doing me harm, I still entertained that he did not intend it, that the pressure he was putting me under was the only way he knew to make contact. There was no reason for Becker to have malice towards me. I wasn't the only one in town who hadn't liked him, and frankly, I'd always been pleasant to him. Polite and respectful at the very least, even when we had disagreed on development and environmental issues around the area.

Many in Deepwell actively held grudges against Becker. People who'd fought against his style of development in vigorous ways. Besides, that type of bloke—the Becker type—isn't generally precious. You need a thick skin to live as he had, not giving a crap about anything beyond business. So, it didn't make sense that he was here for payback. At least not from me.

The lightheaded feeling that accompanies a blood pressure drop washed over me, and I took a gulp of air. It seemed full of rancour, and I inhaled it long and strong. *Yuck.* It was time to get out; it was clearly unsafe. Concentrating on steady breaths—as much as I could manage—I made a run for the exit, pain from my injured foot radiating with each step. As I ran, the pressure continued, and I knew it was do or die. I focussed on the decorative metal gate ahead, painted a rusty heritage green colour. As I approached it, the pressing sensation lessened. The air transformed. My breaths were less obstructed than before. Relief.

Heading straight for the car, I jumped in and locked the door. That act would mean nothing to a ghost, I assumed. But it made me feel safer. I turned the engine over with shaky hands and, after a quick glance to be sure no cars were coming, I took off. A few hundred metres down the street I pulled over. I knew I shouldn't be driving like that. Panicked. I was doubtlessly in shock. The rear-view mirror allowed me to check what was behind me—nothing—but I was still compelled to turn around a couple of times to be sure.

Finally, feeling a little safer, the questions arose in me. Why was Becker targeting me? Was he really intending to kill me? It certainly felt that way. After all, I'd had my airways blocked once before, by Troy, and he had definitely been trying to end my life. It still didn't make sense that Becker would target me like that, though. Was he under some misguided impression about me? Did he think I was his enemy?

I pulled out my phone to call Sayed. Then I realised that I'd kept my plans from him on purpose. Had Sayed known I was going to the cemetery, he would not have been supportive of the idea. He'd have told me that I must take someone with me, him or Jules perhaps. He would have been right, too. I should never have set off alone. I threw my iPhone gently to the passenger seat, fuming at my own stupidity.

The smell had seemed like a complex and changing jumble of pleasant and foul. I shuddered at the ill sentiment it carried as its base note. At first, I was unsure of what I even meant by that. It sounded ridiculous to think that an odour could carry an intent, but at the same time, it made instinctual sense to me. Five years ago, I didn't believe in ghosts. I had never seen, felt, or smelled, a spirit. But my life had changed. Oh boy, had it changed. I had new ways of sensing the world. And I was only at the precipice of knowing what that entailed.

Becker had been brutal, conniving, and money-grabbing. Once there had been a fracas over a couple of properties on which he had placed offers. Leanne told me he'd offered the owners a pittance and pressured them to sign off. Becker never told the owners that a small shopping centre had been approved nearby which would soon increase the property value. Morally, if not legally, it didn't sit well. Word got around, and it took Becker a while to live that one down. He never did get his hands on that land, either.

But the relationship Becker and I had shared in life was barely existent. So why would he be so pissed off with me now, I wondered.

Like a hard slap, a thought hit me. It must have been Becker I had sensed initially, at The Brew, but what if it hadn't been him at the cemetery that morning? Sure, I had been standing by Becker's grave. But there were dozens of people buried at Deepwell Cemetery. Some of them must have been newbies.

The reality was that it could have been anyone's spirit pushing, touching and squeezing me. The thought sickened me.

My body shuddered to realise the dangerous predicament I had put myself in with my secret-keeping and my insistence on going it alone.

I reached for the air-conditioning and dialled it down. I already felt a chill.

Leila. That's who my thoughts turned to. Dinner the night before had been a mess. But that whole fiasco took on a ridiculous air in comparison to the problems I had found on my plate since then. How nice it would be to have someone in whom to confide, I thought. Someone who knew a lot more than I did, someone who understood. Could Leila be my answer? My hope? My teacher?

My breathing settled, reducing to a slow rhythm while the car engine and air-conditioning hummed their white noise. Just then my phone buzzed, its screen lighting up with Sayed calling.

'Hey, darling,' he said brightly.

'Hi. Are things okay there?'

'Fine. Look, the plumber came. He gave the place a good go over, checking The Brew, the courtyard, and the apartment. He found nothing that might cause a smell ... any kind of smell.'

'I'm not surprised.'

'You think it's something more?'

'I guess I do,' I replied.

'Are you nearly finished in town?'

My mind churned. Should I tell Sayed I was at the cemetery, or keep lying by omission? I'd always struggled with the to and fro of rights and responsibilities in intimacy. You didn't want to put too much on someone else, a friend had once told me. To reach intimacy, you have to share, said another. I mean, heck, I'd already loaded Sayed up with my problems, right from our very first date. I didn't want to be responsible for more of that.

No, I decided. I can deal with this. 'Yep, I'll be back in a few minutes.'

'Good,' said Sayed. 'It might be a smart idea to take today slowly after last night. I'll be honest with you, I'm a bit worried that all of this—Mrs Sloper's stunt, and Leila and Cloud and their big mouths—might not be good for you.'

'And you mean?'

'Well, you were so on edge after they left. You didn't seem like yourself, you know? It reminded me of how things used to be.'

The subtle allusion to my trauma and the resulting PTSD was rattling, but I told him, 'I'll be fine. I promise.'

After I'd hung up, I sat wondering why on earth I would give such an oath, especially when I had kept so much from him already.

I thought back to Troy. Days with no idea, or control, over how things would turn out. Just thinking about it, I began to feel the raw horror that had been common in those times. The night of Troy's attack started replaying in my head.

CHAPTER TWELVE

I'm running through the house. Troy is close behind me. Reaching the door, I fumble; the lock won't open. Slippery fingers. Greasy. There's no time. He's closing in, and I can feel his labouring breath reach me. I kick, but it falls on empty space, so I spin around, flinging my hand, closed fist, towards him. By chance, I clip his face, and he stumbles back momentarily. Jesus Christ, he'll be even angrier now. Then the latch opens, and I run.

The cold night air gives me a jolt. All is dark, save for a streetlight overlooking the one curve in our street. I break away from the light. To hide. It's my best opportunity.

'Help me,' I yell as loud as I can—just the once, just to try. Then I fall silent. Not another word now. I have to go to ground; it's the only way.

As I turn towards a yard a couple of doors down, I look back. Troy's shadow is in our doorway. He is struggling to pull on his boots as he comes out the front door. Even from a distance, he's a frightening figure. Not big. In fact, Troy's shorter than me. Sturdier in build, though. His strength isn't so much physical as it is … something else. Something dark, powerful. Oppressive. Something I tried—and failed—to tame in our year together.

As he staggers across the front patio, I see Cleo fly a couple of metres into the yard. 'Fuckin' cat,' he says. The noise of the impact and her screeching sickens me, but I can't yell out. I can't help her.

71

Troy clearly intends to find me, so I dive behind the mock orange bush growing in the neighbour's garden bed. I have my hand over my mouth. 'Cleo,' I scream silently.

Deciding Troy hasn't seen me, I crouch, listening for him and trying to gauge his location. Yet I can barely perceive anything above my own thumping heartbeat. Panic threatens. Will he pick up on that, too? I start to lose control over my breathing. Is Cleo okay? Not enough air.

He's going to hear me. Oh my God, he'll find me.

I'm trying to manage my gasping. I have to. Slowing. Slowing everything down. Breathing in, breathing out. Gentle.

My ears pick up a sound: the cool crunch of asphalt under boots, travelling over the biting air. I'm pretty sure he's heading in my direction.

Breathe softly, Dora, I tell myself. Strict now in my attempts to calm myself down, I lay in a foetal position behind the mock orange. My hands are positioned to help me up quickly. The chill from the ground surges through me—my pitiful flannelette pyjama set is no help. Through my fat reserves, into my muscles, cold floods my bones and takes over my body. Shivers set in.

I see nothing through the mock orange, but I keep checking to the sides from the ground and occasionally above. Is he there? Has he found me?

There's a lull. Deathly silence.

Then, in a rush, the kinetic energy comes before the motion itself. Turning to the side of the bush, there he is, hulking. Despite the darkness, I see his face contorted like I've pushed him too far this time. 'Stupid bitch,' he says, seeming like he might burst with the rage that storms inside.

'No, no, no,' is all I manage.

He steps towards me and I let out a chilling scream that's cut short by his boot landing squarely in my face, damp and hard.

Chapter Thirteen

That night in Rosella Estate, all those years before, I had asked Troy a question: 'Are you coming to Pam and Todd's barbeque tomorrow?' That simple conversation deviated because, unbeknown to me, there was turbulence under the smooth surface of the early evening. Troy had 'discovered' something that day: that I had run into his best friend, Todd, while out shopping. Troy had uncovered the information that, he believed, I had deliberately kept from him. And he had spent the day mulling it over. Ruminating.

When I looked back on it, I imagined the information moving like a current in the shadowy depths of his mind. Swishing this way and that until it spilled nastily onto my shore while The Block aired on television.

'You slept with him, didn't you?' he screamed at me suddenly.

When I woke in hospital days later, I saw my face in a small mirror while being given some consoling words from the doctor. Troy's boot pattern was imprinted quite well in the bruising on my cheek, and my cheekbone was broken. Later I discovered—my family keeping it from me for as long as they could—that he'd knelt down and throttled me, right there behind the mock orange.

Returning to the present, I found myself still sitting in my car on the street leading from the graveyard. 'Troy,' I muttered shakily. But that was then, a long time passed. I began to pull myself together, back to the current day. Troy was the past.

Sayed, The Brew, Doggie and Cleo, my friends and family ...
they were my right now, and my future. I stole a quick look up
the hill, seeing the cemetery gate, and rested my hands lightly on
the steering wheel. I checked the side mirrors and pulled out,
heading for The Brew. Heading for home.

***

'Another thing the plumber advised was to inspect the ceiling
cavity upstairs,' Sayed said sotto voce as I arrived via the back of
The Brew.

'And "hello" to you, too,' I joked, taking off my foggy sun-
nies—nothing like moving from humidity to air conditioning to
fog your glasses.

He gave me a look.

'Okay, so the ceiling cavity? Why?'

'Just in case there is something up there causing the smell,'
Sayed continued quietly, not wanting any of the customers to
overhear.

'Well, why on earth didn't he check that when he was here?'

I was tying on my half-apron ready for the lunch shift that
appeared to have begun already.

'Wrong sort of tradesman, Dor. He's a plumber. There's no
plumbing up there.'

'Smart arse.'

'No, I'm serious. One trade is not another trade. Where
have you been living, Dor?'

'Oh, right. Who do we get to do that, then?'

'I was thinking us. I don't see why we can't do it ourselves.
Save some cash.'

'I suppose we could. But you know, I might go and stay with
Jules tonight, if that suits you. So could we leave it until tomorrow?'

'Girl time? I think that's a great idea,' Sayed replied, passing
me with a full tray in his hand. It always seemed weird that we lived

in a subtropical climate, yet The Brew's customers were all addicted to hot drinks. Not that I could talk. I didn't get started without my coffee in the morning either, even in summer. Vices, right?

Beyond ghostly secrets, Sayed and I slipped back into our effortless style of communication. I was deeply grateful for him and our relationship. Though when I was keeping things from him, I felt some guilt. Lies didn't seem necessary with Sayed. So why was I acting so secretively? Why was I keeping things from this man who'd been a stable, peaceful, happy influence on me for so many years? I watched him stride around the tables for a few seconds, tall and rugged. He was such a sincere person, kind and proper with people. So different from Troy and, to be honest, from many of the guys I'd dated.

In the few minutes' drive from the cemetery to The Brew I had been straightforward with myself. I wondered—though I didn't like the idea one bit—if this could be an episode. It seemed the responsible thing to consider the possibility.

PTSD was a formidable foe. It was a trick, or mistake, in the brain, you might say. Severe fear through a traumatic event occurred, but sometimes the mind didn't register that the trauma had passed. The mind got caught in a loop. I remember the day the psychiatrist sat on a chair across from me at the hospital; I had returned to her for a follow-up several weeks after being discharged. She told me, 'Your reaction to this experience makes complete sense. You are reacting the way many well-adjusted people would react.' I was glad to hear that. Then came the *but* ... Getting 'stuck' afterwards was the problem. My neural pathways had been re-routed, and not for the better.

So, my question, raised by Sayed as much as myself, was something that needed asking. Was it possible that my recent experiences and stresses with Mrs Sloper, Leila and Becker, had created a fissure through which I might lose myself again?

I had to nut it all out, and I needed backup to do that. That's why I was heading for Jules' house.

CHAPTER FOURTEEN

It was after five by the time Doggie and I left. An overnight bag was packed in the boot, and a box with a bottle of wine tucked behind it for Jules. Laura was closing the café with Sayed. I imagined that Sayed and Cleo would enjoy their quiet night together. My husband was personable and social, but he enjoyed having a break, free from disturbance, too. And troubles had been plentiful lately.

Doggie sat in the back seat, settled on his blanket. The smell from him wafted to the front. No bath in a while I remembered, and grimaced. Stealing a look at him in the rear-view mirror, I saw that excited expression dogs get. Sometimes, they were too enthusiastic for their own good, I mused. Only man's best friend could be so thrilled by a trip that was a complete mystery to him. Though Doggie had no idea where we were setting off to when we packed the car and he jumped in, he was sitting there looking like he'd won the lotto.

Pretty soon Doggie would guess we were going to Jules' place. Dogs were smarter than we gave them credit for. With such a keen sense of smell and a brain that can put two and two together, he would work it out, and he wouldn't be disappointed. Doggie loved Jules. Mainly because she took him for exploratory rambles in the forest that surrounded her home. We would never let him run off lead there for the sake of the wildlife, but it was still thrilling for him, with so many unfamiliar smells and things to discover.

'We're doing the right thing, huh?' I asked Doggie. Brown eyes looked at me expectantly.

Taking the north-west road, we went out past the timber cattle yards, overgrown with weeds and grasses in their decades of disuse. The new yards were metal and located to the south. On thinking of the word 'metal', I was, unsurprisingly, taken back to early that morning—the odour, the air, the pressure. I even tasted metal on my tongue momentarily, but then it was gone. Strange, the link between smells and tastes.

There was always plenty of time to think when driving. When passing the cattle yards, I usually thought about my reasons for becoming a vegetarian. I remembered vividly the moment I decided never to have meat again. Linked forever to my relationship with Troy, as though what happened between us allowed me to see things in a different light. I gained a broader understanding of what it was like when your life was in someone else's hands.

My life had been in Troy's hands, yet here I was in the land of the living. A survivor, and then a thriver. Not a victim, but a victor. Of course, I wasn't as positive in the harsh light of day at the hospital, as my cheekbone healed, and detectives and lawyers traipsed in and out—so much horror. On that first day in the hospital, I left the meat on my plate, and I never touched it again. Sure, it didn't stop all the harm and suffering—it hasn't fixed the world—but it meant something to me, to cause less pain. And you know what? I needed that.

Leila crossed my mind as we passed Hunter Street, and before long I saw the sign for Jule's street. Doggie had worked out our destination and was giving occasional low whines from the back. Turning off Vantage Road, I drove eight kilometres through the forest, past the warning signs for 'deer crossing', until we reached Jules'. It always struck me as strange to have deer living in Noosa District. Deer seemed so, well … American. Kangaroos, wombats and echidnas, sure, but deer? Deer were an introduced species doing too well in our native forests.

As I parked the car in Jules' drive, she came out to meet us. Doggie's whining ceased as he threw himself from the rear of the vehicle to greet her on the path. I hugged her tight and handed her the bottle of wine. 'Thank God I'm here,' I said, pulling a face.

'So, it's going to be like that, is it?' she asked.

'Yeah, Jules,' I said with a smile. 'Exactly like that.'

CHAPTER FIFTEEN

Jules and I got started on dinner straight away. I prepped a cos lettuce and other ingredients for a Caesar salad, while she made the croutons and blended the dressing. We found ourselves making light chit-chat only. The funeral took up some time; there was still plenty to say on the matter.

Jules and I sat down inside to eat, even though the cool spot was on the verandah, near the forest's edge. Unfortunately, in the early evening, mosquitos were everywhere.

A glass of wine appeared to go down smoothly for Jules over dinner. I was happy with a glass of water with a squeeze of fresh lemon. After everything that happened with Troy, I found it damn easy to rely on alcohol to get me through. When I met Sayed, I stopped drinking altogether. It seemed easy, since Sayed didn't drink himself, and it had been for the best. When dinner was finished, Jules and I moved the dishes to the kitchen and made a beeline for the couch. Flopping down next to Jules, I sank into the soft seat, brushing my feet against Doggie on the floor.

'So how are things, really?' Jules pressed.

'Completely crazy,' I blurted. 'Or I'm crazy. I can't be sure.'

I felt unsure of myself. Uncertain of where to start. So, I returned to the beginning. I reminded Jules of my feelings in The Brew on Saturday afternoon. 'Obviously, it was Becker. Since we now know that he died only an hour or two beforehand.'

'Right. That makes sense. But …'

'Let's get to the buts soon,' I said, and Jules snickered. 'Honestly, you're so childish.'

'You love that about me,' she smiled.

'So, Becker, at the funeral.'

'Yeah. Disturbing shit, that is.' Jules looked away, then turned quickly back to me, staring.

'It was,' I laughed. 'And he was wearing some stupid t-shirt with a pair of board shorts.'

'You're kidding? Please tell me you're joking! That's fucking hilarious.'

'Yep.' We started to laugh.

'Shit, I hope he can't hear us,' said Jules, pulling up. 'So, I guess the big question is why?'

'Stuffed if I can work it out,' I said. 'Doesn't make any sense to me. But I can report to you that Becker isn't happy.'

'Oh,' Jules said. 'I feel a bit bad now.'

I flapped my hand as if to brush away her concern. 'So, typical Becker. Of course. Like he's railing against something in death, as in life.'

'Controlling is the word you're searching for. Becker always wanted to be the boss of every damned thing. No different now, I suppose. Makes sense that personality won't change after death, right?'

'Exactly. But there's more. Lionel's new girlfriend, Cloud, and her mother.' Jules looked like she knew what I was going to say.

'Talking about all *that* right there at the dinner table? It was weird.'

'Opened her gob and it all fell out. In front of everyone. Awkward,' I agreed.

'Could be a good thing. I mean, imagine a life where you didn't have to mask the real you?'

'Dunno,' I offered. My speech was relaxing along with my body. I took a sip of water. 'Seems the sort of thing I'm always going to have to cover, surely?'

Jules tipped her head and shoulder in a you-could-be-right gesture. 'The stuff about the apartment. Pretty rude. But ... is there truth in it?'

'Well, that's got me confused. Feels like there's some real bad energy there, yeah. After everyone left that night, something happened in the kitchen. More than I've ever experienced before. Fucker pushed me over.'

'What do you mean? Sayed pushed you?' Jules was quick to my defence, but you could tell she didn't really think he would do that. Jules knew him almost as well as I did and knew getting physical wasn't his style. Sometimes she teased me that he was boring, but I know she really loved him, too.

'No. Becker.'

'Why?'

'That was my question! Makes no sense. And to be clear, I didn't see him. Just felt him. Had to be him, right? Who else?'

'Oh, crap. Mother fucking shit balls.'

'Really?' I squinted at her as though I was disgusted, but I was only joking because I was well-used to Jules' foul mouth. Jules looked genuinely concerned. 'Wait, you're serious. What's the matter?'

Let's be real. Ghosts, spirits, the dead—it was hardly comforting stuff. Did anyone, aside from morgue attendants and Leila, really want to be involved in any way with what happened after people died? Maybe it was too much for my best friend to talk about all this.

'Okay, okay,' she said, putting herself back together mentally. 'It isn't good, Dor. Must be tough for you.' Jules still looked serious, not her usual self.

'Why, thank you, Miss Hampton,' I said with a tip of a pretend hat. 'It is tough. I don't know what to do. That's the main issue. Also, there's a tad more to the story. But we don't have to discuss it. You seem like you're at your limit.' Therapy had taught me that you had to be careful with other people's emotions. Just because you needed to talk about something, it didn't mean others were ready—or okay—to hear it.

'No, it's not that. Tell me. Really.'

So, I told Jules about my frightening visit to the Deepwell cemetery. She didn't seem pleased with *that* part of the story. Nor was she happy to know that I'd been keeping most of it from Sayed. 'He's there for you, for God's sake! Why don't you let him help you?' she fumed.

Then I got to the part of the story that bothered me most. It was tough for me to state out loud.

I had struggled my way back to sanity through sheer grit and vigorous effort. To think that I could be losing psychological ground again was as distressing to me as it was embarrassing. But I had to share it with someone, so I told Jules my fear: that perhaps not everything I thought had occurred, had actually happened. 'Jules, what if I'm having an episode again?'

'Oh,' said Jules, long and slow.

We both sat without words for a lengthy moment—the sounds from the forest outside and Doggie's intermittent scratching the only soundtrack.

'What makes you worry about that? You're doing so well. Year by year you're better and better.'

'Yes, but things have been so crazy lately. Triggers, Jules. The shit with Mrs Sloper. Even the whole dinner party debacle. I'm not exactly feeling good. Besides, Sayed questioned me about the same thing today.'

'He did?'

'Yeah. So, I'm just asking, what if? I have to work it out. Otherwise, I could well be running around off my rocker. I have to know what's real and what isn't.'

Jules' head was slowly nodding as I spoke. Then, suddenly, she jumped up. 'Phone's ringing,' she told me. I heard nothing myself, but I guessed that her mobile was on vibrate or something. People get pretty tuned in to their mobiles. Jules grabbed the phone from the kitchen bench and placed it to her ear as she walked down the hall and into her bedroom. Must be important or she would have let it go to voicemail.

I lay back on the couch and stared through the insect screen. Doggie settled at my feet after another scratch, so I reached down to pat him. He turned over onto his back to help me get at his tummy better. 'You're a class act,' I told him as he gave me upside-down side-eye, his teeth protruding a little from his mouth. 'Good boy.'

There was no way I could make out what Jules was saying, but it sounded as though she was having a meaningful conversation with someone. I wondered if it was to do with her painting. She was a tremendous artist, painting mainly in watercolour. Her skills amazed me, but the life of an artist was hard. Jules struggled to earn enough and to find opportunities to show her work in the capital cities. I hoped she was receiving good news.

'So, what was all that about?' I asked when I heard Jules returning to the lounge.

'Eh? Oh, nothing,' Jules said, waving it away. I was sure it was something, but I couldn't press her if she didn't want to share. 'Look,' she said. 'I think what we have to do is try to get all your ducks in a row.'

I was unsure of what she meant. But she wanted to help me sort things out, so I ran with it.

'You do sense spirits. It's weird, but that's real.'

'True.'

'You also smell odours related to the person in question.'

'Well, it's occasional.'

'But there's a history of it. It's not like it's just started for the first time. The physicality—the pushing, the broken clock—that's new. Right?'

I nodded. 'Right. Those are the events I can't be positive about. What if I'm completely bonkers?'

'You're not. I see your point, though. You're saying that you can't be one hundred per cent confident. So, what to do?' Jules appeared lost in thought. 'How to be sure ... how to be sure?' she asked. Of herself, it seemed. 'Dora, I'm not hassling you, but why did you go to the cemetery by yourself, without telling anyone?'

'It seems stupid now, but consider it from my point of view. I've got no idea what's going on, and I didn't want to keep dragging my long-suffering husband into it.'

'But can't you see that when you're not clear on stuff, that's when you need backup? It's the most important time to share and discuss things with others.'

'Honestly, I feel as if no one understands what it's like being me!' I asserted angrily. 'It's all very well giving this great advice, but my life is not average. Leanne isn't in her salon sensing dead people. Sayed isn't haunted by being assaulted by someone he loved. It's all too easy for you guys to tell me what I should be doing and thinking, but you don't know!'

Jules calmly sat back on the couch, maintaining eye contact. After a couple of seconds of silence, she ventured, 'You're finished, then?'

'I am,' I said meekly.

'You're right. In some ways, we can only imagine what it's like to be you. But that's the same for everyone. We all have to guess what it's like for others. That doesn't make my advice wrong.'

I shifted uncomfortably on the lounge, embarrassed by my tantrum.

'We need you—and I'm pretty damn sure I speak for Sayed as well —to keep us in the loop and quit running off to follow up on weird shit, half-cocked.'

I kept Jules' gaze. A challenge because I had done her and my own character a disservice with my outburst. 'I'm sorry,' I told her. She was right. I did have to stop being so secretive. Whether it was an episode again, or I was genuinely being bullied by those who have passed over, I still had to allow others into my world. And I sure as hell needed to calm down.

CHAPTER SIXTEEN

Waking with a start, Doggie's barking sounds far away in some isolated place. My chest heaves deeply for a couple of breaths. I push the sheet down, sit up, and let my eyes adjust to the darkness.

It's lighter outside, than in. My face scrunches trying to understand. The moon must be full or close to it.

Whining carries through the dark. Oh, no. Doggie. What is he doing out there? How did he get out? I check my phone quickly and place it down on the side table. 3.04 am. I leave, slipping on my thongs awkwardly as I head for the door.

Outside, I walk straight towards the forest that surrounds Jules' shack. The air should have a bite at this time of the morning. But it doesn't. Instead, it's still steamy, as though the day has gotten mixed up with night and created a monster climate.

Taking firm steps, one after the other, I enter the woods, ignoring the darkness, and listening for Doggie as I go. The barks and whines are intermittent, but enough to follow. It's as though the incident in The Brew that wounded my foot never happened. Or that I'm completely healed. Glancing down there's barely a mark. Amazing.

Doggie sounds concerned, sparking the worry that he's in trouble, so I pick up the pace. The moist earth cushions my steps as I press on. Following paths worn in by the creatures of the forest, I take in the other calls. Those that come in between Doggie's. Sporadic echoes from the shy, night-time animals.

My nightshirt is soaked with sweat, and I swipe my wet forehead with the back of my hand as I go.

The smell of the rainforest is strong and ripe when you're inside it. The plants are different. Everything is damp and full of equal parts of life and decay. Straying from the path I step over a fallen tree trunk to keep following Doggie's sound. It's harder to walk now. I slip intermittently on the mossy rocks and composting leaf matter, my thongs providing little support. My arm stings from a long, angry scratch on my forearm. I don't know when it happened or how. I ignore it and press on, pushing aside branches and vines as I go.

Must find Doggie. Make sure he's okay. I'm on a mission with just that one thing to achieve. I have to reach Doggie Brasco.

Eventually, I am unsure of which direction to continue. I stand still, awaiting the next signal. A minute later, I hear Doggie's bark ring out through the trees. Doggie leads, and I follow.

The cicadas keep count of my steps and the time, marking both with their beat. Doggie's voice rings out once more. He shouldn't be here, I fret. How did he even get out of Jules' place?

My feet continue in his direction, one foot after the other. Doggie's sounds are close. I've hiked a long way and I sense I might be adjacent to the main road. Panic—further sweat building on my brow and lip. Would Doggie go near the road? Something moves up ahead.

'Doggie?'

The answer comes as a whine as I reach the small area where he sits. Barely a clearing, bushes and vines surround. Doggie stands beside something large and heaving—a buck.

'Hey boy, what's going on?' I say.

Did he hurt this deer? Could he? My stomach roils.

I grab Doggies muzzle and examine it in the available moonlight which streaks here and there through the thick canopy. There's no discolouration around his mouth, no signs of blood.

I let out a gasp as I realise I'd been holding my breath. Quickly looking over the rest of him, he seems unhurt.

Though injured, the buck is alive. Shiny red spills from a large opening on his thigh.

My heart hurts with his lows.

The buck's breathing is heavy, yet irregular. Even with Doggie, and now a human, right there beside him, the buck made no attempt to rise.

I move closer. Was it hit by a car nearby on the Noosa Road? Or further over on Vantage, perhaps?

Touching his neck, the way you would a horse, I feel his smooth and velvety coat. There is an odour. Animal. I stroke, aiming for balance...somewhere between light and firm.

I am unsure if I'm making things better or worse. Crouched down next to the buck, Doggie is seated by my leg. Should I jog back to Jules' to phone for a vet?

The buck's breath is my focus. Then, under the rustling and shrieks of the rainforest—there is silence.

It has stopped. There is no more.

CHAPTER SEVENTEEN

A timber ceiling with uncovered rafters was above me. Daylight. Smacking the bed beside me with an open hand, I realised there was no Sayed. My heart quickened, but a quick look around showed me Jules' paintings lined the walls. Of course. I was in her spare bedroom.

Turning to lean over the edge of the bed, I saw Doggie. Light snoring drifted up from where he lay on the tiles. A small wet patch had formed on the slate from his breath. Doggie didn't stir. He remained in dream world.

In Jules' spare room it was only Doggie and me. No buck. No forest. No last breath. No death.

A dream was all it was. Despite the hyper-real feeling, the buck wasn't real. Lucid dreaming seemed somewhat fitting in that conflicted time. Though the evidence surrounded me to the contrary, a part of me still believed the dream was real. I especially noted the scratch on my forearm, which matched the exact scratch location in my dream. Somehow, I'd incorporated a real event into my dream.

A full account of my night was given over a breakfast of fruits—banana, pawpaw and apple—toast, and coffee. It was easy to keep eating with a jar of the best rosella jam in the Noosa Hinterland on the table. It was made by Mrs Cusimano, Leanne's Mum. She sold various pickles and preserves, including strawberry and blueberry, at the Deepwell Sunday market.

The forest had a life of its own at times, Jules told me. 'That's one of the many things that I love about it,' she said. 'It can affect people in a variety of ways.'

Jules has always said that humans weren't meant to live the way they did now, so far removed from nature. She thought that modern lifestyle caused many more problems with physical and mental health than people cared to admit. Probably because that would mean acknowledging that we fucked up somewhere, Jules always added. And perhaps she had a point.

Once suitably filled with breakfast, I started for home so I wouldn't be late for work.

***

After my mid-morning smoko, I returned to find Annika and her sister, Candy, sitting at a window table. If Annika's kids had had time off for their grandfather's death, then I guessed it was back to school time as of today. I went straight over to them, to see if they'd ordered. Orders were rarely taken from the tables; for the most part, we liked people to call at the counter near the back on their way inside to place orders. But, if anyone needed a little extra kindness, it had to be the Becker sisters, surely. Even Annika. Can't have been an easy few days for them, I thought.

I had spoken to each of them briefly at the funeral, of course. But this was the first time I'd seen them since. I decided to avoid discussing the elephant in the room unless one of the girls brought it up.

'Hi Annika, Candy,' I said with a friendly wave of my hand. 'Have you ordered yet?'

'No.' Annika looked confused. 'That's right. We're supposed to order at the counter …'

'It's okay. Let me take it here today. Not a problem. What can I get you?' I smiled, trying not to seem *too* cheerful. My face was doing backflips, trying to present 'just right'.

'Thanks, Dora,' Candy replied. 'A flat white and a piece of carrot cake for me. Annika?' Candy's voice contained bite. It seemed she wasn't too happy with Annika, though why, on this particular occasion, was anyone's guess. The strangest thing about Annika and Candy's relationship was always that Candy managed to tolerate her sister at all. When speaking of Candy, the word 'saint' was sometimes mentioned. In personality, they had always been so different. Annika clearly took after their father, Bruce, but Candy was a lot more relaxed and likeable. Candy usually took Annika's bad behaviour in her stride and would ignore most of it, from what I could tell. Maybe that was the way to deal with difficult people. Perhaps Candy had really hit on something when she started practising meditation a few years back. She'd even started visiting a Buddhist centre on the coast.

'Cappuccino. That's all,' Annika added. She seemed her usual self: snooty and rude.

Stop that, Dora, I told myself, and thought of the more human excuses possible for Annika's behaviour. Putting on a brave face, perhaps. Most of us do the brave-face routine at one time or another, after all. I'd certainly done the same in times past. But Annika seemed so flippant that day, that I might have doubted there had been any real, life-changing event for her in the week preceding.

'Thanks, Dora,' said Candy. Then she looked up at me and raised the elephant in the room. 'If only I'd been there. I keep thinking, maybe I could have done something. You know?'

I nodded slowly because, well, I really did know what she was saying. Why she was suddenly telling me was less clear. It seemed to come out of nowhere.

'Oh, for fuck's sake,' Annika hissed under her breath. 'Why don't you just come out and say it?' Uh-oh. I held my eyes taut at the hint of an impending scene. 'You think you could have done a better job than me. You could have saved Dad. You would have known what to do. You're a nurse, so of course you would have.'

Candy looked down for a moment, then looked straight at her sister. 'I shouldn't have said that. I didn't mean it like that.'

Still standing beside the table, I didn't know what to do. Walk away to put in their order? That would give the sisters time to finish … whatever was happening between them. Try to help them? Awkward. So awkward.

Candy had worked as an ER nurse, so I could imagine how each of them felt. I supposed Annika was feeling raw, being the only one who had been at home when it happened. But it was hardly Annika's fault that their Dad collapsed and needed medical attention—which she wasn't qualified for—on her watch rather than Candy's. We can't all be doctors and nurses, calm in every crisis.

'He keeled to the fucking floor, Candy. People die.' With that, Annika got up and walked outside.

Biting my lip gently, I guessed it was too late to say, 'I'll get your order,' and walk away. Damn it!

As I watched Annika, she took a few steps towards Leanne's salon, then stopped and leaned against the wall. She lit up a cigarette and took a long draw on it. I didn't know she smoked.

'I'm sorry,' said Candy, looking back up at me.

'No need. She's not leaving you here, by the way. She's waiting outside.' I nodded in Annika's direction.

'Other way around actually. She wrote off her car late last night. Hit a deer on a back road. I'm driving her today, so she's got no choice but to wait.'

'Oh.'

'Unless she wants to walk in this heat.' Candy looked like she wanted Annika to try it.

'Look, I'm really sorry about everything that's happened.'

Candy waved my apology away with one hand.

Wait, wait, wait. Deer on the back road? What back road?

'Near Vantage Road?' I asked.

'Huh? Oh, yeah.' Candy caught up. 'The car's a mess. She really did a number on it. She could have been killed herself. Lucky the kids weren't with her. Must have been a large deer.'

Could have been killed herself? So, the deer she hit died, then? I was stuck on the deer thing. 'When was this?'

'In the middle of the night,' Candy said. 'Annika was out driving around in the middle of the bloody night. And out there of all places,' Candy said incredulously, dropping her head to her hands. 'I'm sorry. I know I should be more compassionate. There are so many questions. That's all.'

'Annika's upset, probably confused, too. She couldn't save your father, and that would cut a person up.'

'Truth is, though, I am blaming her. She's right.' Candy looked up at me. 'We both know it.'

'It's only natural, Candy.' I put my hand on her shoulder gently.

'No, I mean … Annika didn't even *try* to save him. She couldn't or she *wouldn't*? Basically, she didn't try. That's what gets me. What was she doing? Just standing there watching? She didn't even call an ambulance until ten minutes later.'

'What?' I said with more gusto than either of us had been expecting.

'Never mind,' replied Candy. 'I shouldn't be unloading on you. Don't worry about the coffee. Sorry.' Then she got up and walked out.

There were other tables to tend and I continued my work on autopilot. Meanwhile, my head was elsewhere considering the bombshells that had just been dropped.

Did Candy mean what she said, that Annika had not tried to save their father? Is it legal to withhold medical help? Surely you have to—at the very least—call an ambulance for someone who is sick or injured? Plus, my dream. Was it linked to what happened with Annika? And if so, why?

When I got a chance to have a word with Sayed near the kitchen half an hour later, I still had no answers, but boy, were the questions burning a hole in my pocket. I decided that I had to tell him everything I'd been keeping from him. Just not right then. There was simply too much going on, especially there at work. But I chose to share with him the stuff about Annika and Candy. And my dream from the night before.

During a lull, I managed to give him a summary of my conversation with Candy. 'What do you think it means?'

'Can we be sure that's really how it happened? We would need to be sure, Dor. I mean, that's a big thing that Candy's accusing her sister of. Annika's an unpleasant person, but to purposely withhold medical care from her ailing father? That's next-level stuff.'

'Yeah, you're right. To be continued,' I said, rushing to the register where a customer was rapping their fingers on the counter.

CHAPTER EIGHTEEN

Doggie led Sayed and I home after work. Sayed had left Cleo in the apartment that morning, so she would be waiting for us on the other side of the door.

'Don't you think it's weird I had a dream about a buck on the same night that Annika killed one?' I grimaced.

'I would. But you can't be sure she killed it. Might not be the one you dreamed of, either. She's having some bad luck, with her Dad and now an accident. Jeez.'

Sayed avoided saying 'Jesus' in reaction to things, though he did sometimes swear. I mean, he wouldn't be very Aussie if he didn't. Muslims revered Jesus—something which surprised me wasn't better known—and while Sayed wasn't exactly practising, religion was still a part of his life and that of his family. Besides, the habit of not using Jesus' name in vain saved him from getting told off by his parents should he accidentally say it in front of them.

'Sure. But my dream felt super-real.'

Sayed was unlocking the front door while listening to me intently, though with some doubt.

'So, you had this dream at Jules' house—'

'Yes. And I scratched my arm in the forest and woke up with this.' I pointed to the scratch on my forearm. Sayed had already noticed and commented on it when we passed each other in the café earlier.

It was pleasant up on the verandah in the late afternoon when it caught the breeze. I grabbed the broom and gave a quick sweep to some dried jasmine blossoms on the floor.

'You're right. It's pretty weird,' Sayed agreed.

'You want to say coincidence, or picking up on signals or something, don't you?'

'I want to, yes. Still, I don't see how that could be the case if you had the dream last night but only ran into Candy and Annika today. Super-real, huh?'

'Oh, very. You have no idea. When I woke up this morning I was worried about Doggie. But he was asleep beside me, exactly where he should have been.'

'Tell me what happened with the deer again.'

'Well, Doggie and I, we sat down beside it and the next thing we knew, the buck drew its last gasp. Strange how we all have a final breath. Finito. Sorry. I sound like a dork.'

'No, I get you. We're so focussed on everyday life, we don't give enough time to the reality of death. And yet, eventually, God takes every one of us.' I loved his way of thinking sometimes. A little religion, it seemed, could be a beautiful thing. But straight after Sayed said it, his cheeks developed a ruddy tint. 'So dumb. Of course, *you* spend more time than most thinking about what comes in the afterlife. Sorry.'

'It's okay. I've never really thought about the fact that each of us will take a last breath, though. It's implied in the whole death thing. But I never thought about it consciously, even though I see ghosts. I think that's a mistake. We all should.'

'We should. Yes.'

We stood silently for a while and watched Cleo waddle back up the stairs after relieving herself. Even ageing, she was still so cute.

'Dora, thanks for sharing that with me.'

'You asked me to be more forthright with you, and I'm going to try to do that.'

'You know, I'm not sure if this is weirder than anything you already do, and sense, now, Dor.'

'Good point. But it's one more thing. Another concern that I don't understand. More weirdness in my life.' I mock screamed, 'I want normal.'

'That ship sailed a long time ago.'

I gave him a pretend push as I turned to head inside.

Then, stopping to look at him square on, I asked, 'About the Annika and Bruce thing, though. Don't most people know how to give CPR a bit of a go?'

'Not everyone. I mean, you have to take a short course. Like we did at the ambulance service that day. Besides, individuals react differently. She could have frozen.'

'God. Everyone should learn it. Why isn't it taught in schools? We need to do a refresher!' I exclaimed. 'But, yeah, maybe you're right about Annika.'

We were heading up the hall and I was holding Sayed's hand. It was warm and encouraging. 'Why do you think she took so long to call an ambulance?' I was unwilling to let it rest without voicing my most pertinent questions.

Sayed stopped. 'We don't know if it's true, but if it is, she must have had some reason.'

'Hmm. Doesn't it seem suspicious to you? Candy thinks so. Not that she accused her sister of anything specific ...'

'Do you think the police need to investigate?' Sayed seemed to find that idea amusing.

'What the hell are you, then? The devil's bloody advocate? And why was she out driving at two or three in the morning? Out there, on the forest road? Annika killed that deer. I know she did. I'm telling you.' I could feel my heels digging in.

'A big jump from not knowing what happened with the dream to ... I don't know. Okay. Now I am going to play devil's advocate.' Sayed did that occasionally, and he knew I hated it when he did. I rolled my eyes. 'You know why Annika was out driving? Because her father just had a heart attack. And worse, she didn't know what to do to help him. She feels responsible. The car accident might have been just an accident, but it could be the final straw. Maybe she needs understanding and help, Dora.'

'Fine. I feel like a bitch now.'

'That wasn't my intention as you wel—'

We both saw something move in the corner of our visions. As we turned, the front door slammed shut, the force of it causing the bones of the building to shake. I heard the gentle clink of glasses in the kitchen, moving against one another.

'Shit!' said Sayed at the same time as I yelped.

'A window.' Wouldn't have been the first time an open window had allowed air to travel through our apartment causing a ruckus like this. I turned into the lounge, and sure enough, one of the windows was open, its sash raised almost as high as it could go.

The explanation wasn't as simple as I'd hoped, though; nothing in Deepwell was that December.

The window in question was a sash style that we had never been able to raise before. It had been stuck shut with several layers of old paint since we bought the place. It had never bothered us because there were two other windows on that side that we could use.

'You got it open?' I asked, confused.

'No,' Sayed replied bluntly. 'No, I didn't.'

'You didn't lift that up?'

Sayed shook his head without looking at me, then moved over to the window. Examining it, he picked up a few pieces of paint, allowing them to stick to the end of his finger.

Sayed turned, brow furrowed, to ask me seriously, 'Who's been in here?'

'Can nothing be normal around here?' I screamed under my breath as I reached for my mobile.

CHAPTER NINETEEN

I left an urgent message for Lionel, and then the same one for
Jules as well: *Have you been to my place today? Ring me. Now.*

Walking over to the open window, legs twitchy, I was determined to shut it—as though putting the window back into its
default, closed position could put everything right. As I pulled
on the old brass handhold, the frame ran roughly along the
sashes. The movement felt jagged as it caught on the decade's
worth of paint that lined its inner grooves.

'It's shut,' I called out.

'Okay,' Sayed shouted back. He was investigating the rest of
the apartment, determined to ensure our home was safe before
he went out that evening with John. A weekly affair, they liked
to play pool at the Deepwell Hotel every Wednesday—boy's
night. Of course, Sayed had already made an attempt to stay
home and babysit me; it wasn't his style to go out and leave me
when there was any hint of danger. But I had stood firm, and I
was getting my way. First, I'd told him that only my family had
keys, and there was no sign of any break in. Therefore, it was
unlikely to be anything that he could help with, or guard against.
Second, I insisted it was just one of many weird events. In other
words, Sayed cancelling the pub for those few hours wasn't a fix
to what was going wrong in our lives and our home at that time.

'Six of one, half a dozen of the other,' I had told him, resigned to my fate. 'You might as well go. When Jules or Lionel
get back to me, I'll tell one of them to come over and stay with

me. Tonight will take your mind off it all,' I offered as a brighter afterthought. 'You need it.'

So, it was settled. Of course, in the back of my mind sat a tonne of baggage. Inside me, a fountain of anxiety burbled. I'd been pushed about by a spirit and nearly had the life crushed out of me. I'd smelled things that I never wanted to smell again. The clock had fallen, a glass had broken, and as of last night, I wasn't sure whether my dreams were just that, or if they were linked to some new and alien reality that I hadn't asked for—and didn't welcome.

Now, this.

An open window was hardly a worthy scene in a scary movie. It was only by virtue of that window being previously in-operable, that Sayed and I thought anything of it at all. Otherwise, we would each have assumed the other had forgotten to close it. Who cares? No one could get in there. It was a good twenty feet down to the shabby bitumen lining the alley below. It led from the street around the back to our carport, courtyard, The Brew's back door and our stairs.

But there was a problem. I was reasonably confident, feeling it in the pit of my stomach—as well as using my common sense—that the window had not been opened by anyone living or breathing. I tried to push the thought to the recesses of my mind.

Walking over to the bedroom doorframe, I leaned against it to watch Sayed getting dressed. He was pulling on a pair of light canvas pants and a t-shirt. You could call that overdressing—for Deepwell. The gentle waves of his darkest brown hair moved, lifting here and there with the oscillation of the fan. Sayed was a solid man, emotionally and physically. Neither of us were in gym-shape, mind you. Who had the time? But it felt good to be wrapped in those strong arms each day, his muscles holding me in place when I needed it. Gentle and firm.

'Did you hear back from Lionel or Jules?' Sayed interrupted my thoughts.

'Not yet, but one of them will come.' After my initial, urgent, message to call me, I'd followed up with a sitter request. *Because I'm a baby and need backup.*

There was a knock at the door. 'I got it,' I told Sayed. I looked at my watch and decided it would be John. But on the other side of our door stood Jules with a six-pack of Corona tucked under her arm.

'That was quick,' I said.

'Like I have other shit to do. What's going on? Spill.' She started straight up the hall.

Explaining as I followed her, I said, 'I need a babysitter because weird stuff keeps happening and it's Sayed and John's pool night.'

'Cannot believe they still do that after all these years. That's sad. The Deepwell Hotel is like a middle-aged bistro. I mean, I guess the food's okay, but Sayed doesn't even drink.'

'Pool. They like to play it.'

'Mmm. You know if you and Sayed ever split up, John will snatch him up quick as a flash.'

'Good. At least I know Sayed will be well-cared for.'

'Is it okay if I drink these?'

'Of course.' It wasn't like I had trouble staying away from alcohol. I just chose not to drink, because when I did, it could easily get the upper hand.

'Don't rush. It's Jules,' I called to Sayed as Jules plonked herself down on the couch. Placing the other five beers in the fridge, I grabbed a stubby holder for her and leaned into the lounge's doorframe. 'Were you over here today?' I asked plainly.

'No. I've been out pounding the pavement looking for work all day. I need something part-time to keep me going. Art's not paying for itself.' Jules raised her eyebrows in mock surprise.

'Well, see that window there? The one that was always stuck … as in, we have never once been able to free it up. It was open when we got home this arvo.'

'I tried to open it the day we came here with the estate agent.'

'Yup,' I said pointedly as I heard another knock.

On entering, John's face brightened like a child on Christmas morning to see Jules. John always held a torch for her, I reckoned. Then again, John held a torch for many a woman in Deepwell. He'd dated most of them at some point and he wasn't one to have a bad breakup. Quite a skill, I'd always thought. Still, I wasn't going to burst his bubble by telling him I thought Jules had outgrown him emotionally and socially. That would be mean.

'Good to see you, JuJu,' he boomed. John the Baker had lungs that would put a professional actor to shame. 'Nice pluggers,' he added cheekily, referring to her footwear in deeper Australian than simply saying thongs. Classic John. It caused me to look down at the new thongs Jules had on her feet, though. They were shiny with diamantés on the strap. Not her usual style at all.

Looking at the Corona, John said, 'On the turps, ay?', then shouted for Sayed. 'C'mon, mate. There's a jug with my name on it going warm.'

Jules rolled her eyes at John as Sayed came out of the bedroom, dressed smartly and smelling even better. He kissed me and headed off down the hall. The Deepwell Hotel offered the biggest rage you can have without heading for the coast—unless you waited for special events like Show Day, or the Easter Festival. Please don't ask me why Deepwell put so much energy and money into an Easter Festival, but it did. Still, I shouldn't complain. The Deepwell egg hunt held a special place in the memories of many who grew up here, the Hermansens included.

Grabbing my phone, I checked my messages, and sure enough, there was one from Lionel reading: *At work. Didn't come to your place. Come after my shift?*

I quickly replied: *No prob. Jules here now. Ta x*

'It wasn't Lionel, either.' I sighed and slunk over to the couch. 'Jeez, Jules, I really feel like a beer today.'

'It's your choice, but make sure it's a conscious one.'

I took all of two seconds to decide. Before I knew it, I had a beer from the fridge, and a second for Jules. Perspiration dripped onto the table and my leg as I sat down and eased the bottle into its stretchy stubby holder. Mine had a bright and touristy 'I visited Noosa Heads' design, complete with a surfer, a bikini girl, and a seafood platter. Jules' holder had the logo for Deepwell Tyre and Mechanics. I thought of Becker. Wasn't that the same brand that was on his t-shirt at the funeral?

I took a long slug and let the zing of the beer pump through me, my body relaxing into the couch. 'God, I need this.'

If there was a right time to drink, that was it. I looked at my watch. It was five forty-five —definitely happy hour. I decided then and there to run with it.

It wasn't that I was unhappy as a non-drinker. If I was honest, it had been a blessing that Sayed wasn't into the booze. It had been all too easy for me to reach for a bottle during Troy's trial. And, with PTSD dragging me down, it would have been just as simple to stick with the drink to bolster me afterwards. But I had met Sayed and, being with him, I found it easier to choose a healthy lifestyle all round. He was a good influence, gave emotional support and, of course, I was happy with him. I loved him more than anything.

Sayed had drunk alcohol before. As a teen in Australia, he'd tried it—like most kids. Though drinking was generally frowned upon by Muslims, it did happen. Muslims were human beings with free choice and imperfections like any others, after all. It was something he wasn't entirely open about with his family, mind you. In other words, Sayed—like teens all over the world— kept some of his exploits to himself.

I took a long swig of Corona while Jules ran through the businesses she'd left her résumé with: two doctors surgeries, the dentist that advertised 'no-pain procedures', two accountants, and a few specialty stores … so pretty much all of Deepwell. My bestie had been busy, I'd give her that.

'So, I also went to Annika's store,' Jules said.

'You did not!' I said, almost spitting my drink. Annika ran an upmarket clothing store in town called Double Decker. The back of the store had a mezzanine—that was the only link I had ever been able to think of concerning the store name. Double Decker sold okay clothes, plus some accessories and few gift items. It was the most sophisticated store we had, complete with a range of metallic handbags, shoes, and thongs—she called them 'sandals' because it sounded more upmarket. It wasn't my scene; I'm not a glitzy kind of girl.

'I didn't ask for work. I just popped in quickly because I was curious. She was there, working.'

'She was in The Brew earlier, too. With Candy. How did she seem to you?'

It was surprising to hear that Annika was back at work already, given everything that had happened: the accident on top of losing her father. Maybe she and I were more alike than I cared to admit.

'Suppose she wants to keep busy,' Jules replied. 'She had all her Chrissy decorations up. It was like tinsel town in there.'

It was almost like Jules had read my mind. We all like to jump to people's protection. I defended Annika to Candy in The Brew that morning, as Sayed had to me that evening. Now here was Jules thinking the best, coming up with reasons why it made sense that Annika would be back at work.

Then I realised. 'You bought your shiny thongs there!'

Jules crumpled. 'I felt sorry for her, Dor. I couldn't' help it.'

'So, Jules has a heart in there? A soft little hea—'

'Shut the fuck up, woman.'

That's when I remembered that Jules didn't know about the accident, so I filled her in.

'Oh no, that's terrible,' Jules said. 'I do actually feel sorry for her. That's too much for one person.'

'Don't you think it's weird that Candy said she just stood back and let Becker die, though?'

'Well, when you put it like that, yeah. But that Candy's version of it, right? And remember, Candy's suffering, too. She's upset about her Dad like Annika is. She could be looking for someone to blame. I don't know ...' Trailing off, Jules took another sip of her beer.

That was definitely the same logo as Becker's t-shirt, I thought, studying her stubby holder.

'Jules, did you go and ask for work at Deepwell Tyre and Mechanics today?'

'No. Is there a position available?'

'Not that I know of—'

'Thanks for the help, then,' she replied sarcastically.

'Never mind. It was just an idea I had, that's all.' I wondered if Becker had been wearing that t-shirt for any particular reason. What if it meant something? I needed to find out if he had connections with that business.

Or perhaps it meant nothing at all.

CHAPTER TWENTY

Half an hour later, Jules and I had downed another beer each, and I had something more substantial on my mind. I reached for the tequila and cointreau. Why did Sayed and I have spirits in our home, I hear you asking. They were left over from the party we had to celebrate buying the property years earlier. That was probably the last time I'd taken a drink, and now I was getting back on the horse—for better or for worse.

'Holy shit! Watch out!' Jules called after me, sounding decidedly Australian. She always sounded more Aussie when she drank.

I lined the bottles up on the kitchen bench and hoped to hell we had lime. If not I'd have to go downstairs and get some from The Brew. Very professional, Dor. *Totes profesh.*

Reaching into the pantry, I pulled out one of those cheap plastic squeezy bottles filled with lime juice. 'Margarita?' I yelled out to Jules, though it turned out she was quite close by. Then I grabbed two glasses without waiting for her reply.

'Sure,' she said. The glasses were mini tumblers, not margarita glasses. Why would I own the proper glasses, after all? I threw caution to the wind by pouring the tequila and cointreau straight from the bottles. At times like these, one doesn't measure out liquor, I told myself.

I was letting my hair down and looking to forget. I gave the drinks a short stir and took two thorough sips from my own. 'Now we're talking,' I bellowed, heading for the lounge with my hands full.

The next thing on my mind was music; it always was with some drink under my belt.

Heading for the CD cupboard, I spilled dashes of fragrant lime liquid onto the floorboards with each step. The CD collection—if you could call it that—was mostly Sayed's. Though a music fan as much as anyone, I never got around to deciding what music I wanted to own beyond the occasional song I downloaded onto my phone.

I chose Bob Marley's 'Legend' and proceeded to sing my way through the first verse of 'Is this love?' The sound of my voice might have scared away any nasty spirits, I thought, and laughed to myself. Then, Jules and I got to talking about mundane matters, like which home brand jar of olives had the best taste, and how annoying Lionel was for being such a male stereotype.

By the time the second song came on, I was getting unsteady; I wasn't used to liquor anymore. But I raised myself from the couch, set on making another margarita, while Jules opted to go back to Corona.

In the kitchen, I started singing again. I was not known for my extraordinary vocal ability. The music teacher in primary school had pointed me towards the extra-curricular maths group for good reason. I still had great maths skills.

'You're a Hermansen on a bender,' I heard Jules say from the lounge room. Ignoring her was the best idea, I told myself.

Bob was singing 'Get up, stand up' by the time I got back.

'Love Bob Marley!' I called out, much louder than I needed too.

'Yeah. Me too,' answered Jules with minimal conviction. 'Loud,' she added, pointing to her ears. She was wearing earrings with fine silver pieces that jingled lightly and got caught up in her swathes of curls.

Lowering my voice, I continued to sing along for the moment. Then I got up intent on dancing, nearly tipping my drink over in the process.

'Not very sturdy, are you?' I said to my glass as I caught and righted it. The fact that you'd be hard-pressed to find a sturdier glass for a margarita went straight over my head.

Doggie moved over to the corner of the room, out of my way.

Though it had remained moderately sore, the injury to my foot made little difference at that point. A few drinks had dulled the pain.

'Is this really how you want to deal with things?' Jules asked.

'You're one to talk. Hiding out there in your shack most of the time,' I said. 'Oh, God. I didn't mean that. I'm just really stressed.'

'Come on, Dora. What's going on with you?'

There I was at a repeat of the night before, but this time Jules already knew the most of it.

'Look, it's just ... I don't know,' I started, unsure of how much to say.

Her eyes pushed me on.

'Yesterday, at the cemetery ... I know it was silly to go there alone, but it was scary as fuck. So, you know, forgive me if I just want to relax and forget for a bit.'

Jules looked horrified. 'This is going too far. It needs to stop.'

'Yeah, but what am I supposed to do? There's no unsubscribe button for this shit.'

'There must be some way.'

I shrugged my shoulders violently. 'Like I said last night, maybe I'm losing it again?' I waited momentarily, hoping that Jules would get my gist. She said nothing. 'Going backwards with my PTSD. That's what I'm concerned about now.'

'I know. But it's not that, Dor. It's not.'

'How would you know that?' I desperately wanted to trust Jules' judgement on this. No one wanted to be losing it. 'I've got to consider everything. I owe that to Sayed, and to myself. To everyone, really. This is like living in a horror movie.' With that, I threw myself back onto the couch dramatically.

'No wonder you're getting blotto with all that. Especially after the Troy thing,' Jules said, shock at her own words shooting across her face.

'I know. I still can't understand why that old bitch started back up again out of nowhere.'

'Right,' Jules replied hastily. 'The situation with Mrs Sloper. Exactly.'

'I love you,' I said, grabbing a fistful of the couch and using it to drag myself back to sitting position.

'You too,' Jules reciprocated, reaching to rub my back rhythmically.

After a few minutes, and a couple more sips of my drink, I felt better. I jumped up to look through the CDs again. Having lost track of my politeness gland, I pulled faces at what I saw to be Sayed's sometimes questionable taste. 'No. No. Fuck, no.' I said. 'Yes!' I yelled.

I found the exact album that I didn't previously know I needed to hear; I was excited.

I placed the CD roughly into the draw of the player: Florence + the Machine's 'Between Two Lungs'.

'Be careful with his CDs,' said Jules. 'Good choice, though.'

Turning to my best friend, I tried to engage her in the joy of finding the perfect song for that particular moment. 'Hurricane drunk,' I said, pointing to the CD player and emphasising the word drunk.

'What are you? Fifteen years old, Dor?' Of course, the only connection between the song and our current situation was that I was blind.

Pressing on, I began spinning around with my legs wide apart.

'Dora, shouldn't you give your foot a break? Stick it up on the coffee table.' Jules was attempting to 'mum' me, just like Lionel, Wren and I used to do to each other when we were growing up.

But I didn't get mired in thinking about the past, our mother's death, or missing Wren—who none of us had heard from in four months. The alcohol had reduced my sensitivity to pretty much every aspect of my life. Perfect.

I slowed during a gap in the music, handling my glass roughly as I took a sip that left a dribble of sweet liquid on my top.

'Oops,' I said.

'Mmm,' murmured Jules.

Already moving on to another CD, I didn't care that Jules sought to party-poop me. From a Nineties Hits CD, I chose 'I've Got the Power' by Snap and turned the volume way up.

'Turn it down,' yelled Jules, but I noticed she was laughing and struggling to hide the fact. The damage was done. It was all the encouragement I needed.

Breaking into dance again, I maintained eye contact with her.

'Christ, you move like a fuckin' cracker,' she said, shaking her head. Then she jumped up to join me.

We'd been dancing for a few minutes when, mid-jump and still ignoring my poor foot, I burped loudly. Jules glanced at me, but we kept going.

An injured foot was the least of my cares at that point. I just needed a break. 'I'm gonna get myself one more drink,' I slurred, holding up one finger … or two.

'Fine,' she said. 'For fuck's sake, make it your last, though. Here, let me help you.' Jules grabbed my glass, and I followed her. 'You cannot hold your liquor, can you? Sometimes I wonder if you're really a Hermansen.'

'Well, I'm kind of a Bousaid now,' I said. 'Even if I didn't take the name. And I know they can't hold their liquor.' I burped again.

'You're disgusting.'

'Yes,' I admitted.

I set to opening the flip lid on the lime juice bottle. It was harder than it looked. Jules took care, pouring out the tequila and cointreau for me and pretending she didn't notice me arguing with the lime juice.

Still standing at the kitchen counter, I took a small sip of my drink.

'Holy fuck, that is better than the last one,' I announced.

'Here, I'll carry it,' said Jules. Turning for the lounge, she stopped suddenly. 'Jesus. Dor. Quick!'

Doggie was in a steady position, growling at the window—the middle window. It was open again.

Once Doggie sensed us there, focussed on what he saw, he let fly. He began barking viciously until I patted his neck and led him back by his collar.

'Did you hear anything?' Jules asked.

I shook my head. 'Not a thing.'

'I heard it scraping. Fuck, Dora. It's creepy. This isn't right.'

'You heard it open? Well, that's good news for me, I guess.'

'Have you lost it?'

'No need to be a bitch. Maybe I am crazy, but I'm not so cray-cray that my mind had made this up. For me, that's a win.'

'Well, sorry, but Jesus Christ, Dor. We have to call Lionel. Now.'

'Why? Has he taken up ghostbusting?' I paused and looked at Jules while still holding my hand to Doggie, enough to prevent him from starting back up again.

Suddenly I felt bad for Jules. Her face had lost its colour, and she was wringing her hands nervously. For me, it was merely more of the ongoing clusterfuck. Plus, I was intoxicated, and that always softened the blows.

It was a relief to know for sure that no person had come into my home and forced open the window. Clearly, I just had to get more used to the weird paranormal phenomena that was now a part of my life. I got Jules to hold the window while I looked down into the alley, but there was nothing to see there. Darkness and dirt.

'No, we defo have to get Lionel involved in this. Plus, I've got to tell you something. Please don't be angry,' said Jules.

Laughing while I steadied myself on the wall, I said, 'People only say that if they have news that's likely to make someone angry.'

'This is serious, Dor. Troy's dead.'

'Huh? Really? What?'

'That prisoner who was bashed. You didn't see the news?'

'Jesus Christ!' I spat.

I thought for a moment. I *had* seen a headline in the paper.

CHAPTER TWENTY-ONE

Seconds later, Jules' message sank in. Troy, my ex—the man who tried to kill me—was dead.

The newspaper, yes, I *had* seen it briefly. But the news that a Queensland prisoner had been murdered hadn't registered fully at the time. I had been scanning and my eyes had barely grazed the page before I turned over.

Then it occurred to me. 'How long have you known this?' I asked accusingly.

'For a few days.' She was looking at me, worried. For good reason too. How dare she keep something like this from me? 'I'm sorry. But you said you didn't want to talk about him anymore. You've said that a lot lately.'

'Yeah, but he's dead. That's a bit different, surely?' I took a shaky sip from my margarita. 'Who else knows?'

Jules looked uncertain.

'Who?' I demanded.

Jules' exterior crumbled right in front of me. 'All of us,' she admitted. 'Your Dad, Lionel—'

'Oh my God. Sayed?'

'Uh-huh,' said Jules.

There I was living with guilt about keeping things from Sayed when he was hiding something that big from me. Everyone knew that Troy was dead except for me. All of them. Leanne? Of course, she would have known. How did she manage to keep that golden nugget hidden from me?

It was as though the whole town was in on it. Feeling sorry for myself, I became aware that Jules was sending a text—Lionel, I supposed. Good. There were a few things I wanted to say to him. Had Lionel known on Monday when he was here at the apartment for dinner with Cloud and Leila? Or on Saturday when the incident occurred in The Brew?

A sickness pervaded my stomach. Was I missing something? The fact that I was the only one left in the dark made me feel sick. My trust was snap, snap, snapping like a fraying rope. But there was more to it. My gut squeezed in on itself, putting me on edge.

I should have been grateful that he'd died, or at the very least neutral. But instead, I had misgivings. I couldn't settle in my thoughts or my skin, trying to grasp why I was so discomforted.

A few minutes later, the front door opened noisily. John and Sayed came down the hall, accompanied by Lionel. So, Jules had messaged everyone. The moment I saw them, I flipped from upset to positively fuming. 'For God's sake, why wouldn't you tell me that he'd died? You really believed I wouldn't want to discuss that? What the hell, people?'

'Oooh, shit. I'm so sorry,' said Sayed, looking like he might disappear into himself.

'Oh shit is right,' I repeated back to Sayed smartly. But then I had to sit down because I was unsteady on my feet. My face felt red with anger, not to mention the embarrassment of feeling like the last to discover information that everyone else was a party to. As I looked up to examine the faces, not one of them said anything about Troy, or my advanced state of inebriation.

So, I continued.

'You,' I scolded Lionel.' You're a police officer. Shouldn't you have been honest with me? And you?' My eyes turned to John. He wasn't a part of this, but I wasn't going to let him off the hook. He frowned; John wasn't much for confrontation. 'Did you know when you came in to deliver at The Brew the last couple of mornings?'

John nodded slowly, looking slightly mystified.

It was Lionel who spoke next. 'Look, Dora, you've told us time and time again that you don't want to revisit all this. You border on neurotic half the time, so we took you on your word to help you.'

Sayed's head dropped, while Jules gave Lionel a solid push.

'You did not just say that? Blaming your dishonesty on me? Rubbish! You're an arse, Lionel, and I was always going to find out. You can't have believed it would remain a secret. In Deepwell? Huh!'

'No. We weren't considering the long-term. Just trying to put it off a bit. It seemed helpful, what with the way he died, but—'

'This was my way of thinking,' stated Sayed, sitting down next to me. 'Life was already difficult. With everything that happened this week, I didn't want to make things worse. And Lionel's right. You've said numerous times that you don't want to talk about Troy.'

'And you thought that, with Mrs Sloper starting back up, that still stood?'

'Admittedly, we've been conflicted—Lionel, Jules and I. Very conflicted. I mean, of course, Dora, we're as scared as you. Especially the more you told us about what was happening. The physical assaults … I'm out of my mind with worry.'

John took a step back; he was looking a lot more confused than he had been previously.

Hold on. I didn't tell Sayed I'd been attacked. That meant Jules had told him behind my back.

Then, a ten-tonne weight seemed to fall on me. I realised what it was I hadn't grasped before. If Troy was dead, then…

'It could be him,' I said quietly, struggling to get up off the couch. 'All the supernatural stuff that's been happening lately. It could be him,' I screamed.

John was as close a friend to our family as any in Deepwell. We'd known him since primary school. But despite being

Sayed's best friend in the world, we had never let him in on my little secret. Now—whether through drunkenness, sheer thoughtlessness, or just no longer giving a toss—I'd gone and let the cat out of the proverbial bag. Either I had to enlighten John or, the only other option was to write it off as part of my crazy. Great.

'Well, now you know, John. If you thought I was weird before, welcome to your new reality,' I told him, making the decision.

John turned to Sayed. 'Mate?'

'Dora sees …' Sayed began.

'The dead. I see ghosts.' I filled the gap.

'You're not serious?' he said, opening his arms as though pleading for a more acceptable explanation.

'Dor's dead serious,' Jules said to John.

'As a heart attack,' I added with a hiccup.

'It's true,' Sayed began. 'It started after Troy. We don't know why, or how.'

The drinks imbibed earlier helped me to take the moment by the horns. However, I still felt the nausea I'd had in the moments leading to my realisation. Troy was dead. And—worse—his spirit could be hanging around. I shivered. But I didn't have time for feeling ill.

'Look, this seems really bad,' I said to everyone. Sayed rubbed my arms, assuming I was cold. 'The things that have been happening lately. You have no idea. Well, Sayed, you might, since obviously you and Jules have been talking behind my back.'

Sayed looked sheepish. Given my own indiscretions, I should have been more understanding, more forgiving. Sayed wasn't attempting to be duplicitous. He and Jules were simply concerned for me. I had kept things from him for the same reason.

'You should have told me, that's all,' I softened. 'Like I should have confided in you. I could be in real danger if it's Troy rather than Becker. It's a whole different ball game.'

'She's right,' agreed Lionel. 'If Troy was able to come back—'

'Or stay on,' I jumped in.

'Stay on,' Lionel accepted my correction with a frown in my direction. 'Then Dora may be in big trouble. This could be serious. We should have told her.'

John, ashen faced, dropped to the couch opposite me. I tapped my hand lightly on his leg in an offer of support. Poor John. He was sure getting more than he bargained for on that balmy Wednesday.

My addled mind had been chugging like an old computer since Jules told me about Troy. 'That's why she came into The Brew. Oh my God.'

They knew I was talking about Mrs Sloper. The thought of her—and the number of drinks I'd had that night—brought up a small amount of my stomach contents. I managed to control it before I heaved all over the floor.

'Water?' suggested Jules, her face contorting in disgust.

I began to retch. Sayed funnelled me to the bathroom where I unloaded in between hysterical laughing. It wasn't that any of what had happened was particularly funny. It's just that sometimes, when the pressure built up, I laughed. It wasn't a reaction I was able to control.

With an empty stomach, clean face, and my mouth rinsed out, Sayed helped me to bed.

'Where is everyone?' I asked.

'They've gone home. Except for Jules. She'll sleep on the couch in case we need her.'

'I'm going to be alight,' I said.

'Yes, you will be *alight*,' he copied my mistake, smiling at me.

'I mean, in life … with what happened.'

'I know. You will be.'

'Are you upset with me?'

'I'm upset about it all,' he said.

'I was mean. A mean bitch.'

'But right. We were idiots trying to keep this from you. You were going to find out sooner or later anyway. And you should have known for your own protection. I don't know what we were thinking. But you should have been honest with me, too.'

'Mmm. That was stoopid. I'm going to go to sleep now, but will you—'

'Keep you safe? Yup. I think sleep's best for now,' he agreed as he drew the covers and moved the pillows into place.

And as my head hit the pillow, I felt nothing. Nothing at all.

CHAPTER TWENTY-TWO

I had a shabby awakening and had no one to blame but myself. There was no point downplaying it, of course. My head throbbed, and my stomach remained dicey. Despite this, I determined not to let the day get away on me. Jules had left early so I rang her to apologise for my piss-poor behaviour while drunk—two wrongs don't make a right and all that—then I jumped in the shower. Troy was never far from my thoughts. The possibility that I may not have finished with him was impossible to push aside.

By late afternoon in The Brew, as patrons thinned, I was brighter. Sayed and I began our closing routine.

'I'm going up in the ceiling after work,' Sayed told me while serving our last customers. 'Will you give me a hand?'

'Let's not,' I replied. It was the last thing I wanted to do. The whole idea seemed wrong. Why would we want to be up there in the heat and dark after everything that had happened the night before? Over the previous week?

'We need to check it out, Dor. It won't take long. Might as well get it over with.'

I took a deep breath, then exhaled. 'Looks like we're checking the ceiling cavity after close, then.'

Sayed was right, of course. There had been an odour again that morning, so it was impossible to ignore at that point. Plus, we needed to know … if it was of this world … or not.

What started as a burnt smell had become rotten. In the courtyard that day I detected something bordering on fetid. The scent was changing, morphing, and I wasn't a fan. The only reason I noticed was that, feeling overcome during my shift that morning, I had gone outside for fresh air. Some chance.

The mission for the day was to keep busy. But Troy's murder festered in my mind, putting me off my game. When I messed up Leanne's change, and when a cup slipped from my hand, splattering a cappuccino to the floor, he was in my head. Even if he wasn't really, Troy's presence in my blood and bones had been reactivated. I'd rushed outside on the verge of tears. Then, standing by the pipes leading to the upstairs plumbing, the air had turned foul. Like we didn't have enough to worry about, I thought bitterly.

So, I supposed it had been a good idea to do the plumbing check. Next stop the ceiling cavity. But what would come after that? Calling in a priest?

Even after I took time out, my thoughts focussed back onto Troy. Memories of more than just *that* night. I remembered the good times as well, though I railed against doing so. Intimate moments. Like the time we were gardening and, with my hands covered in soil, he'd pushed my hair back gently. His skin, warm beneath a light cotton sheet in the darkness. Sweat and love before the determined hatred threatened our relationship. It hurt me almost as much to remember the affection as it did to know his final act as my boyfriend was placing his hands around my neck and applying pressure in an attempt to cut off life-giving air.

'Couldn't have happened to a more deserving person,' I muttered to myself at least once during the lunch rush while thinking on his murder. Though in the end, I wasn't *really* sure how I felt about anything, let alone Troy's murder by another prisoner. I did wonder how it had occurred, though knowing may not help.

A case could be made that Troy's death was no loss to the community. Not everyone in Deepwell would agree, of course. Mrs Sloper had her supporters, and they came into The Brew from time to time, some regularly.

One of the great things about running a café was that I had to rise above disturbances in my psyche to provide a service for people. There was no wallowing around in depression and fear— not for too long, anyway.

I learned quite a bit about what Sloper's posse thought of me from overheard conversations and occasional slips from my own family and friends. Usually, those close to me didn't offer this information without trepidation, and rightly so.

In the end, it wasn't me to call for death justice. I would never have supported capital punishment. Queensland abolished it in the early 1900s and I still believed that was the correct decision. What would I be like to wish for Troy's death? How would I frame it? As karmic retribution? Universal penance, perhaps? Troy was sentenced to ten years of imprisonment. A state-sanctioned price, and though I wanted him out of my life for good, never once did I wish for his death.

So, sure, it seemed a fitting end, but I never meant for him to be murdered. I googled the news that morning on my mobile. Bashed by another inmate, the *Courier-Mail* said. I imagined swollen, bruised skin. I saw the blood, heard the alarm go off. What did you do, Troy? The prison was 'looking into it', but as yet there were no charges.

I didn't want to sit around feeling sorry for Troy, or myself. In some respects, there had been an end to a problematic instalment in my life. What happened was wrong, but Troy gave up his right to have me advocate on his behalf when he nearly strangled me to death.

I felt even less for Troy when I considered the fact that he would have killed me if the neighbour hadn't turned his television down during the ads. Had he been watching The Block, too? How odd if the advertisement break between a reality show had saved my life.

Fuck Troy, I decided. Someone else could feel bad about his death. Not me.

I had gone back inside The Brew that morning and told Sayed quietly about the smell from the courtyard. Next stop, our ceiling cavity.

Chapter Twenty-Three

After closing The Brew that afternoon, Sayed and I carried a ladder up the back stairs, bumping it into peeling balusters as we went. It was no display home, so we weren't too worried.

Inside, I trawled through drawers looking for batteries for the torch. Fortunately, I found two that fit, though I couldn't be sure how old they were. I'd scoffed at the price of a combined wind-up and solar torch I'd seen in Noosa a few months earlier, but at that moment, I was kicking myself for not having purchased one.

'If I'm not out in ten minutes, call for help,' Sayed chirped. Then he gave me a bear hug and climbed the ladder towards the hatch. Who was he kidding? *Jeez*. Sayed was acting as though everything was completely normal. As though our lives weren't going topsy-turvy, and Troy hadn't just been murdered. Was he behaving like that for my benefit or his own?

'Keep me up-to-date at all times, Mister,' I barked at him.

Holding tight to the ladder, I would make sure a fall wasn't added to the list of current messes. Watching him, I felt overpowering love for the man. What would I do without him?

Sayed squeezed his muscular body through the hatch. It would have been easier for me to go in, but Sayed never considered that and, though I very much wished that he didn't have to do it, even more so I was relieved that I didn't.

On seeing Sayed's legs disappear into the ceiling space, I was suddenly desperate to abort the plan. The dark, cramped nature of a ceiling always gave me the creeps.

'Wait,' I called out. 'What if we ask a tradesman to come and take a squiz? They do it all the time.'

'It'll only take a minute. It's not worth a tradie visit. They'll charge us a hundred bucks just to look.'

'Well, I guess we could wait until someone else is here. Back-up, you know. Should've called Lionel or John over.'

There was no response for a long while. Jiggling nervously on the spot, I chewed at the inside of my cheek. Finally, he called out, 'I can't smell anything nasty.'

'That's good, I guess.' I gave up trying to put the process off. This was happening whether I thought it was a safe idea or not. 'Just be careful. Can you see anything?'

'Not much.'

'Describe what you *can* see,' I urged him, drumming my fingers on one of the ladder's steps.

'Dust and a bit more dust. It's cane trash. It even works its way in up here. I'll be covered in it.'

One of the perils of living in an area that had been sugarcane central was the black soot that settled into every crevice.

'Anything that *isn't* cane trash?' I wondered if I sounded a bit snippy, but it was just stress.

'Nope. It's dark down the back, though. Light's not strong enough. I'll have to go in further.'

'Fucking torch,' I said under my breath.

Looking down at Doggie sitting expectantly by my side, I felt sorry for him. A dog would have no idea of why I seemed stressed. At least, I had to assume he didn't. Giving his head a pat, I listened to Sayed manoeuvring himself on one of the joists.

From time to time, Sayed called out a report. 'Nothing' or 'No smell.' At one point he said, 'There have definitely been rats up here at some point, but it looks fine now.'

Eventually, I could tell from his sounds that he was approaching the furthest reaches, towards the back. My heart quickened.

'Still nothing? You'd have smelled it by now if there was something dead up there.' I waited for a reply.

No reply.

'Sayed?'

Further waiting.

'Come down,' I called firmly.

'Hold on. I just want to check this last section,' Sayed yelled. I was relieved to hear his voice, even though it sounded distant. Due to the reverberation within the enclosed cavity, I supposed. That set my nerves further on edge.

There was a small noise from the front.

'Have you checked the front yet?'

'Yeah. Nothing there.'

'Pretty sure I just heard something.'

There it was again, and not an isolated sound that time. Like a collection of scrambling and thudding noises. As though Sayed was in two places at once. I could hear him crawling from one joist to another to move back towards the hatch. Yet the second set of sounds came from the opposite end of the ceiling, in the far corner.

It's the enclosed space playing tricks, that's all. Sound bouncing around, carrying here and there.

A deep rumble began beside me. Looking down, I noticed Doggie Brasco's hackles were raised. Long, grave growls emanated from him as he stared at the open hatch.

'Shush, Doggie,' I put a shaky finger to my lips. Doggie did as I asked, falling silent. Lucky. His obedience in shushing tended to be fifty-fifty.

Listening, I tipped my head so my ear was facing upwards towards the opening. I stayed as still as I could, my hand resting on Doggie, trying to keep his compliance.

The noise continued; whatever was making it did not sound small. At that moment I was dead sure that Sayed wasn't the only thing creeping around up there.

'Something's moving up the front,' I called out.

'I told you, I checked it. There was nothing there.'

Doggie started to growl again. Panic set in.

'Even Doggie knows there's something.'

'Let me look again.'

I kept my eye on the opening.

'Please come down. Now!' I said urgently.

That was enough for Doggie. He began whole-heartedly barking at the hatch.

'Alright. I'm on my way,' Sayed shouted.

I shushed Doggie again. With Sayed crawling back towards the opening, I climbed up the ladder to get my head through the opening. I needed to see for myself.

'Shine your torch towards the front,' I ordered.

The noise stopped when Sayed did. He scanned the cavity with the torchlight.

'See, there's nothing.' The light flickered briefly, and he tapped the torch a few times.

'Keep coming! Don't stop!'

'Bossy much, Dor?'

'Haven't you heard it?'

'You're scaring me, Dor.'

Sayed started crawling towards me as the sounds from the front started up again. Afraid to give my fear further power by asking Sayed, once again, if he heard something, I soon realised that he had, indeed, heard. Above me he seemed—finally—filled with urgency.

'Move, Dor. Move!' he yelled.

Practically jumping off the ladder, I heard a dull scraping and thudding from above. On top of that, there was the sound of Sayed scrambling quickly towards the hatch.

'Just get the fuck out!' I yelled, throwing nicety out the window.

'What the hell?' he exclaimed, and instead of continuing to move towards the hatch, he stopped again. The torchlight swayed from side to side as he scanned the ceiling cavity.

Then there was a rush of movement; whatever was up there began to move quickly. Was it moving towards me, down in the apartment? Or towards Sayed?

'Argh!' yelled Sayed as he launched himself across the beams towards the only exit from the confined space above.

Doggie's barking was frantic and out of control. His dog breath filled up the house as Sayed spilled headfirst out of the hole and tumbled towards the floor. The top half of his body hit the back of the couch, which thankfully was soft along the back edge. But his legs hit the floor. The collision was stupendous, sending a shudder through the whole apartment. A decorative plate, given to us as a wedding gift by Sayed's relatives overseas, shattered on the ground.

At the same moment that Sayed hit the ground, there was a scraping sound from the window. It lifted a foot, maybe two, and then slammed shut. We all needed to be out of the apartment immediately—I knew that. But Sayed was on the floor making desperate choking sounds and keeping an eye on the hatch, afraid of what might appear. Using his feet, he started to push himself along the floor so that he no longer lay directly underneath the opening.

Doggie ran to the window and continued his incessant barking. I stole a last look at the ceiling's opening, through which I could see the light from Sayed's torch, dropped in those last moments, lolling from side to side.

Then I went closer to the window which was now lowered shut. Sayed grasped for me, but I passed him, leaving his fingers to clutch air. My blood pressure dropped with each step because I suddenly knew what had happened. Even from a distance, I recognised her. But when I got to the window and saw Cleo's face, eyes bulging from the pressure of the window on her neck … it was too much to bear.

A scream came from me. A wail of pain. It couldn't be. Not Cleo.

'Sayed, get up now. We're getting out,' I yelled.

I tried lifting the window, and it raised smoothly enough. I took Cleo's bloodstained body from the sill and rested her in the crook of my arm. Sayed was standing by that point, hunched by the side table.

'Oh no,' he said as he noticed what I was holding. 'No.' His eyes became watery.

'We need to get out. Now,' I said.

Then the smell came. Like a belch from hell, it poured out of the open ceiling, filling the house in seconds.

Doggie's barking was silenced as the smell overcame him.

It was sickening and caused Sayed's stomach to begin convulsing. The heaving was obviously agony for him, after the fall. I was starting to feel sick, too.

Almost impossible to describe, I'd have done anything to avoid taking another breath of that putrid air. With Sayed's arm draped around my shoulders, and still holding Cleo in the other arm, we made our way down the hall.

Doggie hadn't waited for us. He was already scratching at the front door. By the time Sayed and I reached the hall's halfway point, I saw Doggie lower his head to take whatever fresh air he could from the centimetre gap underneath. Smart boy.

We were almost there when my stomach gave out, its contents ejecting with considerable force onto the hall floor. Sayed, who generally had a more robust constitution, continued to retch—more so after I lost my battle. He cried out in pain and clutched his stomach as we navigated the clean patches of floor to get to the door.

Sayed gripped the handle and pulled it towards us, but it was as though someone was outside, holding the door firmly shut to keep us in. We started to panic again—we were trapped, after all—but after ten seconds, Sayed managed to pull the door open forty-five degrees; whatever pressure had been working against us released. The door flew open suddenly, colliding with the wall.

Like a pressure valve had been opened, a strong breeze whistled down the hall. But it wasn't from outside. The air came from *inside* the apartment, and it carried the fetid stench—and us—to the outside.

CHAPTER TWENTY-FOUR

In the courtyard, I placed Cleo's body, near to resting in two pieces, on the edge of a garden bed. Sayed settled in one of the outdoor chairs. He flopped down easily, remaining silent in green-tinged pallor.

'Hon?' I asked.

Nothing.

'Sayed?'

'Mm?' he replied.

Were any thoughts inside his head at all, I wondered. Blank eyes and minimal movement, he had the appearance of an empty vessel.

'We need to get you some ice. A drink of water, too. Stay here. Don't move.'

As I headed for the back door of The Brew, I wondered if I should be leaving Sayed alone. After what happened upstairs, and the way he seemed sitting there, all blank and strange. Quickly glancing back, I noticed his knuckles were white from the death grip he kept on the chair's arm.

My eyes darted back and forth between Sayed and the door to our apartment. Our new reality was strange and frightening. We weren't only scared out of our wits; we had been physically harmed.

Poor Cleo. The window certainly hadn't opened by accident, but had Cleo's positioning in the windowsill been a matter of chance? Or was it part of some hideous plan? I thought of Troy kicking her that dark night.

No time for a breakdown. There were things to take care of and nothing I could do for Cleo anyway. Her trajectory was final. Sayed, on the other hand, needed my support. Taking the keys for The Brew from my back pocket, I unlocked the door and headed for the kitchen. Turning on the tap, I left it to run momentarily because in summer the cold tap ran piping hot at first. Then I grabbed two glasses. The pipes groaned, which was normal. At least something was.

To say that I was shaken by the events upstairs didn't really cut it. I kept checking behind me—above even—and my hands had a tremor. But I was more concerned about Sayed. What had he seen up there in the ceiling cavity?

Outside, Sayed remained seated on the patio chair. I wasn't sure he'd moved even a centimetre in the time I'd been inside. He was muttering something to himself, though, and his voice was weak. As I approached, he offered me a feeble smile that barely touched his laugh lines. When I got close, I realised he was reciting a prayer. Some people, by character or experience, feel the call of religion more than others. Since I had found good and bad people ascribing to most belief systems, I would hardly deny him the benefit of his rituals now. In fact, I found myself envying them.

'You look better,' I exaggerated. 'Here, have a sip.' I passed him the glass and placed a bag of ice against his stomach, moving his hand to hold it in place.

The situation was too big for me. Too frightening. I needed help, so I called Lionel.

As soon as the call connected, I said quietly and calmly, 'I need help. Right now.'

'What is it?'

'Something happened at the apartment. Sayed and I … we …' How do you explain something like this?

'You need the police?'

'No police. We need more than that. You have to bring Cloud too. I'm scared. We can't go back inside the apartment,' I said, my voice beginning to break.

'It's okay. Stay calm. Where are you now?'

'The courtyard. I've got Sayed and Doggie here. But, Cleo, she ...' I began to cry, and Sayed showed his first signs of deeper life when he reached up to touch my hand in response to my pain. My mouth quivered.

Lionel had paused to give me time to right myself, but now he demanded, 'What about Cleo?'

'She's dead, Lionel. It's bad. Real bad. Please come.'

'Jesus Christ. What happened?'

'Not now. Just come.'

'I'm on my way, Dor.'

'Don't come without Cloud. Please hurry,' I added.

Sayed and I sat waiting, side-by-side, in silence. Doggie lay at our feet, his blue-grey chest heaving slower with each minute. I glanced at Sayed's face now and then and was relieved to see his colour restoring. His breathing settled to a normal rhythm, as did mine.

Upstairs, all was quiet. The door to our apartment was open, but we saw nothing from the hall, nor heard anything. The smell, which initially had been quite strong even in the courtyard, had dissipated.

The moments of calm brought me some clarity and determination. I wanted my questions answered. I wanted our home back. I demanded to know what had happened to poor Cleo, and I demanded justice. I was not going to take this lying down. I felt angry, and I was going to fix it.

'How are you feeling now?' I asked Sayed.

'Stomach's better. Yours?'

'Yeah, fine. Quite the chunder, wasn't it?' I said, trying to lighten things any way that I could. Then, in a serious tone, I told him, 'I need to know what you saw.'

'Nothing,' he shot at me.

A long sigh escaped me. 'I get it. You don't want to talk about it. But you know that's not an option. Right?'

'Look. There was something. But I don't know what. What did *you* see?' He seemed exasperated.

'Couldn't see anything, really. But I heard it,' I said.

'Well, there you go, then.'

'Touché,' I said, pausing for a moment. Though I felt terrible for Sayed, I had to keep pressing. Whatever details he held had to be brought to light.

'Was it a possum?' I asked, knowing full well that it was not a possum.

'Sure,' he scoffed.

'Well, what else could end up in the roof? It wasn't rats. Too solid to be even a whole family of rats. I heard it moving. It was heavy.' Then I decided to voice my real feelings. 'It sounded like another person.'

'Fuck, Dora. Stop. Bloody ridiculous.'

Reaching across him, I rubbed his forearm. 'You know I can't stop. We have to get to the bottom of it. For Cleo. For all of us.'

'God knows what it was, okay? Not me.' He seemed fragile. Like he may lash out if I pushed further. It wasn't like him.

Sayed was squeezing Doggie's hair between his fingers, then combing his hand through it. Doggie looked up at him with love in his eyes. Amazing how he seemed to have moved on.

'Look, I couldn't see it. Whatever was there, it wasn't to be seen.' Sayed tightened his mouth and turned away from me.

'But you know something *was* there?'

'Yes,' he replied weakly.

'Sayed, how did you know it was something if you couldn't see it? And you didn't hear it like I did?'

'I just knew.'

Staring at him, I wondered how best to press on. Sayed never wanted to talk about it again. That I could see. But we had a life together. This was our home. What were we going to do? Go back upstairs and hope it never happened again? Wait for

Doggie to be killed next time? Or walk away, leaving our apartment, and The Brew, to the ravages of time, like the publican we bought it from had done? We had to be practical.

When he turned back, he started, 'I don't know how you do it …'

'Do what?'

'Well, it's obviously something … not of this world. It's one of your dead.'

'Well, it's never been like this before.' I felt angry with Sayed now. I thought he was blaming me somehow. Like I'd asked for this or something.

'I could feel it. Alright? Now I've said it. Something …' He seemed as though he was about to overflow. Like the information he'd kept locked up in his head would spill right out of him. 'It kept coming, Dor. I knew it was coming. For me. I was moving as fast as I could, but fuck, I was scared. Do you think it hurt Cleo because it couldn't get me? I'm so sorry.' He dropped his head to his hands.

'Oh, no. No. You don't have to be sorry. I mean, me too. I could hear it, and I was scared too. For you, for all of us. We'll get to the bottom of this,' I told him. I was holding his hand now, trying to support and encourage him. Trying to stay strong about losing Cleo, and trying not to look over to the garden bed because to see her there would be too much.

He nodded, and the support must have helped him open up because he said, 'I did see something, too. You're right. But it wasn't a person or an animal. It was as though when I shone the torch on it, the air changed. It moved. As if I could see …' He was thinking, searching for the right word. 'Energy,' he said finally.

As soon as Sayed uttered the word, the hair on my body lifted like a horror cliché. I ran my hand along my arm feeling the hairs to be sure I didn't imagine it. Sayed noticed too, shock spreading across his face.

With that one word, I became afraid, right to my bones. A chill moved through my body which culminated in a sound like an exhale mixed with a whimper. Any other time I would have been embarrassed. But right then, I didn't care.

At that moment, I couldn't think beyond that one word. It scared me more than anything, although I didn't understand why.

That simple word: Energy.

CHAPTER TWENTY-FIVE

'Dora? Sayed?' Lionel was calling as he came around the corner with Cloud in tow.

'I've never been gladder to see you,' I said, my voice shaky. 'Thanks for coming, Cloud.'

'Okay, what's happened?' asked Lionel.

'It's something awful. Very, very bad,' I began, my eyes fighting back the tears. I proceeded to explain the whole frightening episode, from Sayed's experience in the ceiling cavity, to Cleo's death, to the smell that had almost knocked us out. Lionel's face continued to change as I spoke, until eventually his face was distorted, much like a wince—possibly a disbelieving one.

Cloud listened intently before asking me some questions. 'Was the cat's death part of what happened, or incidental?'

'Well, I'm wondering that myself,' I told her. 'But my gut tells me that it was linked.'

'Do you know who it was?' she asked me next.

'Troy. It's got to be,' I told her. 'Who else would be this evil?'

'Don't get me started,' said Cloud.

'And he never liked Cleo, either,' I added.

'Right. Of course,' said Cloud, as though she knew all about Troy. Perhaps Lionel had told her the full story.

Sayed had remained seated and, apart from a few nods and grunts to agree with things that were said, he didn't add much.

'You doing alright, mate?' Lionel asked Sayed.

'Yeah,' he said. 'I'm all right.'

'I'm going upstairs to take a look around,' announced Cloud.

'It's not that I mind,' I said. 'But it's dangerous. What can we do?'

'Oh no, I'll be fine. I've done this before.'

'I don't feel comfortable about it either,' chimed in Lionel. 'I'll go with you.'

Cloud turned then and very definitively told Lionel that he wouldn't be helping by going upstairs with her. 'I have things under control,' she told him. At that moment I saw a side to Cloud that I hadn't realised was lurking; there was a strength and a hardness that belied the hippy, beach babe look.

'I'll be back down in a few minutes,' she said, taking the first step up to the verandah.

Sayed raised himself from his chair, and the three of us stood there dumbly watching Cloud take each step—worried, but unsure of what to do. Despite my mind spinning with questions, the moments after Cloud's departure seemed to pass lazily, as though a slow motion switch had been flicked. I became aware of the cicadas starting up their call from the bushes now that night had fallen. It was still hot, and my mind turned to Cleo.

'I can't leave Cleo there. I have to do something with her.'

'We need to call the police, Dor,' said Sayed. 'This isn't right.'

'I *am* a fuckin' cop, mate,' barked Lionel.

'Right.'

'For God's sake, Lionel. I've just told you what he's been through. Have some compassion.'

Then I turned to Sayed. 'It's not possible to get the police involved in any official capacity, hon. You must know that.' I turned to Lionel. 'Can you imagine? Your cop friends would think we're all crazy. Probably already do.' Lionel shrugged in a sign of partial agreement.

I bent my knees a little and looked up into Sayed's face. He appeared scared, but a warmth was returning to his cheeks. 'They can't help us,' I said. 'But Lionel, he's here. Him and Cloud. They will help.'

'She's right, mate,' agreed Lionel. 'Cloud will help. I'm sure she will. Now, where are you going to bury Cleo?'

I sighed. There was so much to think about. 'I don't know,' I said, exasperated and teary again.

'How about we freeze her until you decide?' suggested Lionel. I flicked around to look at my brother, horrified … until I realised it was actually a practical and sensible idea. Now definitely wasn't the right time for rushing important decisions.

Sayed didn't look happy about the idea but conceded, 'Probably for the best. We can't put her in the freezer here, though.'

'You don't think a cat in the freezer of The Brew would be good for business?' Lionel tried to make light of the situation. Though Sayed chuckled, a large tear rolled down the side of his face at the same time. 'Help me wrap her, and I'll put her in my garage,' Lionel continued. 'I've got the beer fridge out there, and there's never much else in that freezer anyway. A few bits of meat. I can move those to the inside freezer to make room.'

'Thanks,' I said with a gulp.

Lionel gave me a pat on the back then called out to Cloud. 'You right up there?' The three of us turned to focus on the apartment above, now lit up brightly and shining into the night.

'Fine. It looks fine up here. I think it's okay,' she called back. 'You can come up when you're ready.'

'I'm not going to sleep there,' Sayed said to me quietly.

I felt the same way, so Sayed and I decided we would stay at Dad's for the night. With Lionel watching our backs, we went upstairs, cleaned up the hall, and packed a few things to tide us over.

Downstairs afterwards, Cloud explained that we had experienced a haunting, but she said everything felt normal again. She

137

didn't think we'd have any more trouble. In fact, she believed we *should* stay there, and that there was no need to go elsewhere for the night. But Sayed and I just couldn't do it. I felt the need to be as far away from our apartment as possible, and I knew that Sayed felt the same way. Cloud was sure made of sturdier material than us.

With our duffel bags packed for the first time since our honeymoon years earlier, we headed back downstairs. I wrapped Cleo's body in an old towel I'd brought down from the apartment. She seemed so innocent and frail, all limp on the purple towel. Then Lionel helped me wrap her a couple of times in an outer layer of plastic. Cloud and Lionel gave Sayed and I a little space then. We said a few silent words while holding hands. I cried for Cleo, and for myself, and Sayed cried along with me.

Cleo had been such a tiny kitten when I first brought her home as a high school senior; she'd fit into my hands when I cupped them. I had picked her out myself as a teen, from a neighbour's litter that had only two left. It had been a hard decision since my choice meant one kitten being left all by itself. I had thought that was so tragic. But Mum and Dad would never have let me take both kittens. I thought about Cleo's brother often over the years and wondered where he'd ended up. I hoped that his story had been as happy as Cleo's had … until the end. Cleo had brought me joy and love—and not just me either. The whole family had loved her. I would come home to find her curled up with Mum reading or watching Wren baking in the kitchen. Then Sayed came along and he, too, fell under Cleo's spell.

In fact, I associated Cleo with the beginning of our relationship. It was Cleo who gave me my first opportunity to talk to Sayed, when he had stopped to pat her as she sat there on Dad's brick fence. Sayed had been staying in Deepwell for a couple of months to work with a house painting crew while someone was on sick leave. I liked him immediately and it turned out he felt the same way.

In her younger years, Cleo had been quite the acrobat, always careful about her navigations around shelves and benches.

Later, she lost her edge; I suppose we all do eventually. Now, wrapped up in a neat package, it seemed unbelievable that her life could end this way.

With Cleo's bundle in my arms, I stood up and turned to Cloud. 'Do you think that Troy killed Cleo?'

'Oh, no,' said Cloud. 'Seems like it was just a coincidence.'

'Really, though? Because that window never opened until last night. And when he was alive, Troy tried to hurt Cleo.'

'Sounds like you want it to be that way, Dora. But you asked my opinion.'

'Right,' I said. I looked at Sayed, who it seemed also thought Cloud's comment was strange based on the funny look on his face. Lionel was already on his way to the car, so he hadn't heard it.

But my gut told me that the window, and Troy, and Cleo's death were all connected. He killed her. He murdered my Cleo.

CHAPTER TWENTY-SIX

'I'm glad you came over to stay with your ol' Dad.' Dad was grinning at me, oblivious to the lack of joy on my face. He walked beside me down the hallway, my duffel bag in his hand. Then he slowed his steps to offer Sayed a gentle slap on the back. 'Come on, mate. Let's get you inside and settled, hey?'

It was a friendly show of support based on the bare bones of the story. While Dad knew about Cleo—which I'd told him tearfully on the phone as we left our apartment—he didn't know the rest. 'There's a plumbing problem,' I'd added.

I imagine it was nice for Dad to have us there, even under those circumstances. That he was downplaying—some might even say ignoring—Cleo's death, was not unusual for Dad. He just processed things differently. Mum had passed away many years earlier and since then he'd remained in the family home alone. Though we knew that he missed her terribly, it never seemed to bother him, being there without her. Lionel, Wren, and I had found it difficult to return to the house for a couple of years afterwards, but for Dad's sake we made the effort. Eventually, we all adjusted to life without Mum, and since then Wren had returned for intermittent stints at home. Even Lionel had moved back in on his return from the Police Academy training in Brisbane. In fact, Lionel had lived there with Dad for a couple of years—long enough that the house Mum had kept so well began to look like a bachelor pad.

The Hermansens still gathered at the family home regularly but, despite that, I worried Dad got lonely at times. Dad had been due for retirement a year after Mum's passing, but he kept going to his job at the plant for several years after. My concern about how Dad would cope when he didn't have work to focus him, turned out to be misplaced. Eventually, he retired and the extra time he had was further put towards his love of vinyl records. He also started playing golf for the first time since his twenties. He'd become pretty keen, buying one of those electric golf carts which he kept at home and drove, quite literally, down the street to the club each morning for rounds.

We didn't mind hearing about his vinyl collection; music was a relatively universal human interest, after all. But once Dad started a golf monologue, we siblings would feign group suicide. Sayed would always pretend to be on Dad's side.

Being back in my childhood home, and being with Dad, was comforting. Sayed and I put our things away in the spare room and even placed our toothpaste and brushes in the bathroom. Then we sat down with Dad in the kitchen. I'd warned Sayed not to let Dad in on too much. I didn't want to worry him when there was nothing he could do to help. At the kitchen table, we sipped hot tea and made small talk—mostly about a pressing of Led Zeppelin III that Dad had managed to find in the local second-hand store that week.

I soon became aware that Sayed had gone quiet, sullen even. I tried to make up for it by animating more than I usually would. Twice I made mention of the fact that Sayed was exhausted. 'Long day,' I said. 'Working The Brew and then checking up in—' A knot caught in my throat as I almost said too much. I quickly changed my message. 'With everything, it's just been a big day. Not easy.' I needn't have bothered with excuses, though. Dad probably didn't notice, he was so focussed on telling us the details of his original album find.

'Do you want to get to bed?' I finally asked Sayed.

Sayed replied that he did and so we said our goodnights to Dad and headed for the bedroom. But near the door Sayed grabbed my arm tightly—too tightly—and told me, 'I'm going for ciggies.'

'Oh, honey,' I said, feeling immediate compassion. Sayed hadn't smoked for more than five years. 'Are you sure you don't want to sleep on it? Don't rush that decision, you know? You don't really want to go through giving up all over again.'

'Give me a break,' he said irritably. 'Back soon.'

'Okay.' I watched him retreat down the hall, a little shocked at his brusque message. I did think Sayed would regret it, but I'd said my piece. You can offer advice, but trying to control an adult is a fool's game that always backfires, even when it's 'for their own good'. Sayed was a grown man, and he deserved to make his own decisions. Besides that, I could understand his feelings. I wouldn't have minded a smoke, too.

After pulling on my pyjamas, I flopped down onto the bed in a star shape. I lay there for a few minutes, mulling over what had happened. I felt safe there, in the home I grew up in. The bed wasn't that soft—it was a mattress that had been in the family since the seventies—but a dirt floor would have welcomed me to sleep at that point.

***

I'm walking up the hill. I know exactly where I'm going. My thighs, strong and solid with muscle and movement, are taking the long strides without any trouble.

My feet are bare as I navigate the uneven ground. I can feel the wet soil, dark, almost red. Bunches of grasses grow around rocks in the clearings I pass. In the tree-covered sections, it's darker. No moonlight.

I stop and listen. I hear the low grunts of a possum nearby. I'm about halfway, I estimate. I'm walking up Deepwell Mountain.

There's a scrambling sound in the bushes next to me. I don't care to investigate. I need to reach the summit. My skirt is ripped, there are stains on the front. Is that blood?

It doesn't matter, though—the summit.

I set off again, my breathing rhythmic. My lungs working hard now.

A solid rock covered in moss stands in my path. I walk around it toward the west. Squeeze through, between the rock and some rough bushes, rubbing up against the moss. I'm almost there. I've almost made it.

Tearing forward, I push myself to my limits to make it to the top. I'm hot, my clothing is wet with my sweat now. Or is it blood? No, don't think about it—the summit.

Nearing the top now the vegetation thins out. The night sky opens up to me. Stars speckle the sky. The moon sits precisely where it should. Light spills onto the landscape, and I see the large rock. The rock I'm looking for, the one I'd made the journey for. Large, yet sitting flat on the earth.

I reach the rock. It's top is red, covered with red. And there lies Cleo's body. Fur and blood. It is blood. It must be, and I reach to touch the rock, but my hand touches grit. I rub my hand and turn it towards me to look. It's dirt. No blood, just the red soil that surrounds Deepwell. The red dirt from the farms. The red dirt from the verandah.

***

My eyes snapped open. The darkness was deep and penetrating. I fumbled around on the bedside table for my phone, eventually resting on it and flipping it over. It was 2:03 AM. I rolled over onto my side, realising where I was. At Dad's. No mountain. No hike. No Cleo.

I moved my other hand with a gentler touch on the bed, this time to feel for Sayed. My hand fell on nothing but space and cotton sheet.

I sat up and flicked the lamp on. I was alone.

I made my way quickly to the bathroom, though I knew already. Sayed wasn't there.

The kitchen was lit up, and there I found Lionel sitting with a cup between his hands.

'I'm really sorry, you know.' He looked up at me, worried.

I sat down across from him and reached out my hands to touch his.

'What is it?'

'I should have told you. We all should have … about Troy. We just really thought it seemed like the best idea to leave you out of it for as long as we could. You know? Then, the more time that passed, hours, days … it just seemed harder and harder to bring it up.'

'Hey,' I patted one of his hands to try and get his attention. 'I know. Honestly, I can see how you got there. I was pissed last night, so don't worry about what I said. Not now, anyway.' I rested back into the chair and took my hands back to my side of the table. 'You should have told me, but it's done now. And I should have told you about the problems I was having. It's fine, and anyway, I've got bigger fish to fry right now.'

'What happened at your place, Dor.' He shook his head. 'That's not fine. It's fuckin' scary, mate.'

I nodded slowly. 'It is.' I tipped my head slightly and listened, to see if there was anyone else up in the house 'Anyway, what are you doing here?'

'I just didn't feel comfortable at home. I wanted to be sure you were okay.'

'No Cloud?'

'Nah, she's at home. Hers.' Had something happened between them? I remembered Cloud the night before. She was a little odd. A weird one, like her mother.

'Okay.' I didn't have time to go deeper into Cloud and Lionel's issues. 'Well, we've got a new problem.'

Lionel nodded.

'Sayed's gone. He went to get cigarettes last night—'

'Sayed smokes?'

'No, Lionel. I mean, he hasn't for years, but apparently, he was going to take it up again last night. He left last night, and he hasn't come back.'

Lionel swung into action, cop style. Together we searched the house inside and out. Our car was in the drive exactly where we'd left it. Sayed had probably intended to walk to the local shop, or perhaps to the bottle-o.

Running back inside, I grabbed my phone to check for messages again. There were none, so I called Sayed's phone.

'He's not answering his phone,' I told Lionel. That's when I knew. What I had worried about since the moment I touched the bed and realised he wasn't there. With a punch in the gut, I told Lionel, 'He's gone to the apartment.'

'Why would he do that? He didn't want to stay there last night, so it doesn't make sense.'

'I know, but I've got a terrible feeling. Please call Cloud … and Leila. Get them to the apartment as soon as you can.'

'Okay. You going now?'

'I have to.'

'I'll be right behind you. Be careful, Dor. And Dor?' he raised his voice. 'Don't go inside.'

I was already running out of the door with my keys and phone in my hand. 'Leave a note for Dad,' I yelled. 'And hurry.'

CHAPTER TWENTY-SEVEN

The main road was deathly quiet; there were no other cars on the short drive from Dad's house to The Brew. No light emanated from homes along the way—there were only streetlights, the moon, and my own headlights. Until I approached the intersection by The Brew, that is. Then, I saw the light coming from my apartment.

I pulled up around the back, my tyres screeching a little on the turn into the carport. I was afraid for Sayed. There was no reason for him to return there. Alone, in the middle of the night. No good reason, anyway.

I wished that Lionel was there already, to support me. Should I wait for him? No. I had to go in. Anything could be happening inside the apartment, and I decided that was as good a reason to go in as to wait. Sayed was up there alone ... and that was the best-case scenario. The reality was that he probably wasn't alone. Who—or what—Sayed might be with was the problem.

Why would he return here after what had happened the night before? What drew him back? Lionel was right that it made no sense.

My decision was made. I had to go in. Sayed may need help, and I was the cavalry.

When I got out of the car, the air was cool compared to our usual daytime temperatures. Come to think of it, it was even cooler in comparison to the typical December evening temperatures. The temperature always drops a little in the few hours that lead up to dawn, I told myself.

I approached the back steps, and a chill crept over my body.

My intention was to move as silently as possible until I could assess the situation. Then I could decide on an action. I took my first slow step. My muscles came to life as I placed my foot on the steps, skipping one each time. Adrenaline was pumping through my body. My muscles felt hard and worked fast. I could feel my body like never before, as though I was controlling every action. I remembered the dream: Cleo. The mountain. The blood. No, it wasn't blood at all. It was the dirt — Deepwell's red soil.

Despite my slow, steady pace, a few of the steps squeaked. Nearing the top, I couldn't hear much at all. The front door—always a misnomer being located around the back—was wide open. Light streamed down the hallway, odd shadows were playing on the timber floor, the red dirt stain appeared patchy as always. I stood a little to the side, poked my head around the frame and listened. Nothing.

I called out, 'Sayed.'

I waited, but still heard very little: an occasional creak—typical for an old timber structure—and insect sounds from outside in the dark. Wait, was that a groan?

'Honey? Sayed?' I called, a little louder this time.

There was no answer. I had to go in. My decision felt as horrific as it did inevitable. If Sayed was injured or stuck, I had to help him. I wouldn't be able to live with myself otherwise.

I scanned the courtyard downstairs, then I stopped and listened for any sound that might suggest Lionel was almost there, that maybe I wouldn't be alone in this horror show. There was nothing but crickets.

The first step inside the apartment was the hardest. After that, I felt like my choice had been made. It was a case of following through on what was already in progress.

I walked slowly and softly down the hall, checking the door to the unused accommodation wing as I passed. It was located about halfway down the hall, and it was closed, but not locked: precisely as we usually kept it. I stole a quick look inside the wing's hallway, but nothing looked out of place there, so I shut the door and continued.

As I approached the wide opening into the lounge, my focus was drawn to the floor. Detritus was strewn across the floorboards and, as I turned into the lounge, I saw an even worse picture. Books open, their pages bent and torn, CDs and cases smashed onto the ground. A potted plant that we had barely managed to keep alive indoors was lying sideways on the floor, its soil spread across much of the room.

I took a deep breath. 'Sayed? Where are you?'

From the other side of the lounge, I heard someone else's breath. Heavy breathing that put me further on edge.

'Did you do this, Sayed? Who did this?' I called out loudly.

There was a grunting noise. It was short, but I heard it nonetheless. I couldn't tell where it came from, but I spun around quickly, trying to catch the owner of the sounds. There was no one there. I moved slowly through the lounge, finding that no one was on the other side of the lounge suite, despite what I thought I'd heard.

I poked my head into the kitchen. No one. I went in, and I opened each cupboard, checking inside while remaining as far back from the cupboards as I could. There was nothing extraordinary inside the kitchen cabinets, and I realised nothing had been touched. That room looked exactly as I'd left it. The lounge was the only ransacked room.

Back through the lounge, I started for the bedroom. That's when I saw it, and the hair on my body felt electrified. My breath was stolen momentarily from my lungs as my heart sped out of control. I looked up at the hatch. It was open again.

There was no ladder or piece of furniture underneath that might have helped anyone to climb up there. The couch was a full metre away.

I let out a cry and took a few steps backwards. 'Sayed? Are you up there?'

He wouldn't have gone back up there, would he? He had to be in the bedroom, surely. I waited and heard nothing beyond the same, deep breath. I started doubting myself in that moment; maybe it was my own breath ...

'Sayed? Answer me, damn it!'

Was the ceiling hatch open when I came in? I thought back. I'd been concentrating on the floor, the mess. It probably was open when I walked in. I felt sickened, realising I'd most likely walked right underneath it without knowing.

I walked forward a metre, still keeping my distance from the opening. 'Sayed!' I called angrily.

Someone moved overhead. Like they were crossing from one beam to another.

'Fucking answer me, Sayed!' I yelled. My lip quivered. The sound of heavy breathing emanated from the open hole.

I moved over towards the wall. I felt safer having one side of me covered. If it was Sayed up there, he must have lost his god-damned mind. But how would he get up there, without a ladder? And if it wasn't him ...

I shuddered. Every moment the situation felt worse, more horrific.

It was clear I needed to get out of the apartment, but should I check the bedroom first? The hatch was in the hallway at the door to the lounge. There was only one way out of the apartment, and that was by going underneath the sinister black hole of horror. Even the bedroom was on the other side of it.

I decided that the bedroom would have to wait until Lionel and the others arrived. It was clear that I had to get out. I couldn't remain upstairs while I waited for back-up; solo investigation didn't feel like a safe option. Even as a group, safety felt debatable. I stood and took a few calming breaths.

Just run to the hall. Turn and head for the door. That's all you have to do.

I took a last deep breath. As I started to run, I heard movement on the beams above me again. I didn't stop, though. I wasn't stopping for anything. Keep moving. That's it.

Passing at high speed under the open hatch, my shoes slipped a little on the floorboards, surfing me a couple of feet. But before I had a chance to start running down the hall, something caught me. My head stung, a searing pain.

Looking up, I saw Sayed hanging upside-down from the hole, his legs remaining inside the ceiling cavity. His eyes were bulging, red, and focussed on me. His hand had gripped my hair. Some strands, torn from my head, now fell limply towards the floor. Sayed looked so different. I found myself doubting it was really him. His teeth were gritted as though he were undergoing some dreadful pain.

I screamed at the top of my lungs and flailed with my arms, my hands hitting at him. But Sayed had such a good grip on my hair that I couldn't see how to break free. 'Let me go,' I screamed at him without looking. I was afraid to take another look at the monster he'd become.

At that moment, Lionel called out. The thump of feet on the stairs had never sounded so beautiful. Sayed—or whatever that was—must have heard it too. He let go of my hair suddenly, which allowed me to continue my escape down the hall to where I met Lionel at the door.

'Run!' I screamed as I rushed past him and down the stairs.

At the bottom of the stairs stood Cloud and Leila. When Lionel reached the courtyard, I collapsed into his arms. Sobs worked their way from my body rhythmically and intensely.

'What happened?' Cloud was asking.

After a moment I began to tell them what had happened, through my cries. Cloud and Leila gave each other knowing looks as I told them about the ransacked house, Sayed being up in the ceiling again, and him attacking me on the way out.

Finally, Leila said, 'He's inhabited. Sayed's got someone inside of him.'

'Like channelling?' I asked, still struggling to breath.

'Oh, no, no. Not like that, unfortunately. This is difficult. But we can help him.'

There was a lot of talk after that, mainly between Cloud and Leila, but Lionel joined in at times too. Finally, Leila turned to me and told me, 'We are going to get Sayed back, but it's going to be hard. Difficult work. We have to work together. All of us.'

'I'll do anything. But I don't know what's going on. What's happened to Sayed?'

Leila looked at me long and hard. 'You have a spirit in there, right?'

'I think so, yes.'

'You felt it.'

'You smelled it too, remember,' added Lionel.

'Right,' said Leila. I just looked and listened.

'Now, did Sayed come into contact with that spirit?'

'Oh my God. Oh my God,' I repeated. 'The ceiling. He went up there to look for the problem. By himself. And something happened.'

'I'd say so, yes,' Cloud spoke now.

Leila added, 'Sayed found whatever was causing the disturbance at your place and he wasn't ready. He couldn't protect himself. And that spirit found Sayed. Perfect.'

'What do we do?' I begged. We had to fix this. It wasn't fair. I'd already suffered through so much in my life, and Sayed was such a good person. He didn't deserve this.

Chapter Twenty-Eight

Leila and Cloud pulled up in the laneway beside The Brew in Cloud's maroon sedan. They had just returned from a supply run to Leila's house. Lionel and I had stayed behind to keep an eye on the apartment. We had sat in the car where, from the back seat, we could see the door of the apartment.

So much had happened since I woke up in Dad's spare room at two o'clock. It was nearly three-thirty as Leila and Cloud bundled a basket and two bags from the boot. Standing in the courtyard, Leila began shuffling around inside them. She drew out some drawstring bags made from rough, red fabric. Drawing the bags to her face, she drew air inwards before expelling the breath over the bags.

Leila began reciting a prayer over the bags as she held them close to her lips. I couldn't work out what language it was in, but it wasn't English. I knew it wasn't French or Arabic either. They were the other languages Sayed spoke so I would have recognised them. Leila then handed a bag to each of us and told us to put it in our pocket and keep it there, out of sight. Mine had a crunchy feel, and as I squeezed it into the pocket of my jeans, a herb-like smell wafted upwards. I recognised rosemary, but there were also more pungent scents involved.

Leila looked at me. 'Angelica, rosemary and bay leaf,' she said quickly.

I nodded. It was as though Leila had read my mind.

'Protection,' she added, reading me a second time. I nodded again. At this point, I had no choice but to accept that Leila knew what she was doing to help Sayed. I thought of him then, my husband and my protector. Now I had a chance to protect him. Well, it was a bit late for that, but I had an opportunity to correct the wrong that had befallen him. I had to gather my strength.

'Now we create shields,' said Leila.

'Out of what?' asked Lionel with a scrunched-up face. 'Do we really have time to make shields right now?'

'It's a mental process. Not physical.' Leila sighed. 'Join hands.'

'Is that going to be enough?' Lionel spoke again, and this time Leila looked exasperated. I could tell Lionel was anxious about the whole process. He was a man of action—a practical man, who enforces the law.

I spoke up, too. 'I'm more worried about the fact that we should be up there now helping Sayed. Shouldn't we be doing something more than creating pretend shields?' I recognised immediately how rude I had sounded. I regretted not choosing my words more carefully.

Leila frowned and continued with a serious face. 'If you want my help, you have to trust me. What is in your apartment is powerful, and we need to create psychic protection. Physical protection is nothing, understand? You can go up with a gun, but that malevolence could use that gun against you. You need something stronger than a gun or a knife. You need to be strong inside. Strong emotions, strong thoughts, strong gut. Physical weapons can't help you here.'

Lionel and I were silenced by that.

'Right,' I said finally. 'Yes. I'm on board.' I looked at Lionel. 'You too?' I asked. He nodded and swallowed.

'Good,' said Leila. 'Stand in a circle. Concentrate on every step of the process. You get out what you put in.'

The chill I'd felt before when Sayed had used the word 'energy' went through me again. I refocussed, trying my best to do as Leila instructed. We stood facing each other in a circle, my protection bag forming an uncomfortable lump in my jeans.

'Stand with your feet flat and take a few deep breaths. Breathe from your stomach. In, out,' said Leila, lengthening the in and out so that we could easily follow her instructions.

I wondered if we really had time for meditation, but I held my tongue.

Leila paused for a few moments, then continued. 'Begin to feel the energy coursing inside you. Tap into it. Rub your hands together in front of you then hold them an inch apart. Feel the energy between them.'

The uncanny thing was this: when I did what Leila instructed, I *could* feel that energy. Without a doubt, it was there between my palms. It was an incredible feeling, and it helped me to trust her.

'You can feel it now, and you're going to let it build up. Gather more and more energy from your own body. Let it gather into a ball of power that you are holding between your palms.'

'Are we meant to see this ball?' piped up Lionel. I rolled my eyes as Leila answered him through gritted teeth. 'No. You feel it and imagine it.'

Just then there was some noise from the apartment, but Leila snapped quickly, 'Keep your focus on the energy. Don't worry about anything else. That's under control for now.' It was hard to bring my mind back to the energy after that. Was it Sayed? Was he okay? I continued breathing—in, out—and imagining my ball of light.

'You should have a large ball of energy now, right in front of you.'

I *could* almost see it. And I could definitely feel it there, shining pure and bright. It was magnificent, even amid this dire situation.

'Now, you're going to expand that light and bring your physical body inside it. The energy will surround you. It will be your armour. Imagine it,' Leila raised her voice a little and seemed to direct her instruction to Lionel. 'This energy will protect you from what we face upstairs. Believe that.'

I hoped she was right. Leila was finishing, and I sensed she had opened her eyes, so I did the same.

'We're going upstairs now, and you need to continue to follow my lead. Do as I ask. You hear?'

'Yes,' said Lionel and I at the same time.

We started up the stairs as a group, with Leila at the front. Cloud followed, then me, and Lionel took the rear. Taking these stairs with fear in my heart seemed to be becoming a habit—and not one I was happy about.

On the verandah, we paused. The door was pinned open, and we could see down the hall. The hall light was still on and, now that I knew to look for it, I could see that the hatch was still open.

Leila took out a small ziplock bag full of red powder: the brick powder she had talked about on her first visit here. Sayed and I had scrubbed and scrubbed, but the red stains on the doorway's entry were simply too engrained. Now Leila added a new line across the threshold. But won't laying another line trap whatever it is inside?

As if Leila had heard my thoughts again, she said, 'Before, it was to keep the evil out. Now, we want to keep it in. We're going to capture it.'

Within seconds of Leila laying the powder, the door began to close slowly with a light creak. Leila put her hand out to stop it, pushing it back against the wall again and securing the latch on the wall.

I had no idea how Leila managed to stay so self-assured. Years of occasionally sensing spirits had not prepared me for them stickybeaking into my world and affecting the physical things around me.

'Hold the door as you pass. For safety,' Leila advised as she stepped over the threshold and began to walk down the hall. Each one of us followed, slipping into the apartment quickly and quietly, while lightly pressing our hands to the door as we passed.

I looked back at Lionel and grimaced; he nodded. It felt like we were walking into fire.

When Leila reached the ceiling's opening, she slowed. We all lined up behind her, as though she were our shield, while she rummaged in her bag. Finally, she took out a crucifix, and the scene suddenly took on the feel of a paranormal film. Were we going all religious now? Leila didn't seem the type to believe in God or to partake in organised religion. Perhaps she just pulled out all the stops when she needed to. I could relate to that. Not Christian? Who cares? Where are the crosses? I'll take one, too.

Leila held the cross up towards the open hole, just like a priest during an exorcism.

'Stay behind me as you move into the lounge,' she told us.

I wasn't overly keen on entering the lounge room again, since I'd already been trapped in there, but it was happening anyway.

'What about checking the bedroom?' I asked Leila. 'In case Sayed's in there.'

'I'll do that,' she said squeezing forwards without taking her eyes off the hatch.

So, Lionel, Cloud and I moved past Leila into the lounge room where, with more space, we didn't have to stand in single file.

'Jeez, Dor,' Lionel exclaimed on seeing the lounge room.

'Yeah, he's a hell of a decorator.'

Cloud smirked, but I was intent on keeping an eye on Leila as she entered the bedroom. I could see her busying herself in there before checking the bathroom. 'Nothing here,' she called out.

I began to feel relief … until I realised what that meant. Sayed remained *up there*. 'There was no ladder here, you know,' I started explaining. 'When I arrived here tonight, I mean. The ceiling was open, but there was nothing underneath that he could have climbed up onto.'

'Chances are he doesn't need a ladder right now,' said Leila.

I wished she hadn't said it. I already had fleeting thoughts in my mind about how Sayed had gotten up there without a ladder, what that could look like … I stiffened briskly at the thoughts running through my head.

Then—although I didn't want it to happen—my lower lids filled with tears.

Lionel noticed and put an arm around me. 'It's going to be okay,' he said supportively, but I could tell he wasn't sure.

Cloud was busying herself, I noticed. She doled out a collection of crosses from one of Leila's bags—one to each of us—then began placing herb bunches around the lounge room. It really did feel like a movie set. At any moment, I imagined objects might start flying around the room, and Sayed would scream obscenities then projectile vomit all over us.

Leila took charge; she could be quite a leader when she got going. From a spot in the bedroom doorway, almost underneath the opening, she took a few deep breaths. She didn't ask us to do the same, but I automatically followed. The cross was clasped firmly in her hand, her knuckles white. You could feel she was collecting her power again. I followed suit.

Then she looked up and began talking. 'Show yourself. Don't remain hidden. Show yourself to us. No more hiding in the darkness.'

There was a small movement on the beams above, as though someone had started but then stopped just as quickly.

'Or are you afraid? Scared to face us? We're the ones with the power here.'

'She's cajoling. Calling it a scaredy-cat, and trying to make it come down,' Cloud whispered to Lionel and me.

It? That was my husband, I thought.

I glanced worriedly at Lionel, who shook his head as though he wasn't happy with the situation either. It was fair to be unhappy about pretty much everything going on around us that night, but what were we going to do about it? Lionel and I were already working blindly, with only Leila and Cloud to show us the way.

'Show yourself. Show yourself, you monster from hell. Show yourself ...'

Leila continued to repeat those words, over and over, for what seemed like many minutes. Her cross was held up high as though she really believed it would protect her, or all of us.

Finally, there was a flicker by the hole that caught my attention. It was light in colour, or was it a light? Then I saw something reach out. My eyes bulged in their sockets. A pale finger curled around to grip the border of the hatch—first, the one, then two, three and four. They grabbed on tightly.

Leila continued. 'Come! Don't hide like a coward. Coward! Show yourself.'

Overhead, a sliding sound began, and more of the body came into view. There it was, slipping out of the ceiling and towards the floor, towards us. At that point, I couldn't say with any certainty that it was my husband. I was referring to the body as 'it' in my head. This was not a man. My mouth hung open. How could I explain what I saw?

Its skin looked thin, so you could see more blood vessels. And the limbs ... it was as though Sayed had been taken apart and reconstituted. This time, it was not falling; it was creeping out, as though in control of everything. The body seemed all limbs.

Overcome with nausea, I rushed to the kitchen sink and filled it with the pain of what I'd seen, while gripping my stomach.

Lionel was yelling, ramping up. He sounded hysterical—not a good look for an officer of the law. 'Jesus Christ. That's it. We have to call an ambulance. It's gone too far. He needs help, or we're all going to prison.'

'No,' Leila said. 'No. They can't help him now. Only we can.'

I didn't know to what extent Lionel bought Leila's assertion, but he seemed to quieten. I turned to look, once again, though my gut didn't want to see it. I had to see squarely what we were up against. The sight was resting on the floor underneath the hatch. It was alert but quiet. My husband's thick hair was still visible, plastered to its head.

Then, I caught a glimpse of Leila. Far from being in charge as she'd seemed earlier, she appeared out of her depth. That was hardly what I needed to see. The only thing I'd had to fall back on was the belief that Leila knew what she was doing and could handle this; now my hope seemed dashed. Maybe this was too much for her.

I glanced instead at Cloud, whose expression offered more promise. She looked in her element. She might even have been enjoying herself.

Then the noise came.

It was gentle through the quiet. So soft we could almost have missed it—a murmur travelling over the airwaves. I tried to control the shaking in my body so I could listen. It was coming from whatever it was that had slunk from the ceiling cavity. That I knew. I stole yet another glance but had to look away quickly. What I saw there wasn't something I could understand.

A swishing sound from its voice box accompanied each syllable, but I was sure I heard words.

'He's speaking,' I whispered, to myself as much as to Lionel, Cloud or Leila.

I finally felt there was something I could do, and I jumped on it. In a situation like that the best you can hope for is to have a purpose. My job, I decided, was to understand the message.

The monstrosity was speaking, but the words were near impossible to understand at first. Was it speaking to me? I stole another look. Its eyes seemed to be looking my way.

'Ehh eees oh ucck nuthh een.'

I turned my ear towards the sound and mentally blocked as much as I could from the surrounds. I chose not to think about the fetid odour that now permeated the room, and I ignored what Leila, Cloud and Lionel were doing around me.

I listened closer, deeper.

The feeling coming from my core was that this was my time to step in.

And I heard it. As the monster got better at using Sayed's poor, wracked body to communicate, I heard the message loud and clear: 'You a piece of fucking nothing.'

'Oh my God,' I said aloud, without even meaning to. 'It's Troy alright.'

CHAPTER TWENTY-NINE

The moment I realised—and voiced—that this monstrosity was Troy, it threw its head back and laughed sharply. It knew how I felt, and I knew that it knew.

And how did I feel? Desperate and impotent pretty much covered it. I had been transported back in time, to a stage of my life when I had no power. When I didn't know how I'd ever been able to move forward and have a life. When, at one point, I'd fleetingly considered suicide.

Putting out feelers, I connected to the energy in the room. It seemed I was tapping into unknown abilities. I realised that, in this form, Troy had an awareness of my thoughts and feelings—and not just mine, either. His power was extensive. His repulsively monstrous look contradicted his ability to know us: an ability that could be the end of everything. He could break us.

The worst thing was that he'd stolen my husband from me. He'd taken Sayed away and made him into something I couldn't understand, and certainly couldn't love. He was killing him.

A small stream of yellow liquid oozed from the side of its mouth. Its skin was cracking, like lava fissure vents, hot and painful looking. I rushed back into the kitchen to purge. But as soon as I emptied my gut, I spun back around. No way was I giving Troy a chance to sneak up on me a second time. Leila, Cloud and Lionel remained dotted around the living area. Lionel had a taser in one hand and a cross in the other, while Leila still held her cross. Cloud, well ... what *was* Cloud doing? Not much it seemed.

Troy was a monster. This thing certainly wasn't my husband. That they could be one and the same was impossible. I may still have been able to see Sayed's face when I looked carefully, but his expression was gone; his life force and character were buried so deep as to seem non-existent. Was he dead already? I gasped, taking a closer look, unable to form an opinion. The body in front of me was not put together in the way it should be. It wasn't medically possible.

It—I was determined it wasn't a person anymore—began to move, to sway. It was on the ground, on all fours. Glassy eyed, looking in Lionel and Cloud's direction, it focussed on Lionel. 'You were the afterthought,' it told him. 'They never wanted you, did they?'

'Fuck off,' Lionel retorted. His fingers adjusted on the taser.

'Even when your Mum died of cancer, she forgot to mention you.'

'That's not true, and you know it, Lionel,' I countered.

'I know,' he replied. But his face gave away his true feelings. That monster was knowingly plucking at a nerve for Lionel. Mum had practically wasted away to nothing the day she sent for us, knowing her death was near—'us' being Wren and I. Mum had forgotten to mention Lionel. But she was ill; she wasn't thinking straight. It didn't mean anything. The rest of the family knew she had meant the three of us. She loved Lionel just as much as she loved Wren and me. Any sensitivity Lionel felt over this was bolstered by another, partial truth. Lionel wasn't planned, and our parents had considered termination. Of course, they didn't do it, and Lionel should never have even known about it. It wasn't for a young boy to learn something as damaging as that. But small towns sometimes do away with niceties. Dangerous gossip escapes, and it can harm.

'Troy's an arsehole, you know that. He always was, Lionel. You know Mum loved you. A happy surprise,' I shouted at him. Mum had always described Lionel's birth like that.

Lionel was staring directly into the monster's eyes, which seemed like a bad idea to me.

'Look at me, Lionel,' I said. 'A happy surprise.'

He nodded gently in answer, but he didn't turn. It seemed he was stuck there, looking into the eyes of the very monster trying to harm him—just like I had been for so long.

Then, without warning, Lionel smashed his own face with his hand a few times. Fortunately, the taser didn't go off. His breath was ragged. Lionel was losing it.

'For God's sake, do something,' I screamed at Leila.

Leila remained stock still on the other side of the hatch, in the hall. Frankly, I'd have felt safer if she were right next to me, and that's saying something given how unsure I was about her character.

Leila started talking again. 'Let these men go. Let Sayed go. Lionel, too. You don't own them.'

For some moments, I stood back, watching only.

Then it turned to focus on Leila. 'Stupid old bitch. You have no idea who's with you and who's stabbing you in the back. You know nothing,' it hissed.

'We know who you are, hiding there. Demon,' Leila said.

'Are you saying Troy's a demon?' Lionel asked. Or was she simply describing Troy's behaviour as being like a demon? That was some next-level shit that I definitely wasn't ready for.

'Jesus on a stick,' I said under my breath.

'This is not Troy,' Leila said, eyes on Lionel and me. 'Well, not entirely.'

'Not Troy?' I was incredulous. 'But I recognise him. You have to be mistaken.'

'This is something much craftier. Troy is there, yes. That's why you recognise him. But the main force here is much stronger and more evil than Troy could ever be. It's using Troy's violence and hatred. And his stupidity. But it's not actually Troy.'

It laughed again, spraying an arc of opaque spittle over the floorboards.

'But …' I began, but I couldn't finish because I was brutally disoriented and dizzy—as though someone had taken me and spun me around until I lost all direction.

'No!' Leila roared. Then she caught my gaze, stared into my eyes without a blink and told me, 'No good can come of this discussion right now. Trust me.'

Leila knew more, but she did not want to say it aloud, either because of the demon, because of Troy, or perhaps because of Lionel, Cloud and I; I wasn't sure, but I got her message loud and clear. With that understanding, I decided to keep following her advice. Leila and her knowledge had got me thus far. It wasn't time to push back on it. Instead, I leaned back against the wall for support momentarily and scanned the room. Lionel's face was round and ashen, resembling the moon. Cloud looked, at the very least, disconcerted. Not exactly in control of her feelings for the very first time I had noticed that morning. So, her strength has its limits, then.

I accepted that the demon was not Troy—or at least, not Troy entirely—even if I found it hard to believe. It continued to laugh at all of us, its body contorting and jerking with the chuckles. I saw this mostly from the corner of my eye, wanting to keep an eye on it, yet unable to cope with looking square on. Its throat was the dark purple-red of bruised skin, and its eyes were inky and full of nothingness. But the face was so deathly pale—so much worse than Lionel's—that I worried for Sayed's life.

Leila took a small bottle with a screw top from one of her knapsacks. The oil looked to be infused with herbs; I could see little flecks of dark green leaves floating inside the clear glass. She took off the lid and screamed at the top of her lungs.

'You must leave that man alone. He hasn't harmed you.'

It was then that the monster moved a little towards Lionel. Watching it unfold, I saw Cloud's face change: a return to the confidence I'd noticed in her earlier. She was smiling. Shouldn't she have been worried out of her mind? A goddamned demon was inching its way towards her boyfriend, for goodness sake. I was finding Cloud as exasperating to try and understand as her mother.

Leila motioned for Cloud, Lionel and I to get into a circular formation around the demon as she screeched, 'You have no power here. Go back to hell.'

Then Leila yelled again. Only this time it wasn't at the monster rocking in front of us, but at her daughter. Everything began to speed up, rushing like we were inside a jewellery box and someone had overwound the ballerina.

'What are you doing, Cloud?' Leila was upset about something. Cloud remained silent, but the smile was wiped right off her face. 'Make the circle, girl!' her mother called to her.

Instead of moving into the circle we were forming as a group, Cloud moved out a little—away from Lionel, away from all of us. Another strange and unhelpful move on Cloud's part. Especially now, at the time that her mother, Lionel, and I needed her. Not to mention Sayed, who was fighting for his life. Was Cloud being affected by the power Troy and his demon were wielding? That thought was frightening. Or was she simply stubborn and refusing to follow her mother's orders?

The demon turned a little towards me then, its face changing, showing its increasing monstrousness. Being in the sights of a demon wasn't something I ever wanted to repeat. While I pondered, it leaped at me and pushed me down. I fell hard to the timber floor. The house shook. Hands reached for my neck, those same fingers I'd seen curl around the hatch. They tightened around my neck, constricting my windpipe and prompting a struggle for breath.

Lionel and Leila tried to drag it from me. Once again, I had someone trying to snatch away my breath, my dreams, my entire life, from me. That Sayed was connected to this in some way was not something I considered. I honestly didn't think of this monster as having anything to do with him in those moments.

The next instant there was a release on my neck, but I felt a throbbing pain in my upper arm. Lionel was yelling, 'Get it off her!'

The demon had attached to me, and a familiar deathly smell suddenly overcame us all. Its festering teeth were sinking well into my upper arm. When I realised my stronger arm was free, I lifted my right arm and began hitting at its head and face. Though I didn't want to cause any permanent damage—my husband's life was at stake, after all—I fought as anyone would. Not a woman of enormous strength, I aimed a few solid punches. Turns out, it could bleed.

Meanwhile, Leila returned to her prayers. She was focussing her energy to overcome it. Simultaneously, Cloud seemed to have righted herself enough to help Lionel try and get the demon off me. Finally, though the thought repulsed me, I squeezed my thumb into one of its eyes, causing it to shriek and recoil a bit.

At that moment Leila yelled, ' Go away from her, creature from hell, or I'll deal with you!' and we were splashed with the bottle's contents. The demon removed its teeth from my arm, just as quickly as it had planted them. It took its weight from my body and spun around.

It all happened so quickly, but I had seen a change I wished I hadn't—you know the expression you can't 'unsee' it. But there in my mind were visions from which I could not escape easily. The images of the body of my husband returning were bittersweet. Joy mixed with horror. One moment, the body of a demon, drawn-out and terrifyingly unnatural, then the next, his limbs returning to arms and legs as nature had intended them. The form of the man I loved was back. Beaten up and shaken, but no longer so ill-formed that it turned my stomach.

The way his body restored itself was incredible. His skin, cell by cell, was put back together into one piece that covered and protected him. His bones were set out once again in a pattern that one could recognise as human.

Sayed, as I felt able to call him again, tried to get to his feet but stumbled.

Cloud rushed to Leila's side to help her, but Leila turned away from her. In one hand, Leila held a dark jar that I had not seen before. On the side table, there was another identical jar. The herbal oil infusion was gone now, and Leila was screwing the lid on the jar she had and holding it with care.

'Are we okay?' I asked tentatively.

'We are,' said Leila, smiling.

When Cloud attempted once again to help, Leila turned to her. 'Don't,' she hissed. 'You leave it to me.' I wasn't in the best frame of mind, but one thing I did notice—didn't I?—was a tiny curl in Leila's lip when she spoke to Cloud. That second suggested a narrative unfolding, something of which I had no knowledge. But if Leila said we were safe now, then I had to believe her.

CHAPTER THIRTY

Standing in the lounge room that morning, Sayed was like a lame horse trying to raise itself from the ground. I didn't have time to follow up on whatever I may have noticed unfolding between the mother and daughter duo. Lionel offered his hand to help me to my feet. 'You okay?' I asked him.

'Hmm,' he muttered, clearly not okay. Neither of us was, but I had to turn my attention towards Sayed who was still not able to get off the floor. He needed help, but we hadn't exactly run to his aid. Lionel and I were the closest people to Sayed, yet our bodies remained locked in fear.

I took a few slow steps towards my husband, who was on the ground underneath the hatch, and glanced at Leila for help. She nodded her head just a tad as if to say it was safe to go to him.

Sayed looked a mess—so pitiful, naked on the floor. With Leila's approval, I rushed to my husband and helped him to sit.

What I had seen that morning remained clear in my mind, though.

Had we all been hallucinating? For a person's limbs to change like that, from human to something so … inhuman. It was impossible. It had to be impossible. And then they reverted again. Though the transformation had happened over seconds, it seemed as though it had occurred piece by piece over hours.

I had seen the event, but I still couldn't fully accept it. I didn't want to.

'How do you feel?' I asked him, brushing his damp hair back from his face with a gentle hand.

'I'm okay.' As he looked at me, lines of tears welled along his bottom lashes, more so on the eye I had recently poked. 'I'm so sor—'

'No, baby. No. It wasn't your fault. *I'm* sorry,' I told him with conviction. 'Do you understand what happened to you?' It seemed such an odd question given neither Lionel nor I understood it. Perhaps Leila and Cloud did, but Lionel and I … we were lost. Sayed nodded, but I couldn't be sure he understood what I was saying, let alone his situation. 'Something overtook your body.'

'I know who it was,' he said. 'He came for you. But it wasn't just him …' Sayed's brown eyes, like rich soil, looked as though they might pop right out of his head if he continued.

So, I stopped him. 'Can you move your legs okay?' He opened his arms and legs out one by one. Incredibly, it seemed there were no broken bones.

'They're sore,' he told me.

'They would be,' I replied. 'There's so much bruising. I need to take Sayed to the hospital now.'

'No,' Leila said. 'You can't. What will you tell them? That you saw your husband change into a supernatural? That a non-human entity possessed him? Good luck!'

'Well, I …' I was stumped. I wanted Leila to be wrong, but the more I thought about it, I realised she was on the money. 'After what happened he needs medical help, surely?' I trailed off weakly, my shoulders slumping under the enormity of the problem.

'No. Sayed will be fine. Some pain relief and rest, that's all he needs.'

'You can't be serious?'

Noticing my disbelief, Leila added, 'You have a lot to learn about the supernatural realm, Dora Hermansen. What happened was an unearthly event. The cure, then, has no basis in the earthly realm. You're trying to frame this using your outdated understanding of how the world is. It's time to wake up. All you need to do is treat him for aches and pains.'

Though it wasn't an easy thing to accept, what Leila was saying sounded logical. I had just seen my husband's physical body change so much that it should've killed him, yet there he sat, breathing and attempting to apologise to me. He lived.

I advised myself to continue following Leila's advice.

'Okay. I get it,' I said.

'The other thing you need to know is that beyond the non-skilled humans are the sensitives. You, me, Cloud: witches, psychics, middlemen—which I think is what you are. Some are born, while others, like you, develop an ability along the way.'

'A middleman?'

'Like a medium or ghost whisperer.'

'But I can't even talk to them.'

'Yet,' said Leila bluntly, turning away and busying herself packing things up.

I went and found two ibuprofen tablets in the kitchen cupboard and gave the sink a quick rinse—feeling particularly thankful that my puke had been mainly liquid. I shuddered as I filled a glass with water.

Raising the glass to Sayed's lips, he seemed to appreciate the water. I helped him take several sips before introducing the medicine, figuring he might be dehydrated, not to mention sporting a sore throat. After the noises I'd heard coming from him during the possession, I was pretty sure that his throat would be raw. He swallowed the tablets with some difficulty. I remembered the voice, the strangeness of it all, but pushed it aside. I needed to focus.

With the tablets swallowed, I went to get a t-shirt and shorts from the bedroom and helped Sayed get dressed. I took his face in my hands, gently so as not to scare him. I had a long look, particularly at his eyes. It was him. It was definitely him, so I gave him a kiss on the forehead and leaned my own forehead to rest on him momentarily.

'What happened here tonight … it was … I'm so happy that you're okay, honey. You are okay, aren't you?'

Sayed was slow to answer me, taking another sip of water, then giving me a meek nod. He looked so terribly worn out, yet the warmth was returning to his skin. The cracks that had broken his skin earlier—when he was something else entirely—were gone completely. Was it magic? A miracle, perhaps? It seemed to have more to do with hell and the devil, than with anything God-like.

'Let's stand you up,' I suggested. While Sayed remained unsteady, he made it to standing by holding on to the side of the couch.

Leila was nearby with a black candle, its flame dancing with the air currents moving through the apartment from the open door and hatch. Leila was frowning with concentration, as she let wax drops fall around the lid of a jar.

'We have to seal it,' she said, matter-of-factly.

'But what is it?'

'Of course, sorry. Inside this jar is the demonic force that attacked us tonight. Captured for good. Now we seal it and place it where it can't hurt anyone. That,' she pointed to the side table where a second jar sat. 'That's Troy.'

I felt a coldness as I looked at the jar. It appeared empty.

'So, Troy's stuck in that little glass jar?' I asked. Leila nodded. 'Good. So, what happens now?'

'Now we go out to my place to bury it. We all have to be there. I need the energy. But *I'll* bury it,' said Leila, taking an *almost* imperceptible glance towards Cloud.

'Then what?' I asked.

'Then? You're free.'

Relief washed over me. Free? Free from this! I wanted to scream it.

CHAPTER THIRTY-ONE

On the drive out to Leila's, my mind wandered to Cleo, and I felt a wave of burning anger towards Troy. As if he hadn't caused me enough heartache! It was unspeakable that my beautiful cat could go out like that, by Troy's hand. It was so unfair—such a brutal ending for a peaceful soul.

Cloud had gone in Leila's car, leaving Sayed and me to get a lift in Lionel's ute. Lionel was shaky but managed the drive. I wondered if his training had helped him any that morning, although I was sure they didn't prepare officers of the law specifically for brother-in-law possessions by angry exes and evil demons.

I sat in the back seat with Sayed so I could tend to his needs, although in reality there was little practical to do. Still, I gave my best effort by helping Sayed hold a few icepacks in place, and I figured I was providing moral support. I had time to marvel, again, that he was sitting there without a cut or broken bone—barely a scratch in fact. Sayed was whole and able to walk around. Sore, yes, and definitely uneasy. But after what had happened to his body, to be in one piece … if that wasn't a sign of supernatural workings, I didn't know what was.

I wondered how fully Sayed understood what had happened back in the apartment. The world as we knew it, was changed. Or, more likely, we had realised once and for all that the world was never as we thought.

I was on steadier ground than Lionel or Sayed, which I supposed was because they were non-skilled, as Leila had explained it. Meanwhile, I was a non-born sensitive. Not that I'd used my abilities to their full potential since I got them, of course. Yet, there I was after a nasty encounter with pure evil, and I was feeling something odd. Was that … a sense of awe? I do believe it was. I was enjoying the idea that the world was full of the supernatural. Though it was scary, I felt the excitement and rush of power that came with your world suddenly opening right up.

I came quickly back to earth with a yelp from Sayed. A pothole had caused me to push just a little too hard with the icepack I was administering. Sayed was still nursing bruises from his tumble out of the ceiling the day before. Now he had bruises on top of bruises. It would take those a while to heal.

'Sorry. You poor sweetheart.' I adjusted my arm so that if the car shuddered again, it would be less likely to affect the pressure level with which I held his icepacks. Then I rested my head on his shoulder gently, so that our heads were almost touching.

On arrival at Leila's, we bundled out and milled on a small grassy area in front of her verandah. The day remained cloaked in darkness, but a promise of golden sunrise flickered through the forest—some welcome beauty after the ugliness of the night.

Fortunately, Leila's home on Hunter Street had no visible neighbours, because we must have looked a suspect sight: the five of us standing in the yard, all dirty and scrappy. I wondered what would happen if someone called the cops on us. Then I remembered that Lionel was the police. Still, if a cop car pulled up, would Lionel being on the force make our situation at that point better, or worse? I really didn't know.

Leila got to work. Step one was dropping a biscuit crumb line of herbs in a circle around us. When the line of herbs met, she directed us to form another small circle. I was learning that circles were Witch Studies 101. The other thing was that to get supernatural tasks completed, you often needed to pool energy from several individuals. The power wielded by movie and television witches seemed a myth.

Our small group formed the familiar circle. This time, though, Leila told us to focus our energy on containment of Troy and the demon.

I wanted them to stay gone—forever—so I directed everything I had in me towards the circle. Leila held the jars, which looked to be blown from strong, thick glass.

'You'll never see the light of day,' Leila began. 'Your life is within these glass walls for eternity.' Leila broke the circle, then, and we all followed suit. She stood there with the jars in her hand, their black wax seals thick around the lids.

'It's burying time now, deep, deep in the ground. You stay here,' Leila added, glancing at Cloud. She walked off, tucking the jars of evil against her and grabbing a spade on the way past the rusty shed. Soon, her dark shape disappeared into the trees at the back of the property.

It sure appeared that Cloud had pissed her mother off somehow, and Cloud was being edged out of proceedings. We'd done everything as a group, but now Leila had taken charge of the burying of the jars. While the vibe in the human world raised questions, the feeling in the non-human world was deathly quiet. There were no unearthly sounds, smells, or creatures, which was a huge relief. I found myself imagining a world where my abilities simply disappeared, never to bother me again, in which I could go back to my life with Sayed, running The Brew and living without distraction.

Cloud barely spoke. When Lionel tried to comfort her, he received trifles in return. I thought it should have been the other way around. Cloud, who was more experienced with the supernatural, should have been comforting her boyfriend.

'Is everything okay, Cloud?' I asked her.

'Fine,' she replied roughly. Sayed and I exchanged a glance. We all knew what *that* sort of 'fine' meant.

In Leila's absence, I settled Sayed on a verandah chair. Lionel sat down on the steps, and I offered a chair to Cloud. She didn't answer, seemingly lost in her thoughts, her cheeks ruddy. Could she be suffering a problem that extended beyond mother-daughter issues? I thought about trying to talk to her again but decided it wasn't the right time.

Instead, I took the seat next to Sayed and wrapped my arms around him. There was a chill in the air at that time of the morning, yet Sayed had nothing more than the light clothes I'd dressed him in before leaving home. I was wearing pyjamas from the night before: three-quarter length pants and a t-shirt.

'How long do you think your mother will take?' I asked Cloud.

'Fuck. I can't stand newbies.' Cloud looked away, out into the green expanse of the side garden.

'Cloud—' Lionel began to chastise her.

'I'm sorry. But Jesus!' Cloud was looking at him like she was trying to drum up support.

'You mean because I don't understand about magic?'

'Magic? You don't know what you're talking about. But bravo for illustrating my point so precisely. You got your skills later, so you were always going to be a newbie for a while. But you ... you didn't even bother to learn.'

'I couldn't. There wasn't anyone who could teach me.' My voice quavered, more from embarrassment.

'You didn't even want to learn. You said it yourself. So, you're worse than a newbie.'

Lionel stepped up again. 'That's not fair,' he told Cloud. 'It's not. You need to stop it now. Dora's just been to hell and back.'

'Yeah, okay, I know. Sorry, Dora.'

'It's okay. Tonight was full-on for all of us. I'm sorry that you had to be involved.'

Cloud looked to where we had last seen Leila, a small entryway into the forest. Lionel put an arm around her, attempting to pep her up. After a few seconds, she seemed to arrive back on earth; she turned and gave him a weak smile.

'Sorry, everyone,' said Cloud. 'I'm just stressed. Ignore me.'

I offered Cloud a smile, then rubbed Sayed's back gently with my hand. I knew that Cloud had a point—I hadn't wanted to learn. That much was true, but why she came for me like that I wasn't sure. We all sat in silence until Leila's return. I was glad to see her as I had started to shake a little in the dawn air. Cloud was rubbing her legs and Sayed jiggling his. Lionel fared better with long pants.

The first thing on my mind was whether everything had gone to plan, and Leila said that it had. 'Now, we ground. It lets go of the excess energy,' she told us. We gathered in a circle once again. I made sure not to stand next to Cloud but—being such a small group—it backfired, putting me directly across from her.

'Stand with your feet flat and imagine you have roots leading into the ground below you, connecting you to the earth. You can feel the energy of the earth and your own energy become one,' Leila told us.

Stealing a look, I saw everyone had their eyes closed, except for Cloud who was frowning at me. I clamped my eyelids shut again. I wondered why Cloud was taking out her problems on me but I couldn't spend more time contemplating; I needed to focus.

'Let the excess energy from tonight drain out, through those roots. You do not need it now. The evil has been captured and removed. You are free and safe, and all negativity is draining from you. You are being filled with positive, white, light.'

As Leila spoke, I tapped into her steady voice and felt it. I felt the negative drain away, and I felt the positive grow inside me, spreading its solid, earthy tendrils through my body and mind. When Leila snapped her fingers lightly and announced that it was done, I felt freer for sure. I was almost happy. I glanced at Cloud, and her face looked softer, too. It made sense that she had been stressed, but I was sure her emotions, like mine, had been stabilised by the grounding.

As we left, Leila gave Sayed a tub of herbs and told him to drink it as tea. 'This will help you heal.' Turning to me, she advised, 'You can keep up with ibuprofen and icepacks. Do not go to the hospital or to a doctor, and do not explain this story to anyone. You need to know that we don't look kindly on sensitives who blab.'

'We?' I questioned.

'The skilled. Do you understand what I'm saying? You can't go telling just any non-skilled person about the supernatural world.'

'I do. I understand.' At least I thought so. Those of us with different skills needed to keep them under wraps.

I took the tea—a collection of sticks and leaves from the forest in a glass tub it seemed—and Sayed, Lionel and I started towards the car. On the way, a few bell-shaped flowers caught my eye. They were highlighted by the day's first light rays and were a delicate purple. I stopped to look at the sturdy stalks growing in Leila's front garden. I reached for one, intending to gently cup it for a closer look, but Leila hissed at me, 'Don't touch them.' I glanced at her, one eyebrow raised. 'Don't smell them either,' she barked.

I threw my hands up, palms outwards, to show her I wasn't going to touch her precious flowers. I was getting quite tired of these controlling and contrary Cowles.

A minute later, Sayed, Lionel and I were in Lionel's ute heading for town. Though I was grateful to Leila and Cloud for what they'd done for us, I was so relieved to be done with the whole horrific night—from the savage possession of Sayed to the strong personalities of the two women and whatever troubles they had bubbling between them.

'What's going on between Leila and Cloud?' I asked Lionel.

'What do you mean?'

'Come on. You're the law. You have to have noticed.'

'Give me a clue at least.'

'Don't worry,' I said and rolled my eyes. 'Stay clueless.' Useless, I thought with a chuckle.

I stole glances towards the forest as Lionel drove and thought of everything that had happened. The supernatural attacks, poor Cleo's death, the hideous smells. Metal. The penny dropped. The metal: prison bars. That had to be it. I turned to share it with Sayed, but he was silent beside me in the back seat, holding my hand tightly, and I decided it wasn't the right time. 'Are you going to be okay, Lionel?' I asked, leaving Sayed to relax.

'Yeah. I'd like to go back to Dad's, though. Might stay there a couple of nights, you know?'

'I do. It's a good idea.'

'Why don't you guys come back with me?'

I remembered, with a sudden sharp pain in my chest, what Sayed and I were returning to. But Leila said we were safe now, and I didn't want to hide away at Dad's. I wanted to take back what was mine, to meet the event head on, to make the apartment ours again, and to get everything back in order as quickly as possible. My life was The Brew. *Our life.* I didn't want this debacle to fan out and take up more of our mental space, and our business. Of course, I had checked with Sayed, but he too was keen to stand strong and not give in to our fears.

'No,' I said with surety. 'No, we're going home. We're not going to be scared out of our own home.'

Lionel looked unsure and told me that I should call him if there was anything that even remotely suggested trouble. 'You're crazy, you know that?'

Lionel and I laughed, and Sayed rested his head on my shoulder and closed his eyes.

'I'm going to sleep and then, when I wake,' I announced, 'I'm going to clean the crap out of the apartment. Get rid of the dirt, and everything that's broken. I'm going to remove every last hint of last night's clusterfuck.'

CHAPTER THIRTY-TWO

It was past lunchtime when I woke. Sayed was still asleep beside me. Technically, that meant we'd managed to get a full night's sleep—length wise, at least—and that seemed like quite an achievement, given we'd slept in the apartment.

Before bedding down that morning, I'd messaged Laura to ask her if she could get to The Brew early and open up. Sayed and I usually did that ourselves, but I knew that Laura was capable. She was planning to call in Jules to help her; Jules would be a little confused as to why this was necessary, but I was pretty sure she would do it if she could.

A stream of light entered through a crack between the curtains. Sayed and I had tried numerous times to prevent it—even clipping the spot together with a bull clip—but the area was quite stubborn.

Sayed grumbled a little as I woke him. 'How are you feeling?' I asked.

'Eh.'

'I figured.' I smiled at him. 'I'm going to get up now and start giving this place a spring clean. But I think you should get some more rest.'

'I can help. I made the mess after all.'

'Erm, I don't see it that way. You've just been through ... well, we both have ... but actually, it's because of me. Wouldn't have happened if it wasn't for Troy, would it?' I said, though I couldn't be sure that was true. I had explained the entire night to

Sayed so that he knew it from the outsider's point of perspective as well as his own. In return, Sayed shared his version, which I had to admit was much more confusing since he had little memory of being at the apartment. Just odd snippets of nastiness that he'd picked up about Troy and the demonic force that was inside him. Sayed knew nothing whatsoever about why he had returned home that night. 'No, I think you should rest up,' I said finally.

'You didn't invite this, Dor. You've got to get over Troy being your problem. Troy is responsible for the havoc he wreaks. And the violence he brings ... brought. Brought,' he repeated firmly. 'Yep, I'm helping.'

My head tipped in acceptance. I could tell he'd dug his heels in. Sayed and I had a lot in common when we got down to brass tacks.

'So, we just get up and set the place back to normal, then?'

Sayed looked around the room and smiled at me. 'Uh-huh. Let's put our big-boy pants on.'

'Nooo,' I whined. 'Please stop.'

'I know you hate that expression. But it's exactly what we're doing.' Sayed looked happy for the first time in almost twenty-four hours. 'Now, pull up those pants,' he teased.

'Eww. Stop,' I said, pushing him playfully so he flopped slowly onto the bed. He had me laughing against my will, so I leaned down and kissed him, taking care not to hurt him. His lips were soft and comforting, and I felt overcome with gratefulness that I had found someone so good to spend my life with, after such a dangerous start.

'So, about the clean-up,' I said. 'I do the strenuous bits, and you're just the assistant. Okay?'

'Okay,' said Sayed and kissed me on the cheek as he eased past me to the bathroom. I could see the pink and blue bruising that fanned out across his torso—a good reminder to keep getting Leila's magic tea into him.

Cleaning the apartment would be an immense process and so, I hoped, it would provide catharsis. We could have called in a professional cleaner, of course. If we'd come up with a good enough explanation as to how our home ended up looking like one—or both—of us had lost the plot and wrecked everything, that is. With a professional cleaner, Sayed and I could have worked that day, rather than leaving The Brew to Laura. Or we could have let Laura and Jules take care of everything and continued to rest. The latter was probably the more sensible option since I was sure Sayed and I would need more than a night's worth of sleep to recover fully from what had happened.

The biggest argument for doing the cleaning myself, though, was that I *needed* to. I really did need to tidy and scrub, and dump items that were ruined. In doing so, I would be helping remove emotional and psychological residue from the disturbing events of the week. There was something about cleaning that cleansed and released if you let it.

I was pretty sure that Sayed felt the same way. We had a similar pattern of thinking. I knew in my bones that setting our sights on the clean-up was a part of our healing process. It would help us to feel comfortable in our own home again.

The first thing we did was close the hatch cover. Of all the chores we had ahead of us, this was the most formidable, and the most important. I approached it with my heart thumping in my chest and an ice-cold feeling creeping over my limbs and into my body. But, within seconds, I had slipped the little wooden door snuggly into the square hole in the ceiling, and it was done.

Then, as much as was physically possible with his tired and sore body, Sayed was right there with me. Sweeping, moving the bin around as needed, and wiping down surfaces, he was a good assistant. We tidied and scrubbed until the homemade cleaning spray spread the scent of eucalyptus through the apartment.

Sayed also had his own little fire to put out. The fact that he'd missed Friday prayers in Brisbane hadn't gone unnoticed. It was the first time in all the years that Sayed had lived in Deepwell that he hadn't attended the Friday—Jummah—prayers and visited his family afterwards. Worse, he hadn't called them. He could hardly tell the Bousaids the real reason why, either. 'Yeah sorry, Mum. I was just fighting off possession from a demon working in tandem with Dora's ex. See you next Friday, though.' In the end, he told his parents that he had contracted a stomach bug. After a night of nasty sickness, he told them, he'd been so tired that he'd slept through and hadn't even woken in time to warn them.

Throughout the afternoon, I felt my blood pressure lower, and my tense muscles relax. Everything was returning to normal—relatively—and the relief was exquisite. The closer our lounge room looked to the way we were accustomed to seeing it, the closer I felt to safety. I was finding my strength as I wiped and scrubbed.

I was gaining some understanding of my situation, too. While scraping soil, and who knows what else, out of the edge of the hardwood coffee table, I had time to ponder my skills with the dead. I had been able to sense the deceased for many years now and had flatly refused to consider it a gift in the real sense of the word. Cloud was right. I had hidden from it, run from it, and avoided spirits as much as I could. At every turn, I had shirked any responsibility that others might feel if they had my abilities.

It was deflating to think that I had made a choice that wasted years of my life. A selfish choice, too. I hadn't wanted to know about those people, those ghosts, in need. So, I blocked it all. Still, was I really prepared to see my ability as a gift? I wasn't sure, but I needed to learn more about it. Leila, as bothersome as I found her, had inspired me. Though seeing a possession was hardly a glowing drawcard, it was empowering to feel that I could deal with things instead of remaining a victim. When I left the hospital after being assaulted by Troy, I took a self-defence class. Not exactly the same thing, sure, but what if my best defence in this new supernatural environment was to develop and use my ability?

Sayed was vacuuming the floorboards and the rug in front of the couch. I got his attention.

'I want to take this more seriously from now on.' He looked confused. 'Sorry. What, you can't read my mind?' He laughed and spread his hands open, agreeing that he could not.

'The "skill" I have,' I said, making air quotes with my fingers. 'I think I need to take it more seriously, learn about it. Stop running, you know?'

Sayed began a nod that ended in a shake of his head.

'Is that going to be okay with you?'

After a moment or two, Sayed rested the vacuum on the floor, stepped closer and held my shoulders. 'I'm not one hundred per cent comfortable with this.' His head hung before continuing. 'After last night? Really?'

'It seems to me that the best way to be protected from something like last night happening is to be ready.'

'You think it can happen again?' He looked horrified.

'I'm not saying that. No, I'm not.' I needed to be more careful with my words.

'Then, what are you saying?'

I sighed inaudibly and sat down on the edge of the coffee table, not even caring if I got grime on my pants. 'I guess I'm saying that I want to be ready for all possibilities.'

'See, I just think that after last night we should divorce ourselves as much as possible from whatever shit goes down in the spirit world. I mean, my Nanna was into all this, the djinn and stuff. It's scary.'

'If I'm honest, it's more than just being ready for whatever comes.' I took a breath and then said it. 'I want to do something with what I've been given. Otherwise, why do I have this sense? If I'm not supposed to use it for something.'

'My sister, you know she has the knack ... but you don't see her inviting it. Right? Why? Because it's bad. There's so much evil out there.'

I was nodding slowly. Everything Sayed said made sense. After he had nearly been killed, it was hard to deny his point of view on this. What had I been I thinking?

'You're right,' I said. 'It's crazy to follow through with something that could put us in further danger. It's not fair on you, either.'

'So, you're decided?'

'I'm decided,' I said. I nodded and smiled. 'Okay. Shall we get this done?'

'Definitely,' said Sayed reaching for the vacuum.

***

By late afternoon, the apartment looked spick and span. Although we had lost some books, plants and crockery forever, I was pleased with the shiny results of our work. Sayed was taking containers of rubbish to the skip. He insisted that he felt much better, even going so far as to claim he could barely feel his injuries. Just what had Leila put in that herb tea, we wondered; I was going to ask her that question.

It wasn't long before I began to doubt my decision to separate myself from the whole ghost world thing. After all, I was working on a new plane—one on which humans and animals weren't the only ones in existence. Humans now came in various flavours I had never dreamed of. Some could predict the future, others allowed the dead to speak through them, and in that new world it was perfectly normal that I could see ghosts. Even if I'd wanted to, I couldn't unsee it all. It was too vast and life changing. I gave the kitchen cupboard a light kick. 'Damn it!'

Bubbles from the kitchen sink caught my eye, reminding me of the broken glass from Monday night. 'Boy, a lot can happen in five days,' I said under my breath. Then I took to the dishes and the bubbles receded with each item I washed. As I dried a couple of serving plates that wouldn't fit on the drying rack, I smelled a mild, yet unmistakable, odour. Confident it wasn't just 'nothing', I spun around to see: only the fridge and our kitchen table. Very déjà vu. I laughed, and stepped backwards so I could lean against the small section of wall our kitchen offered.

To accept this other world was one thing, but to be comfortable with it was another entirely. My heart was a rabbit in my chest. At this rate, I'd have a heart attack before the year was out.

Then it began. Energy, and pressure, in the air around me. My thoughts sped up. Troy ... had he escaped? A few slow breaths brought clarity. Breath in. Breath out. In, out. It didn't feel like Troy. It didn't have the mean edge to it. No, this was different. Yet I had felt it before. This was Becker.

I began to settle, my breath returning to a regular rate. Becker was better than Troy, I reasoned, even if Becker was needy. My hasty thought was cut short as my new awareness brought into sharp contrast that Becker was simply a ghost in need. He couldn't help it. I felt a new compassion that had previously eluded me. I didn't know Becker's exact reason, but here he was, persistently calling me again.

I could then tell which past times had been Becker, as opposed to Troy. Troy had pushed me in the kitchen, and at the cemetery. Troy had nearly squeezed the life out of me as I ran from the graveyard. It all seemed so clear suddenly. Becker created pressure too, but it wasn't a health risk.

My love and care for Sayed meant something, but I didn't see how I could deny Becker my help—not when he had come to me so many times, and when I might be one of the few people who could help him.

When Sayed returned from dumping the rubbish, he knew something had happened.

'I have to help Becker,' I rushed to say. 'He's still here, and he needs something.'

'What? What does he need, Dora?'

'I don't know. I have to find out, though. Becker needs me to fix it. Can you understand that?' Sayed nodded slowly. 'Can you forgive me?' Reluctantly, he nodded again.

This was my chance to do something new and useful with my skill. But how could I find out what he needed?

CHAPTER THIRTY-THREE

Another night of solid sleep was well-received by Sayed and I. My husband seemed even more like himself after the extra rest. Overnight, his muscle aches had reduced so far as to be minor annoyances only. Incredible.

The night before, we'd reached an imperfect agreement on my helping Becker. In bed, the discussion had continued regarding the best way to help, and we decided I would ask for Leila's guidance.

'We've seen the extent of what can happen now. Imagine trying to deal with more events like that through trial and error. We could get killed,' Sayed had said.

When I got up that morning, I threw on a sundress and sandals, skipped the shower, and grabbed my bag and keys. I was heading for Leila's.

'Back for work in about an hour,' I called to Sayed as I headed for the door.

Leila met me on her front verandah. 'Everything alright?' she asked warily.

'Who is it?' I heard Cloud call from the kitchen.

I offered a wave to Cloud as she snuck a look through the door. 'Oh it's you,' I heard her mumble.

It was then I realised how rude I was to turn up without warning, and so early too. Still, those were desperate times, and Leila invited me inside despite everything. 'Sit down then. Tell me what it's about. Do you want a cuppa?'

I took a seat. Leila lived in a Queenslander, the quintessential style of home in our state. The ceilings were about fourteen feet high; it was believed that the height, coupled with raising houses on stumps, made for more comfortable living in the tropical and subtropical climate. But the reality didn't always hold up. Stunning as Queenslanders were, they were often outperformed by modern buildings.

'Sure, tea would be nice. A dash of milk, one sugar,' I replied to Leila, who in turn called out the order to Cloud. 'Sayed's had an unbelievable recovery. I mean, if I hadn't seen it myself, I would not have believed it. What was in the tea you gave him?'

'Nothing much. A few herbs.'

'Well, "nothing much" doesn't really explain why Sayed's body has repaired itself miraculously.' I sat steady, wondering if she would answer.

An audible sigh emanated, then Leila said, 'Look, you don't try to cure a spiritual issue with antibiotics, or a sensitive's magic with a medical procedure. That wouldn't make sense.'

'No, I guess it wouldn't. So, you're saying that the herbs were magical. They weren't just herbs?'

'Boy, you ask a lot of questions.'

'Actually, Leila, that's why I'm here.' I thought I'd better get on with it before she lost patience with me. 'I sensed someone in the apartment again. I thought it might be Tr—'

'Not Troy. No.'

'But,' I continued, drawing it out to make the point about Leila's impatience. 'I realised very quickly that it wasn't Troy. Turns out I *can* tell the difference.'

There was a scoffing sound from the kitchen. Personally, I was proud of my achievement. I wasn't going to tell Leila that, though. Leila wasn't the nurturing type. I had to wonder how Cloud had gotten on as a youngster. I imagined her bringing home a first-place certificate in spelling or maths, thrilled with her win, to find her mother barely cared.

'Alright,' said Leila.

'I think it's Becker. He needs something, but I don't know what it is. Also, you seem to think I should use my sense, my skills, in some way. So, I want to. I want to help him, but I don't know how.' I scrunched my face, as you do when asking for a favour you weren't sure would be well received.

'You want *me* to help him?'

Cloud joined us in the lounge with cups and a blue teapot on a tray.

'No,' I quickly corrected the misunderstanding. 'Actually, I want you to help me help Becker. I want to learn more about …' I struggled to even describe it. 'About this world, the sensitives, the supernatural, my skills. Then I can help him.'

'I'm not a teacher,' Leila said, dismissing the idea with a swift wave of her ghostly white hand. Leila was the opposite of Cloud; Cloud had the burnt toffee tan and naturally bleached hair of someone who spends a lot of time on the beach, and Leila appeared as though she'd stayed inside the house her entire life.

I was disappointed. I had assumed—since Leila was so scornful of how I'd handled my ability so far—that she would be more open to helping me.

'You'll need to find someone else,' Leila said as she reached for the teapot and poured the first cup.

'It's not like I have lots of choices at this particular juncture. I can't google a supernatural class. Wait. Can I? Maybe I could choose someone through the listings in the paper. There are other psychics in the area.'

'No,' Leila answered quickly and suddenly. 'You can't trust most of those people. Charlatans, ninety-nine point nine per cent of them. Good thing, actually. That's exactly how sensitives have gone unnoticed for this long. Most people ultimately assume we're all untrustworthy liars because most of those claiming to be us, are.'

'Well, that's all well and good but where do I go then? How do I weed the real from the charlatan?' Not so long ago I hadn't believed in psychics, mediums and tarot readers either. But when you suddenly develop the ability to see the dead walking around, meet a few witches and a demon, well …

Leila looked bothered, as though she were calculating and trying to make a quick decision.

I felt I had a chance to convince her. 'Look, I know your skills are real. You know what you're doing. I've seen it. I'm eternally grateful for what you and Cloud did for Sayed and I the other night. So, please, help me.'

Leila raised her voice now. 'I've helped you enough. I don't want anything to do with that whole Becker thing.'

'Yet you attended his funeral. You cared enough then. What's changed?'

'Look, Mum doesn't want to talk about this. Can't you see that?' said Cloud.

'I don't even know him. It's not my fight.' Leila was talking to herself, but then she appeared to close up.

Was it that she didn't want to help *me*, specifically? An annoying newbie, as Cloud had put it. Or was it something to do with Becker himself? It's not my fight, she'd said. What fight?

I pushed on, asking, 'If you didn't know Becker, why did you attend his funeral?'

'She was doing the right thing. Just like you. Nothing more,' Cloud said stiffly, collecting her sun-kissed locks and tying them with an elastic band.

'Leila, had you ever met Becker before his death?'

'You need to leave now. I don't want anything else to do with this whole mess.'

So, it was a mess, now? 'What mess?' I asked.

'Please go.'

'Fine.' I got up and started towards the door, annoyed and quite confused. Heading for my car, I stopped again at Leila's front flowerbed. Those flowers caught my eye again. The stalks were swaying gently, even though there was no breeze to speak of. Those little purple bells screamed for my attention. 'What is this flower?' I asked. Leila brushed me off last time, but I wasn't going to give up so quickly that morning.

'Never mind,' dismissed Leila.

Those pretty blossoms were always calling to me, so I turned back to Leila, repeating firmly, 'What is it?'

I was propelled at that point by something that wasn't entirely positive: pride. I had a rumbling perturbation with the way Leila and Cloud were disrespecting me. They were treating me like an idiot who had no idea what she was doing. Okay, so there was some truth in that—I really did have little idea about this new world. Still, there is no excuse for such consistent rudeness. I'd had enough, and I frowned at Leila stubbornly.

'It's wolfsbane. Please do not touch it. I've told you before to just leave this alone. Why are you pushing, girl?'

That made me extra curious. 'Wolfsbane? Sounds like something spooky. To do with werewolves or something.' I smiled at her to lighten the mood.

'It's poisonous. That's why you shouldn't touch it. Nothing to do with werewolves. We don't have those in Australia.'

Cloud, who had been standing near the front door, rolled her eyes angrily at her mother.

'I was joking, for God's sake. Wait,' I gave her a questioning look. 'You're not trying to say that werewolves exist somewhere? People who physically turn into a wolves?' If Leila wanted to distract me from her stupid flowers, she'd done a great job of it. 'Leila …?' I clapped my hands together to get her attention.

All I got was a sweeping arm movement, as though I should head to my car and go. I stood stock-still. When Leila reached her door and turned to check on me, she sighed dramatically. I had remained standing exactly where she'd left me, a few metres from the bottom of the stairs, right next to those damned flowers. 'You ask too many damn questions, you do.'

'You won't help me. I get it. You don't want the trouble.' My arms crossed in opposition to her attitude, and I moved my head from side to side gently as I spoke.

'Look, there are no werewolves in Australia, Dora. We don't even have actual wolves.' Leila scoffed as though the thought were utterly ridiculous. 'Aside from the few who holiday here, from overseas.'

My mouth slackened, and I dropped my hands to my side. To say I was shocked didn't cut it.

'Werewolves holidaying? Is Australia a popular destination for the werewolf?' I came back at her sarcastically. Yet, I knew she was serious because Leila wasn't one for fun and games. Frankly, I wasn't sure Leila had more than the most basic certificate in practising humour.

The thought of werewolves taking a break in Australia was not something I was going to forget too soon. Did they surf? Enjoy long hikes? Or visit the outback, perhaps?

I nodded slowly. Leila was dead serious.

As fascinating as the whole werewolf thing was, it was a distraction. It seemed crazy, but I had bigger fish to fry. It was clear that Leila was hiding something regarding Becker; she knew more than she was willing to tell me.

'Tell me about Becker,' I demanded.

Leila fumed, but at that point I did not particularly care. Her anger was further proof to me that I was on the right track. I was onto something, and I just had to work out what it was.

As I fully realised Leila's duplicity about Becker, I also noticed that one of her precious flowers was missing. A stalk had been snipped away, low down near the soil.

'One's been removed,' I said bluntly.

Leila exploded. 'Why are you even here?'

That was enough for me. I hightailed it to the car, glancing back only briefly from the safety of the front seat. Leila was making her way up the stairs while Cloud was silhouetted in the front doorway. I felt Cloud's gaze as I pulled out of the drive with a small skid of tyres on the gravel.

CHAPTER THIRTY-FOUR

Pulling over a kilometre down the road, I googled wolfsbane, which I found out was also called Aconite, Monkshood, or Devil's Helmet. It all sounded pretty dark. Maybe it *was* something to do with the werewolves Leila mentioned. It sure sounded creepy enough.

So, Leila was not going to help me with my Becker problem. I tried my best to recall anything she had said about sensitives in the past that might help me. Leila was a witch. But she was also a medium like me, a person who could sense ghosts. Leila was the channelling type of medium, the creepy kind in my opinion. I was a middleman—a term that applied to men and women—so I should have been able to communicate with Becker. But, of course, I had ignored my skill and never learned how to put it to use. Now I really needed the ability, and I felt like a colossal failure.

Thinking about werewolves was making me nervy. I took a quick glance around before returning my focus on the search listings.

Wolfsbane was also called the queen of poisons. It affected the heart, killed in minutes to hours, and there was no antidote.

What if Becker hadn't died from a heart attack? Obviously, it was assumed that he had, but what if he had been poisoned? I had no solid reason to think that was the case, other than a few individual facts that seemed suspicious to me. One, that Leila grew this wolfsbane plant. Two, that a stalk of it was missing. And three, that Leila got antsy at the mere mention of Becker's name. That seemed especially suspect for a woman who claimed not to even know the guy.

Those were some pretty good reasons to at least ask the question. What I was really considering was, could Leila have poisoned Becker? The idea was shocking.

My eyes returned to my mobile. *How to tell, how to tell ... how ... there it is. Not easy to know if someone has been poisoned with wolfsbane. Initial toxicology report might appear negative.* I wasn't sure how, in this day and age, a doctor could miss a poisoning. But that knowledge sure would make wolfsbane flower an enticing choice for someone wanting to commit murder.

I had forgotten something, though: motive. Leila's behaviour told me she was hiding something, but wanting to kill Becker was a long jump. Until you recalled Becker's character, that is. Perhaps Leila was staunchly anti-development, or extreme about wildlife rights? Maybe Becker had it in for sensitives? Hey, maybe Leila just hated arseholes.

Deepwell was a small town with very few murders. Could it be hiding a poisoner? Deepwell had cradled Troy, after all. The key, I decided, was to discover what the connection between Leila and Becker was.

I pulled off the gravel curb and headed straight for the Becker's to see whether Annika or Candy could shed any light on the mystery.

The Becker house was an imposing design. Naturally. Two storeys with ostentatious pillars at the front. After knocking, I saw a shadowy figure approach through the frosted glass panels. It was Annika. Her face was worn, and the dark circles under her eyes hinted at a lack of sleep. Yet she jumped into hostess mode without missing a beat.

'Hi, Dora. To what do we owe the pleasure?' Then, not waiting for an answer, she ushered me inside.

'Are you doing okay?' I asked her.

'As good as I can be.' The broad smile pasted across her face didn't reach her eyes.

'Annika, would you mind if I asked you a few questions?'

'About?' We arrived in the vast, open living room and Annika motioned for me to sit on a wraparound lounge. I could hear the squeals of children—Annika's I assumed—just out of view in the yard. Abutting their home was a vast tract of bushland. Becker had spearheaded so many pushes for development in Deepwell. Still, I bet he wouldn't have wanted the bush beside his own home sold off for a new housing estate.

Candy appeared from the hall. 'Hi,' I greeted her.

'Oh.' Candy looked taken aback. 'Hi, Dora. What's happening?' She slumped down on the lounge, dressed in white pyjamas that reminded me of the first time I had been at their home. Years before, I had attended a garden party there, where guests had to dress in white. There was a table set up for the cheese platter, and—I'm not kidding—some guests were playing badminton in the yard.

'Well, I just wanted to ask something ...' I was unsure about the efficacy of having the sisters together, but that was how the situation played out. 'Annika, do you know Leila Cowles?'

I watched Annika for non-verbal information and even stole a couple of quick glances at Candy. A gentle twitch at the corner of Annika's mouth with the mention of Leila's name was a positive response. Either she knew her, or was uncomfortable with the question—or both. Regarding Candy, I could not tell.

'Look, Dora, my father just died. I don't have time for this.' Her hand made a sweeping motion in front of her. 'Whatever this is.'

'But you do know her?'

'I ...'

She does know her, I marvelled, feeling very clever. Just say it, Annika, I hoped silently. When no further information was forthcoming, I asked, 'Tell me, then, did your Dad know her, too?'

Annika's face paled, suggesting she wasn't so much pissed off at my rudeness for barging in and asking impertinent questions, as she was scared of something.

'I knew *of* her, sure. Her daughter …' Annika's voice trailed off, her face hardening. She pulled her ponytail even tauter. 'Well, she read my cards at the market one weekend. Said I had good things coming. Good relationships. Good money.' Annika huffed lightly and flopped her hands into her lap, looking despondent. 'I remember thinking puh! I just paid you thirty bucks to tell me what I already know. But now it looks like she was wrong, doesn't it? Sneaky little charlatan. Dad's dead and everything is in ruins.'

It made sense that Annika would have strong feelings about Cloud's reading, given what had happened since.

Candy scooched over to Annika, touched her sister's leg and shushing her. Was she trying to help her, or to prevent her from giving herself away? I couldn't tell.

I turned. 'Candy, did your Dad know Leila Cowles?'

Candy answered me. 'Not that I'm aware of, Dora. I mean they would hardly have had many opportunities to come into contact with each other. They didn't exactly run in the same circles of people.' Candy was matter-of-fact, and her meaning was clear. Had Annika said the same words, it would have been a put down aimed squarely at Leila.

'Yeah, I thought that, too,' I admitted.

'I don't understand why you're here,' Candy continued. 'Why are you asking these questions?'

'I'm not here to upset you. I … I … can't tell you why just yet. It's just a hunch I've got about something. Candy, do you think your father really died from a heart attack?' As soon as I'd said the words, I knew it was a mistake. What was I thinking? I had no right.

Annika jumped on it right away, too. 'I need you to leave,' she spat. I had made a grave error; I had gone too far.

Annika looked shaky now, and her bracelet was jangling on her wrist.

'I definitely think it's time for you to go,' agreed Candy.

'Yes, of course. I'm so sorry. I don't know what I was thinking.' I started towards the door.

'I mean, what the fuck, Dora? What are you even suggesting?' Candy was shaking her head, confused and angry—and rightly so.

Annika, who remained in the background, tore into me. 'Do you think you're a policewoman, now? Having a constable brother doesn't give you any powers over me, Eudora Hermansen. Don't you have coffee to make?'

'I'm sorry,' I said one more time as I rushed outside. Candy slammed the door behind me. I got into my car with my heart pounding and a thin line of sweat across my brow.

I heard Troy's voice inside my head. An old conversation replaying, as they did at times.

'Dora, you work at a fuckin' supermarket. It's not like you're a surgeon.'

'I'm not saying that. I just …'

'I just. I just. You just what?' He laughs heartily.

My stomach drops to my feet.

'You're being mean again, Troy. I'm not willing to put up with this. I'm not.' I try to stand up for myself. That's what I'm supposed to do. Boundaries. I read about them in a book somewhere. You have to enforce your own boundaries as no one else is going to.

'Put up with what? The truth? You're really fuckin' thin-skinned if you reckon I'm mean to you. Jesus! I'm just saying you work in a store. You're not a rocket scientist. Am I wrong?' He leans in closer to me, over me, so I can smell his dank sweat. 'Am I wrong?' he asks harshly.

I think about it. I do work in a store, Troy's right about that. So why do I feel as though I want to crawl up into a little ball and disappear forever? It's not what he says, but the way he says it.

Snap out of it, Dora, I told myself. That was all over. It was history. It was gone. He was gone.

I was sitting in my car across the road from the Becker family's home. I'd just made an arse of myself, but I was going to be okay.

I was back in the present.

I'd had no right barging in there, asking impertinent questions like I did. Annika fought back in her usual fashion, and rightly so, but it triggered me. Nothing more. 'Troy is past. Troy is gone,' I repeated to myself a couple of times.

Once I reached a state of equilibrium, I started analysing my unsuccessful visit. I had been wrong to turn up there, but there was something between the lines I couldn't grasp. Was it possible Annika was simply embarrassed that she had visited a psychic? It may have been seen as silly by some, or even crazy by others.

No, I thought. There was something more than that. Annika was genuinely rattled by my questions. My gut feeling was that she had met Leila, not just Cloud. She didn't want me to know it, and she was afraid.

Perhaps the trip was not a complete fail. I had come to the Becker house with suspicions about Leila. Now you could say that Annika's behaviour—and even Candy's—were adding fuel to the fire. A picture was forming.

I was determined to follow this through. I moved my car over to the next street, so as not to draw attention from the sisters, and I hit the call button.

CHAPTER THIRTY-FIVE

Yes, my brother is an officer of the law, Annika. Now, let's see what he has to say about your fear of Leila in the wake of your father's death?

Lionel's voice came through the phone. 'What's up, sis?'

'Plenty. I need to talk about Leila. And Annika. But mostly Leila. And possibly Candy, I don't kn—'

'Whoa. Hold up. Are you okay?'

'I'm fine. But this is serious.'

'It may be, but I have to say you're coming across as frantic. Is everyone safe?'

'Well Becker's not safe, is he?'

'What?' I heard frustrated breathing through the phone. 'Where are you? Do you need me to come and get you?'

'I'm around the corner from the Becker's residence.'

'You're what? Why?' Lionel sounded exasperated, but I figured he'd soon change his tune when I told him the whole story. 'Look, head to The Brew. I'll meet you there in five to ten,' he ordered me.

When I arrived back at the café, Sayed was about to open the front door to customers. I gave him a summary of my morning before I saw Lionel pulling up. Sayed didn't exactly get on board, but I didn't have time to try and convince him, nor did he have time to elaborate on his disapproval. Sometimes running out of time was a handy thing.

I lead Lionel into the courtyard where I hoped we could speak without the town eavesdropping.

198

'The beginning, please,' said Lionel.

'It started at Leila's this morn—'

'What on earth were you doing at Leila's?'

'For God's sake, Lionel. I'm telling you the story. Let me.'

'Sure. Sorry.'

'Right, well, I went out to her place because I wanted her to …' I lowered my voice before continuing, '… help me develop my ability a bit.'

'Christ, Dor. I would have thought you'd just want to stay away from all that shit.'

'That doesn't seem like an option right now. Since the … *event* the other night, I've had Becker call on me again. There's something wrong with him. He's really upset about something.'

'He was always upset about something.'

'I know, but this is different. You have to trust me on this. Something's going on here.'

'What do you mean different?'

I sighed. What did I mean? I wasn't even sure. 'Look, I don't know how to explain it. I just know.'

'So, you know in some weird supernatural way?'

'Don't say it like that. It's real.'

'I know. I don't have to like it, though.'

'You and me both!'

We laughed awkwardly.

'Okay, so you've got a ghost who needs something, and you went to ask Leila for help.'

'Yeah. But it didn't go as I'd hoped. Leila's hard-nosed sometimes.' I expected Lionel to chastise me, but instead he silently nodded in agreement.

'Was Cloud there?' he asked.

'Yeah. I have to say, Cloud doesn't seem to like me.'

'Eh. You'll get used to her.'

'Whatever. Anyway, Leila refused to help me. Said she doesn't want to be a teacher, or she's not a teacher, I don't know. But as soon as I mentioned Becker specifically, things got weird.'

'Tell me about the weird.'

'Well, she doesn't want anything to do with Becker. But she's a channeller, a medium. It's her job, right? It's literally what she does. So, why is she so anti-Becker? I wanted to find out if she knew him when he was alive, so I went to see Annika and Candy.'

Lionel's eyes widened in judgment of me. 'So, you went to question them a week after their father died? After Leila had already told you she didn't know Becker?'

I drooped a little. 'Don't. I already copped it badly from Annika, and I know I deserved it. But I'm onto something. I am. I don't think Becker died from a heart attack.'

'What? That's ridiculous.'

'Is it? When I asked Leila about Becker, oh, boy, did her demeanour change. Then, when I asked Annika if she knew Leila, and if Becker did, Annika wasn't happy. Honestly, she seemed scared. I think she's scared of Leila.'

'She's probably just upset. Her Dad dropped dead in front of her just last week.'

'I know.' I bit my lip. 'But I have more. Leila grows a poison plant in her garden. Did you know that? It can kill people, and it's hard to trace forensically.' When he said nothing, I added the final blow. 'When I asked Leila about the flower, she was mega cagey, and I noticed that one of the stalks had been cut. There was one missing.'

'She's a witch, though. She's into all kinds of herbal shit. Doesn't make her a murderer.'

'Poison, Lionel. Wolfsbane. It actually kills people. I'm thinking that Leila *did* know Becker somehow, or that she knew of him and didn't like what he was doing. Maybe she's anti-development. It's been such a hot issue in this town.'

'So, you think she bumped him off with a flower from her garden? I'm sorry, but it's all so far-fetched. It's not enough to investigate. My boss will laugh me out of the station if I go to him with this.' I slumped down onto the patio chair. 'Look, it was a clear heart attack according to the death certificate. Trying to re-write it as murder, it's—'

'But forensics don't always pick up that poison. That's what it says on the internet.'

'Do you hear yourself? The internet? Come on now. Just leave it alone. Let Becker's family grieve in peace.' I folded my arms across my chest, and my jaw tightened. 'Jesus Christ, Dora. It's like you're trying to ruin my relationship with Cloud.'

'Is that why you don't want to follow this up?'

'No!' Lionel's face filled with colour. 'It's because you've got sweet fuck all to go on!'

I could see it would be problematic if Lionel started investigating his girlfriend's mother for murder, though. I sighed loudly to make a point.

Lionel was shaking his head at me. 'Do you have anything else to tell me?'

'That's it.'

'Well, you've told me nothing I can use. Come on, Dor.'

'Lionel,' I whined. 'You have to look into it.'

'How about I be the judge of that? Wait!' He put his hand up in front of my face. 'Wait. I'm making a judgement. The answer will be in soon.'

'Stop it, you idiot.'

'Oh, here it comes. The answer is no. A big fat no. I, Lionel Hermansen, will not be starting an investigation into *nothing*. But thank you so much for wasting my precious time this morning.'

I wasn't going to be drawn into a fight with my arrogant brother, so I said nothing more.

'I've got to get to work. Can you just stay out of trouble for one minute? I'll call you tonight. Hopefully, you've straightened out by then.' He walked off.

'Dickhead,' I said under my breath.

With Lionel's refusal to take my pressing issues seriously, I set to work in The Brew. Saturday mornings could get busy, so it was all hands on deck.

In a quiet moment, I asked Laura about her girlfriend, Sam. They had been a couple for nearly two years. Sam was a few years older than Laura and had worked out at the plant since she graduated from high school. She might know something about Becker, I figured. At that point, I was grasping at anything that might shed light on the situation. I needed something to make Lionel take notice.

'Sam never liked Becker,' Laura told me. 'But, honestly, it's not like she knew him well. Most staff at the plant rarely saw him. If they heard from management, it was usually through Tristan, rather than Bruce. I know Sammy thinks Tristan's a tosser if that's helpful.' Tristan was Annika's husband and, of course, Bruce Becker's son-in-law.

'Not really helpful,' I said. 'We all think that.'

'Well, from what I can tell, Sam didn't like Bruce for the same reasons as most of us. He was difficult, and she didn't approve of his cut-throat business dealings.'

It was commonly felt by the town's residents that Becker's business dealings—privately, not within the plant—were grey in nature. He wasn't considered the most trustworthy guy, and yet he was practically running Deepwell.

I took a couple of orders out that Sayed had prepared. Then Leanne came in and I started making her regular order for her. She waited until I'd finished with the coffee machine before she started talking.

'I hope you two haven't been sick, Eudora?' Leanne waited for an answer, but with my mind elsewhere I didn't catch on quick enough. 'We missed you yesterday. It's been a long time now since you had to take a day off work.'

'Oh, of course. Yeah. I mean, no. We weren't sick. We just had some other business to take care of.'

'I'm glad to hear it. Is Jules going to be put on the permanent roster?'

Jules had waitressed before, but not for many years. 'Do you think she'd make a good addition? We're not adding her on just yet. But if business picks up, I'd like to.'

'I think she'd make a fine waitress here. She did good.' Leanne gave me an encouraging nod then made her way to a table because there were two other customers lined up behind her by then.

I was pleased to hear that. Now all Sayed and I needed was for business to improve. In the past, we'd thought of various ways we might be able to increase our profits or add value to the café. Laura suggested adding a second-hand record store in the back. She painted a groovy picture with crates full of albums, and a player that would run the music through The Brew's existing speaker system. Then customers could make sure the records played okay before they bought. 'While they're here for coffee, they might flip through the records. And while they're checking for that vinyl they really want, maybe they'll buy a coffee, too,' Laura told us. Sayed and I hadn't jumped at the idea because, well, what did we know about selling music? But Laura had wide musical taste and knowledge. Other than my father, I couldn't think of a single person who knew more about music than Laura, and she was only in her early twenties.

For Sayed and I, it seemed that the best way to increase business would be to update all our equipment and furnishings. Then again, there was something sweet about our haphazardly decorated little café. The Brew had a mismatched retro charm with a hint of bohemia and a dash of kitsch. That could be seen as a plus, couldn't it? 'If people want a chain store look and service, with brand new matching laminate tables, maybe they need to go to Coffee Town. We offer a genuine, small-town service here. It's personal,' I'd told Sayed, preaching to the converted. Anyway, we couldn't afford an update like that even if we'd wanted one.

'Dora, can we talk?' Cloud stood before me in light blue shorts and a singlet. She was gorgeous, and I could see why Lionel was smitten.

'Sure. Let's go out back. Laura,' I called. 'I'll be in the courtyard a moment.'

Cloud and I settled on the patio chairs. 'I know you aren't letting this whole Leila-Becker thing go, but you have to.'

'Lionel?' I asked. He obviously couldn't keep his mouth shut. Cloud nodded. 'He discussed this with you? Look, I know Leila keeps saying she doesn't want anything to do with this, and well, neither do I really. But a man is dead. Maybe you need to do the right thing.'

'You don't know what you're doing, Dora.'

'Then tell me! Tell me what I am doing.'

'I need you to leave it. There's nothing I *can* tell you.'

'We could go around and around like this all afternoon. But, I repeat, a man is dead.'

Cloud leaned back in the chair and sighed. I could tell she was thinking of the best way to start pushing her point again. 'You think Leila did something, but she didn't. She didn't do anything wrong.'

'Fine. Prove it. Right now all I have is clues pointing towards your mother. And when I ask her about Becker, she seems ... well, guilty.'

Cloud's lips pouted. She tucked her hair behind her ears and leaned forward towards me. 'You're making a mistake, and you need to stop. Now,' she said in a growl.

'Are you threatening me?' Cloud said nothing; she kept her gaze up. 'I know you love your Mum and I get that you're trying to help her. I do. But she needs to come clean.'

I stood up to leave and noticed that Cloud's eyes looked red. I suddenly felt sorry for her. She looked mournful, like a child needing affection. But what was I going to do? A suspected murder wasn't something I could overlook, and that was precisely what Cloud was asking me to do.

When I got back inside, Sayed was folding his apron ready to visit his parents in Brisbane. The trip was in place of his missed visit the day before. I think his mother needed to see that her son was okay. I gave him a firm hug. 'Give my love to your Mum and Dad, okay?' He nodded and said, 'Please don't do anything else until I get back. I'll see you later tonight.'

I saluted him and hoped he wouldn't ask me to promise. I had no intention of stopping my investigations after what had gone on that day with Lionel and Cloud.

As Sayed left through the back door, I grabbed my phone and texted Lionel: *What are you doing tonight?*

Five minutes later, his text came through: *Dinner with Cloud in Noosa. Unless you need me?*

I replied: *Nevermind. All good with me. Enjoy.*

Perfect, I thought.

CHAPTER THIRTY-SIX

After Laura and I closed The Brew, I had a quick shower. The sky was deepening in colour. Sayed was in Brisbane, visiting his family, and it was time to enact my plan.

I drove out towards Leila's house on Hunter Street, taking the back roads. Then I turned onto Vantage Road and drove from the opposite direction to my usual route. The key to my plan was that it was also the opposite direction from the one Cloud and Lionel would take that evening. When I saw the Hunter Street turn off ahead, I backtracked to park on a nearby shoulder that would be off the road, yet wouldn't draw attention to my car. Fortunately, that section of Vantage Road was quiet anyway.

As I sat there with darkness encroaching, I planned what I would ask Leila. Could I get her to admit she was involved? And, if I could, what was my plan then? I had no clear answer to that. Yet I'd come that far, and I wasn't going to turn away. A couple of cars passed, their headlights already on to protect them on the dusky country road. Then I saw a maroon sedan pull out onto Vantage from Hunter Street. I saw a flash of blonde hair and knew it was Cloud; I guessed she was meeting Lionel at his place, or at Dad's.

I took a couple of deep breaths. I was nervous. Whatever you do, do not accept the offer of a cuppa this time, I told myself. It suddenly occurred to me that no one knew of my planned visit to Leila's. I shuddered at that thought, and grabbed my phone. Staring at my favourites list, I made a quick decision: Jules, it was. I had not fully updated her on the shit-show my life had become, so Jules was the least likely to freak out. I sent the text: *FYI on my way to Leila's right now* and received the reply: *Erm. Ok. WTF?* I switched my phone to silent and took off towards Leila's.

Walking from the car, I got straight down to business. 'You need to tell me exactly what is going on, Leila. Something's not right and I'm not going away.'

Leila had been sitting on a bench stool on her verandah when I pulled up. 'I told you I want nothing to do with all of this,' she called back.

'All of what, though? What don't you want to be a part of?'

'The thing with Becker. It's nothing to do with me.' She looked haughty as she turned her face away from me.

'Isn't it? You seem adamant that it's not connected to you, yet … the lady doth protest too much, methinks.'

Leila's exterior started to crumble and what I saw underneath was perplexing. I had kept my distance, keeping a clear path to the car and my keys in my hand, ready for a fight. I'd expected that if Leila did break, it would be in anger. But what I saw didn't look like anger. Leila appeared to be afraid of something —prison, perhaps?

I gave another push, intending to provide Leila with no option but to spill her guts. 'I won't stop until I find out,' I warned her. 'I already went to see Annika …'

At the mention of Annika's name, Leila's mouth quivered and I noticed her fingers rubbing on the fabric of her skirt. The woman was anxious to say the least. 'May the Gods help me if you don't let up,' Leila said, her voice taking on a pitch I had not heard before. 'You're going to get me killed. Both of us, even.' Leila quickly scanned around. 'Come inside,' she said.

'I don't think so. I'd prefer to stay right here.'

With her hands fidgeting at her sides now, Leila continued to scan the area. She *was* afraid, and not just of getting caught. Why was everyone in Deepwell so scared?

Feeling sorry for her then, I coaxed. 'Leila, I think you're already in trouble. You're hiding something, and I know you've got those poison flowers in your garden. You're a witch, so I'm guessing you know exactly how to use them, and I don't think Becker died of a plain old heart attack. If you want me to try and help, then I need you to tell me the truth.'

With that, she came down the stairs. I took a step away from her. Leila noticed and scoffed lightly, but stopped where she was all the same. In a quiet voice, she said, 'I can't get mixed up in this. If Annika …'

'Why Annika?'

'She's the one. If she finds out I'm talking to you about this, well … Hell, if you've already spoken to her, then maybe she's coming for me now.'

'I'm going to need more explanation than that I'm afraid.'

'She's the one holding a secret.'

'Okay …'

'You have no idea what you've got yourself into with this,' said Leila, a direct copy of Cloud's message for me. 'Annika came to see Cloud a few months back, to have a tarot reading done. I was here, too, but I stayed in the kitchen. On her way out, Annika stopped at the wolfsbane, just like you did.'

'It surprises me that someone like Annika would know anything about wolfsbane. Nail polish colours, or term deposits, maybe,' I added, feeling bitchy.

Leila twisted the side of her mouth when she realised I wasn't adding anything serious to the conversation. 'Oh, she knew nothing about wolfsbane, believe me. "What's this beautiful flower?" she asked me. Just like you did. I told her not to touch it. I told her that wolfsbane's extremely poisonous. I warned her.'

'Oh my God.'

'Yes. Now you see. Then, just last week, Annika came banging on my door in the middle of the night. Cloud wasn't here.

She was with Lionel. But Annika didn't care. "I need you to talk to my father for me" she yelled at me, near to hysterical. I thought maybe she'd lost her mind, with trauma, you know. What with her father …'

Now that Leila was talking, the words were coming easy.

Though still unsure of Leila, I tried to soften my face a bit as I listened intently.

'I didn't let her in. I told her I couldn't help her. But on the way out, that girl stopped again right by those flowers. I wasn't sure what she was up to.'

'What? What did she do?'

'After a few seconds, she let out this sound. From right down here.' Leila gently punched her stomach. 'So painful to hear. Then she turned and gave me a look. You know how they say a look that could kill? Well, that was it. Then she just got in the car and tore off. Now, do you see?'

'You're telling me that Annika Cotter killed Becker, her own father. You think she came back at some point and took one of the blooms?' I felt energy begin to swirl around me.

'Becker's here. I feel him,' I said. 'Do you think that means we're on the right track?'

'Probably,' replied Leila. 'But I still don't want any part.'

This had to be what he wanted from me: to find out the truth.

'If Annika wanted to kill her father, why was she upset about it? That part of the story doesn't make sense.'

'It's not easy to kill someone, Dora Hermansen. It was her own father. I'm guessing she had mixed feelings in the aftermath. The reality, you know.'

'Yes, I see your point.' So I had been really wrong. If I was to believe Leila—and I did at that point—then she was innocent of anything except mistakenly offering information to someone who then used it to commit a crime. Her reluctance to get involved in this was actually fear that Annika might come for her next. I could see why Leila was so frightened. Annika had a scary edge to her; she always had. Plus, if she knew we were on her tail, there was no telling what she might do to protect herself. Now I had not only placed Leila entirely within the firing line, but myself as well.

I had a thought. 'Leila, what night was it that Annika came to you wanting you to speak with Becker?'

'I'd say it was Tuesday night. Well, Wednesday morning really. It was well after midnight.'

I strained my brain, trying to think back to the night I dreamed of the buck. That was the night Annika had written off her car. She was probably roaring away from Leila's when she hit the buck.

Annika was running scared, and Leila and I should be, too. 'We have to take this to Lionel. It'll be enough for him to present to the sergeant. Neither of us will be safe until she's in custody,' I said.

'Is that what Becker wants?'

'How would I know what he wants?' I blurted. I could feel my face reddening as I realised the implications of what I'd said. I was responsible for my own lack of usefulness in this situation. 'Anyway, it doesn't matter if he wants this or not. A murder has been committed, and the police need to know. You're involved already. There's no backing out.'

Leila looked frustrated but her facial expression eventually settled on resign.

'I'll call Lionel. He'll know what to do.' I was dialling before I finished my sentence.

'What is it? I'm just arriving at the restaurant,' said Lionel, sounding annoyed already.

'You need to take notice now. It wasn't Leila. It was Annika. I'm telling you, Becker was murdered. I'm here with Leila right now. She knows the truth.'

'Annika? Hold on. Cloud, I have to take this. I'm going outside.' I could hear Cloud fussing in the background amid the clinking of cutlery and crockery in the restaurant. 'Okay. How does she know this? Does she have any proof?' returned Lionel.

I put my phone on speaker so that Leila could hear the conversation too. 'Annika knows about the poison flowers Leila grows in her front garden.'

'Poison flowers. What a fucking stupid idea,' grunted Lionel.

'You're on speaker, Lionel.' I mouthed sorry to Leila.

'Nice one, Dor. What else?'

'So, there's a flower missing, like I told you earlier today,' I reminded him pointedly. I continued to tell Lionel about the night of Annika's accident, how upset she was.

Finally, Lionel said, 'Please tell me you've got more than that.'

'Well …' I started.

'It's not enough, Dora. Goddamn it! What do you think the law is? You've got to have real proof. Not intuitions about poisoned flowers in someone's front yard, and women crying in the night.'

'Fine, forget it,' I said and hung up. I turned to Leila 'It's you and me, Leila. We're on our own.'

'Then you need to get Becker involved. You can ask him what happened and what we should do. I can't do it the way you can. You have the power of communication, even if you haven't worked it all out yet. You know that deep down, I think.'

'I'm not sure that I do. I've got next to no idea what I'm doing.'

'You have real power in you. Now's the time to put it to use. I'll help you.'

Those were the words I'd wanted so much to hear. I was overjoyed that Leila was on board, though my expression of it was tempered by the situation that we found ourselves in. We were now embroiled in solving an actual crime and life felt a lot more dangerous than it had that morning.

CHAPTER THIRTY-SEVEN

'The thing is,' Leila was telling me when we were settled inside, 'You have everything you need inside you to hear exactly what these spirits are trying to tell you.'

I had just been telling her of ghosts I'd seen: confused and upset people by the supermarket and the library in town, occasional sightings in the street where I would turn and walk the other way. Now I had to live with the guilt of it.

'You don't need to develop skills so much as tap into what you have already. As I said before, you are holding a lot of natural power—'

'Did I always have it?'

'Probably some, yes, but what can happen is a person with an in-tune mind can have their skill levels pumped right up through an extreme event. I'm sorry to mention it, but it's probably related to what happened with your ex.'

'Why, though? How?'

'Some things we don't know. We may never be able to say. Or maybe, in time, science will be able to explain us, the way it has explained some of the workings of the non-skilled.'

'The non-skilled?'

'All the humans with no supernatural skills whatsoever.'

'Okay.' I was pleased to have learned something new. 'Unskilled. Got it.'

'No! God, never say that. Non-skilled is the term. Don't say un-skilled. That's a slur.'

Oops, I thought, as I slid into the couch.

Leila had offered me a cup of herbal tea, and I had accepted. I no longer feared her, no longer suspected her. I took a sip. 'So, how do I tap into this power then?'

'Well, it's all fascinating.' Yes, it would be to Leila, I thought. I'd seen how animated she became when the topic turned supernatural. Leila continued. 'So, it's all about confidence and relaxing into what is already there within you. When the dead realise that you can see them without fear, then the communication part will be easier to manage. No doubt you've been scared in the past.'

'Correct,' I replied. Could I do what Leila was asking of me, I wondered. After all this time? I had to be brave and open up my world. It didn't matter what I feared might come my way. In the short-term, I had to do it for Becker; in the long-term, I wanted my life to be a useful one where I used my gifts for good. Onwards and upwards, as they say. Still, it was a far cry from being a business owner, a café manager, or a wife.

'So, the main thing is not to show fear?'

'The number one thing, yes. If you approach with fear, it can over-excite the spirits, or even enrage some. They need to be able to relax, as well. Remember, this is much more difficult for them than it is for you. Also, confidence in yourself is important. Remember these are spirits who have a problem. Otherwise, they wouldn't still be here. They'd be somewhere much more pleasant than this. They need help. So, these ghosts will be more comfortable if they sense that you are a solid person who might be able to handle their issues.'

'So, what you're saying is that I need to become a ghost therapist? I'm not sure if I'm cut out for that.'

Leila laughed. 'Oh, I think you are. Don't worry.' But I *was* worried. I had Post Traumatic Stress Disorder. I was fragile. I wasn't a professional; I was the patient. 'Are you worrying?'

I realised I had been sitting looking horrified.

'You really think I can do this?'

'Yes. Here's what we'll do. Tomorrow night we'll have a séance at the plant. That will be a good spot to get information from Becker because it's *his* place. He'll be comfortable there and it will make the connection easier. We'll need a few people involved because the more energy we can ramp up, the better. Not that you always need huge amounts of energy. This is just because you're—'

'New,' I jumped in.

'Yes.'

I grabbed my diary from my handbag, not because I was in danger of forgetting the date, but to keep a list of instructions from Leila. 'Okay, who do we invite?'

Leila gave me a funny look, glancing at my diary and pencil at the ready, then back to me.

'Cloud, obviously. Lionel …'

'I think he might be out. He hasn't been very accepting of my ideas on this murder business, so far. Now he's irritated with me, so I think we might have to count him out.'

Leila grunted. She obviously wasn't happy to hear it. I hoped that I hadn't made things difficult for Lionel. Then again, Lionel was acting like a colossal idiot. That was his choice.

'I have plenty of people, skilled sensitives, that I can invite. But it's short notice.

'What about my friend, Jules? She already knows about me, and I'm sure she would help if I needed her.'

'Okay. Yes.'

'And Sayed, of course. If he feels up to it.'

'That makes five of us. It might be enough. I'll bring anything else we'll need,' Leila said.

It seemed like we had a plan. On my way out, I turned to Leila. 'You need to stay inside tonight. Keep your door locked. Please tell me that you will. Who knows what Annika is capable of.'

'Don't worry about me. You take care too, and keep your car doors locked on the way home.'

***

When I arrived home, Sayed was inside. I parked in the carport and with my doors still locked, then I took out my mobile and called Cloud. This was not the time to feel awkward about calling someone I didn't know very well for the first time.

'Dora? What can I do for you?'

'Look I know it's a bit unexpected me calling like this, but I need to give you a heads up. It's about your Mum. She's okay, but she could be in danger.'

'The Annika stuff?'

'I know you're with Lionel and I know how he feels, but this is real. I think you should go home as soon as you can and stay with Leila. She shouldn't be alone.'

I hoped Cloud would be on board through concern for her mother's safety.

'Lionel told me about all that. Honestly, I think you're barking up the wrong tree here. This wasn't murder. Becker died from natural causes, Dora. No surprise or mystery.'

'Let's say you're right. But, just in case, could you humour me and stay with your Mum tonight?'

'I'll see,' was Cloud's noncommittal answer. Then I could hear Lionel getting involved in the background.

Great, I thought. That's all I needed. I could hear snippets of what Lionel was saying: 'not this again' and 'dog with a bone'.

Closing the call, I couldn't help but wonder what had gotten into the people of Deepwell. Sure, Deepwell had its secrets, its gossip, its tales. But I'd never known the town to be so wrapped up in dangerous threads that if you pull one several others come unwound. It was beyond a joke.

My new life was really serving up drama on a platter—first, the supernatural world, then a murderer walking around free. My plan was to channel Detective Poirot to make sure the truth came to light, and the first step was Leila's séance.

CHAPTER THIRTY-EIGHT

Unlocking the door to the apartment, I was surprised to hear two voices. I had assumed Sayed would be alone, or with just Doggie for company, but a female voice trailed down the hall. I knew exactly who it was, too, and I picked up my pace to meet her in the lounge.

'Aww, it's so good to see you,' said Ameerah, the broad smile on her face a perfect match to Sayed's.

Ameerah Bousaid was Sayed's younger sister. While their other sister lived in Brisbane with her husband and their brood, Ameerah had settled in Noosa Heads two summers before when she got the position of head chef at the River Bar and Restaurant at the Coco Palms Hotel.

We gave each other a big hug, her thick, wavy hair tickling my arm as I leaned in. The front of Ameerah's hair was completely covered in a striped scarf that ended at the nape of her neck, twisted there, then trailed down her back along with her ponytail. It was her signature style.

It had been a long time since I'd seen Ameerah. Noosa Heads was only twenty minutes away, but it was a considerable undertaking—not to mention a big career achievement—being the head chef of a premier restaurant.

'How on earth are you here? Saturday's one of your busiest nights at work, surely?'

'It is. But I can't work at the moment. Not allowed back until next week.'

'Oh my, that sounds mysterious.'

'It's not. I burnt my arm.' Ameerah pulled up a loose cotton sleeve to show me the plaster.

'Damn.'

'Yes, you've both been in the wars,' Sayed said. 'I've filled Am in on a lot, Dor.'

'I see,' I replied stiffly, unsure of what reaction to expect, given how close the Bousaids were. 'Just how much?'

'Pretty much everything,' said Sayed, his face screwing up, ready for chastisement. But I didn't have time for that.

'Okay, well, I know you said not to do anything until you got ba—'

'But you did?' Sayed crossed his arms and gave me a look. I knew from past experience that it was part serious and part light-hearted.

'Lionel is dismissing everything I've found,' I continued. 'I can't count on him, an officer of the law, for anything right now.'

'What have you found?' Ameerah asked.

I gave them a quick rundown on how I had believed that Leila was the culprit because of the flowers and her general odd-ness—there was definitely a lesson there for me to learn on not judging people because they did things differently. 'Then it came to light that it wasn't Leila at all. It was Annika. Annika knew about the flowers, one is missing, and she's acting suspiciously. Again, I brought all this to Lionel, earlier this evening, and he doesn't want to know about it. It's up to Leila and me now.'

'Oh-kay …'

'Look, I've got Leila on board now. I'm happy about that, actually. Finally, she's agreed to help me, and we have a plan.' Then I turned to Ameerah. 'This is where things are going to get a bit weird. I'm going to talk about ghosts and stuff.'

'Actually, that's why I'm here. I want to help.'

'No, I mean *really* weird.'

Ameerah laughed. 'Sayed filled me in, Sis, and frankly, I'm already on board. I'm sure Sayed's told you about our Nanna?

She always spoke of the djinn, the ghosts living parallel to us humans. They're even mentioned in the Quran. Of course, we can't see them, but they can see us.' I nodded, and Ameerah continued. 'Most of our family ignored her rantings about ghosts. Nanna always told us she could see them, but I was the only one who knew it was true. Because I saw them too.'

'Oh my God, you're a sensitive! I have a trillion questions for you, but first things first. I think you can help us. Will you be here tomorrow night?'

'If you want me.'

'We always want you here. It's just … there's something a bit scary happening.' Sayed and Ameerah both gave me the same questioning look and waited for a proper answer. 'Leila and I have planned a séance for tomorrow night. We want Jules and Sayed to be there. The idea is to gain information from Becker, and find out how we can help him. I think you'd be a great help, Am.'

'Why do you need Jules and me there when we can't speak to ghosts?' asked Sayed.

'Leila says extra energy in the circle will give us a better chance of success. That is, if you are okay with this. Everyone would understand if you didn't want to take part. Cloud will be there to help, of course. By the way, I'm not sure I like her for Lionel anymore,' I admitted to Sayed. 'Anyway, no time for that now. So, how do you feel about this? We can do it without you.'

'I wouldn't say I'm comfortable,' he grimaced. 'But I can do it.'

Ameerah piped up. 'Do you expect it to be dangerous?'

'No, I don't think so. The thing is, Becker's been hanging about looking for help for a week now. He wants to tell me something, and I'm pretty sure his message will be useful. Becker wasn't exactly known for his sweet nature, but I don't see any reason why he would be a direct danger to us.'

I felt uncomfortable remembering the possession, when Sayed—and the rest of us—had indeed been in grave danger. I flushed a little.

'It's okay,' said Ameerah perceptively. 'Sayed told me about the other night.'

It was both an embarrassment and a relief that Ameerah knew. My cheeks flushed deeply. 'I'm so sorry,' I told Ameerah. 'I never intended for Sayed to be hurt like that.'

Ameerah scooched over to me on the couch and put an arm around my shoulders. 'No one is blaming you. Least of all, Sayed. It must have been a nightmare, and I understand.'

I felt the heat of tears welling. Wishing more than anything to hold them back, I waved my hands in front of my face. Finally, I managed and straightened myself up. 'Okay, the only way to fix all this is to push on. Be strong and push on.'

'Dor, what about leaving Jules out of it? Perhaps Ameerah, since she's a … what did Leila call them?'

'A sensitive. You're a sensitive,' I said, smiling to Ameerah. 'I am.'

'So, since my sister is one of you,' he pointed gently towards me, 'Maybe you could leave Jules out, and Ameerah would be enough. Energy-wise.'

'What do you think?' I asked, addressing Ameerah. 'You're more experienced than I am, after all.'

'Are you kidding me? I'm in.'

We all laughed. Obviously, some people thrived on weirdness. For a good ten minutes after that, I picked her brain about sensitives. Her information was more forthcoming and relaxed than Leila's had ever been. I asked how long she had known, how she felt about it, in what ways she used her abilities, who knew about it, and so on. It was a revelation to hear that sensitives were just as real—and as secretive—in the cultures beyond my own. Then came the big question, at least the one of the moment. I waited until Sayed had gone into the kitchen to switch the kettle on. 'Do you know about werewolves?'

Ameerah leaned back but kept my gaze. 'Why? What do you know?'

'I heard mumblings about it. Are they real?'

Ameerah leaned in and spoke sotto voce. 'Yes, and you don't want to mess with them. They're super-secretive, and don't like those outside the community to know about them.'

'It would endanger a werewolf, I imagine. But are they a danger to us?'

'Yes, and no. Weres are formidable creatures, but not evil, you know? They're strong, and they're good at sneaking around. They're shy, I suppose. They rarely get caught out.'

'Leila told me that we don't have them here, except those who travel here.'

'Yes, that's true. Kind of. We don't have actual werewolves because, well, no wolves.' Exactly as Leila said. 'But they can travel on planes when they're human. So, they occasionally come here, and a few have even stayed. Do not ask me why, but they seem to enjoy surfing. I know there are at least two living on the coast right now. One comes into the restaurant sometimes.'

My mouth dropped open in a most embarrassing fashion. Ameerah looked towards the kitchen to check on Sayed. Fortunately, he had decided to do a few dishes, so we continued.

'She always orders steak or roast. Anything meaty.' We giggled.

Then we had to change subjects because Sayed arrived back with a tray of tea.

'What have you girls been discussing behind my back?' he asked cheerfully.

'How wonderful you are, bro,' replied Ameerah, and Sayed and I laughed.

CHAPTER THIRTY-NINE

The Deepwell Water Treatment Plant ran 24/7, so it was lit up like a Christmas tree. The running noise travelled the half a kilometre to us, through the forest. Leila scurried about, setting up incense and candles and laying out cushions in the small clearing. Had this been a daytime picnic with friends, it would have been a bohemian event that I would have remembered and cherished. But Leila, Cloud, Sayed, Ameerah, and I were there for a séance.

Now and then I heard the creak of metal from the water treatment structures. The sound was unnerving, but I guessed quite normal.

When I looked in the other direction, beyond the glow from our group's torches and the candles Leila was lighting, I saw endless darkness. I knew the general area well enough. There were kilometres of forest before you came upon the seaside towns of Tewantin and Noosaville—at least that had been the case decades ago.

Being there that night was the natural progression of accepting my ability, I reminded myself. I had to push on, and I was grateful to have three people with me who knew a hell of a lot more than I did. My preference would still have been for my brother to take his job seriously, by acting on my suspicions, but it was too late for that. Instead, here I was, about to take part in my very first séance, in the middle of the bush no less. Should anything go wrong—and I could think of a hundred possible ways it could—what were we going to do then? Call Lionel? At that stage, what on earth would I tell him? In many respects, the séance seemed like a terrible idea, yet here we were.

Given what Sayed had been through in the preceding days, I was confident I had the best husband in the world. I also had no idea why Ameerah had decided to turn up and get herself involved in what seemed like an event any sane person would run from. Was her life so dull that she needed a shake-up? Still, I was grateful. Energy-wise, the more, the better.

'You don't have to take part, you know?' I said to Sayed quietly.

'I sort of do,' he replied, and I knew what he meant: he wouldn't let me go alone. Best husband in the world. I saw a flash of him early that Friday morning as he slunk down from our ceiling, and shivered.

'You cold?' Sayed asked.

'No. Fine, honey,' I replied. Those memories and visions would have to sit with those of my relationship with Troy, I supposed. After all this, I would lock them away. No one got through life without pain and heartache, I told myself. I was no better, no different, from everybody else.

I remembered something I'd heard years ago: it's not what happens to you, but how you deal with it. It hadn't helped me that much in the short-term; the trauma I'd been through had enveloped and controlled me so strongly. But, as I took my first, tentative steps out of those dark times, that's when I was able to take that idea and develop it. I had made it a part of my life, and now, with this new direction I was taking, I would try to espouse it further again.

My attention was snatched away by Leila who handed me some insect repellent, then began to explain the process for the evening.

'Now, we sit in a circle, close enough that we can touch, but not close enough to crowd each other. In the centre will be this pen: Becker's pen.'

'How did you get that?' I asked.

'Never mind that,' said Leila. I glanced around the circle and found that Cloud looked very put out. Their mother-daughter relationship sure was a complex one, I thought again. Leila continued. 'We gather our energy, each separately. Then we pool it, drawing it in and using it to reach out to Becker. If Becker comes—'

'He will,' I butted in. 'Sorry. But I can feel him already.' No one was more surprised at my forthrightness than me.

'Then, I will start to communicate with him, and then you, Dora, need to try to tap into Becker. See if you can start to talk to him.'

My stomach fluttered at the thought. The events of three nights previous were palpable—my husband all twisted, the whole thing so very wrong—but this wasn't the same thing. That was evil. Becker, he was just a pain in the butt who needed my help. This was my chance to shine.

'Do you expect any danger tonight, Leila?' asked Ameerah, clearly wanting a second opinion. All power to her.

'This isn't my first time at the rodeo,' said Leila seriously. I stifled a smile. Leila used some odd turns of phrase, but her rather annoying disposition was growing on me. 'There is a slight possibility of something going wrong, always is. But Cloud is experienced, and we know what we're doing. All you need to do is follow our instructions and stay focussed. Don't panic.'

Ameerah and Sayed seemed pleased enough with that answer.

Leila had a preparation routine that involved a lot of body shaking and flicking movements, her hands skimming across different body parts. It was an odd display that looked more like an Olympic sport warm-up. When she had finished, she raised her hands to the sky and began reciting. I wasn't sure if it was a prayer, but I quite enjoyed it. At that point, I felt more enthused about the whole process, and my trust in Leila grew. It felt almost like a spell—she was a witch, after all. More likely, this part of the process offered me a sense of the spiritual for which, perhaps, I had been longing. Something for me to unpack later anyway.

As we settled into place, the intermittent noises from our surrounds continued: the plant, the rhythmic cacophony of insects, an occasional mammal or marsupial scrambling or calling, the creak and rustle of branches, leaves and vines. A musty smell from the forest floor wafted occasionally, but for the most part, all I could smell was the sweet spice from an incense stick that had been stabbed into the dirt beside me.

I breathed deeply. I could feel the air being drawn into my throat and travelling deep down into the bottom of my lungs. My stomach enlarged. Then it was expelled back into the humid night. A mozzie buzzed near my ear, but I tried to focus on Leila's words. I leaned into the experience. My personal energy gathered. Unlike the night of the possession, when I was full of fear and desperation, this was a smoother process. I knew what to expect, and I knew Sayed would be okay. I slipped into an alert yet relaxed state. Leila—initially a difficult woman to trust—was now my guide, and I let her lead the way completely.

'Are you there, Becker?' Leila said, her strong voice calling into the night.

By then, I could feel his presence all around us.

I smelled nothing beyond the forest flavours, though: the dampness of the soil and moss, stones, some grasses. But Becker's energy—that pressure—encircled me.

'I feel him,' Leila said.

'Uh-huh,' said Cloud.

'Me too,' added Ameerah.

'We sense you there,' Leila told him. 'And we're here to help. Dora, you go now.'

Yikes. Talk about throwing me in at the deep end. I felt awkward, suddenly unsure of what to say or how to speak to Becker. I was ... well, self-conscious.

'We're here as friends, Becker. We, umm, we want to help you. We know you're upset, err, about something. That's why you haven't moved on.' There was no answer, and I wondered how to continue. I gave Leila a questioning look, but she pushed me on with a nod. 'Try to speak to me, Becker.' I shrugged my shoulders at Leila, and she nodded again. 'Can you do that for me? Can you tell me what happened?'

The air around us pressurised, as though the world was imploding. It was the same feeling as at the cemetery on Tuesday, only this time less threatening—because I wasn't alone in a graveyard most likely. But, of course, this time it wasn't Troy. The strong reaction from Becker wasn't so much bad or painful as it was useful. I knew he was there, and I was ready to find some answers.

'Becker, if you can't find a way through Dora, you can speak through me. I give you permission,' Leila said.

Great. Here we go, I thought. She's about to use my least favourite supernatural skill so far.

As soon as Leila had uttered the words, the air moved. My hair was in its usual plait, but the wisps that fell around my face fluttered. I gathered them and pushed them back, behind my ears. At the same time, the whoosh of air blew out several of the candles. Becker had clearly decided to take Leila up on her generous offer.

Ameerah and Sayed looked grave. It was evident that Ameerah wasn't ready for this, and I realised that I should have given her fuller warning about Leila's penchant for channelling. I reached over and rubbed Ameerah's shoulder a couple of times before placing my focus back on the séance. Cloud moved forward quickly to relight the candles using a long gas lighter; the smell of snuffed candle permeated the air.

As soon as Cloud sat back down, she looked towards Leila. My gaze followed. Becker really had taken her up on the offer. All Leila's features remained, of course. Her pale skin, almost translucent, glowed in the candlelight. She was wearing a dress made from patches of fabrics, velvet and cotton, in maroon, red, and purple.

But her thick red hair had risen through a static charge. Something in her face had changed, too. Was it the way her features moved? I'd encountered this before with people I came across, often in the café. I would see someone that reminded me of another. Studying them, I would be unable to find any single feature shared with the other person. Yet, somehow, something in their whole being was similar. People really were more than the sum of their physical parts.

For a few seconds, very little happened. Then Leila's face animated. She looked shocked as she gazed from one of us to the next. It looked like something had gone horribly wrong.

'Oh my God,' I exclaimed.

'It's okay,' said Cloud. 'Becker, it's okay. You're inside Leila now, and you can speak to us when you're ready.'

Then I realised. Nothing was wrong at all. Becker was where he needed to be, and Leila was just fine. Becker had merely gotten a fright when he realised that Leila was channelling his spirit. It was intriguing to realise that a ghost was subject to confusion, misunderstandings, anxieties, and fears, the same as those on the earthly plane. Who knew what else was occurring in the spirit world?

Becker began to use Leila as a conduit. His face—or Leila's, depending on which way you looked at it—turned from fear to urgency. He wanted to speak. Why was he waiting? Was he unsure of how to proceed?

We all followed Cloud's lead, waiting patiently. No one gave Becker advice. We just sat there. My instinct told me to share some words of encouragement. Finally, I told him, 'It's okay, Becker. Just relax and—'

'Shut up,' barked Cloud. 'You don't know what you're doing, and I don't need your help.'

Cloud really wanted me to remember that. But I had a gut feeling that led me on.

Trying to ignore Cloud, I said to Becker, 'Relax. And when you feel you can say something, say it. Remember we want to help you. We want whoever did this to you to pay.'

226

Cloud was fuming, and that worried me.

After a minute, which felt like an hour, Becker's mouth began to twitch gently, though I could tell from the look on his face that he was struggling to make even that tiny movement happen. Then came a noise; air was expelled, close to a grunt.

Becker's rented body went stiff. He was frustrated. I felt sorry for him. He may have been an arse in life, but he no longer had life, did he? Besides that, he didn't deserve to have that life snatched from him. And by his own daughter ... how much more can a person lose?

'Heylpme,' he boomed suddenly, taking all of us by surprise. Even Cloud jumped. In fact, she looked concerned and got up off the cushion she'd been sitting cross-legged on.

Then, using Leila's tongue and lips, and moving them haphazardly, he said, 'You he-help me.' He was understandable enough. The message was clear, despite his lack of coordination.

'How? How can we help you?'

Cloud was silent, sitting with a furrowed brow. Becker was stuttering, but I couldn't make out what he was trying to say.

'What is it, Becker?' I asked. 'You can tell me. I'll try to help you. I told you that, and I mean it.'

'Dora,' Cloud hissed, but I had decided to do what I could at that point. From where I sat, it seemed like Cloud was doing nothing to help the situation.

'It's okay, Becker,' I said.

'No,' he said, his words getting clearer by the minute. 'Danger.'

At that, Cloud rushed in and began shaking Leila. 'Mum, wake up.' She turned to us 'He's right. We're in danger. We need to get out of here.'

I jumped to my feet along with the others. 'What is it?' I asked as Sayed and Ameerah looked on, horrified.

'Gather what you can. Mum, wake up.' Cloud slapped her mother.

'What. What happened?' Leila was groggy. 'Is it done?'

'We have to get out of here. There's something wrong, Mum. Someone's here in the area. I can feel it.'

Cloud would have better sensibility than I did, me being a newbie. I felt nothing different. But if I'm honest, it all felt strange to me. I would have continued to focus on Becker and his communications none the wiser. When he spoke of danger, I assumed that he was talking about something to do with his murder, his killer.

Sayed was collecting candles and placing them into the cardboard box that we'd come with. The site became a flurry of activity.

Leila asked Cloud. 'Do you think someone followed us here?'

'I'm worried in case it was Annika,' Cloud admitted.

I certainly didn't need to be told twice. No way did I want to mess with a murderer out in the sticks after dark, even in a group. Grabbing pillows and stuffing them into a sizeable, un-bleached cotton bag as quickly as I could, I was soon ready to flee.

'Are we ready? Ameerah asked, her face pale.

'I think so,' said Leila. 'Let's walk back to the cars. Stay close. Once there, we'll decide what to do.'

We walked single file for most of the way; it wasn't easy to spread out on the path that led back to the road—to call it a path would be generous, in fact, given the number of obstacles. Leila took the lead, and Sayed insisted on taking the rear. His reasoning was that he was the tallest, and probably the strongest. He, therefore, felt he was the best person to fight off a real, live human. 'If it were a spirit trying to get us again, then I might see it differently,' he said.

There was no doubt I was in the thick of it lately. Ghosts, demons, and a murderer possibly stalking us through the bush. I wondered how close Annika had gotten, assuming that it was her. What might she have done if her father had been able to keep talking though Leila? I took a moment to rest in the disappointment that I had been unable to communicate with Becker myself. Still, it was a start.

At the road, far enough from the plant that our cars wouldn't have been seen, we stopped and shone our torches around to ensure we had not been followed. None of us could see anything out of the ordinary.

Leila flicked a pointer finger to draw us close. 'The graveyard,' she whispered.

So it was that we drove into town, to Deepwell Cemetery.

CHAPTER FORTY

The street was intermittently lit by houses and the streetlights near the cemetery entrance. It was eight-thirty by then. Being back in town was a relief. Visiting the graveyard at night, not so much.

We were grouped by the cemetery gate when Cloud suggested we just 'leave it for now.' It was too dangerous, she intimated.

'I'm really worried, Mum. I don't think it's a good idea to continue,' she was saying quietly. 'What if Annika's followed us? Plus, I don't think you're up to it.' Cloud turned to Sayed and I. 'Mum's weak. I don't think going again will be good for her health.'

I certainly didn't want to do anything to harm Leila.

'Leila, how are you feeling?' I asked. I lightly touched her arm, but she grabbed it away.

'Fit as a fiddle. Let's go.'

'You're sure?'

This put mother and daughter, again, at loggerheads. Leila would have her way, though. So, Sayed, Ameerah, Cloud, and I followed her down the street a little way. It was decided; we were pressing on.

'It's always locked by this time,' said Leila, nodding towards the main gate. I nearly laughed out loud at her—as though coming to the cemetery at night was common practice for her. Thankfully, I caught myself. Leila, I felt, would not have seen the funny side.

We would have to jump the fence, it seemed. Leila chose a spot to the left of the gate where the bricks had a nice flat top. It made it easy to swing your legs into position for the jump down. I was astonished that Leila could do this so easily; obviously, it wasn't her first time jumping this fence. Not her first rodeo, I mused. We all made it over the wall and, before long, we were heading towards Becker's grave.

Cloud wore a sullen look. Worried for her Mum, or peeved she hadn't got her way? Who knew?

Loosely gathered around Becker's grave, Sayed and I stood a little closer together than the others. I immediately felt Becker. 'He's here.' Sayed gave me an encouraging smile.

'Good,' said Leila. 'No candles. We don't want the neighbours calling the cops.' We formed ourselves into a circle as Leila sprinkled herbs around. We were ready to begin.

Though we had been through the motions less than an hour earlier, we had to repeat the process. I had now prepared myself several times, and I noticed that it felt more natural each time. Grounding—a process of connecting fully to earth, and tapping into the energy around us, and in us—was an enjoyable process for me. In fact, it was very similar to tricks that the psychologist had taught me to try and ground myself in the present after I developed PTSD.

As I felt the sensation of connecting to the soil beneath my feet, it was almost physical. We pooled our energy, and I could feel it physically swirling around me, like being caught in a churning ocean. Then Leila said a prayer and began to address Becker, just as she had done back in Vantage Forest.

This time, Becker entered Leila's body without fuss. Almost immediately, he began to speak through her. Becker's words spilled forth with barely a warm-up.

'Help. Annika. Danger.'

'We know Annika did this to you,' I said. 'But tell us how we can stop her. Point us in the right direction. We need proof.'

'Danger. Help. You, too.'

'You mean Annika is in dang—'

'He's not making any sense,' Cloud cut in. 'I knew we shouldn't have continued with this. And look at what he's doing to Mum.'

'Annika's dangerous, right? Or Annika's *in* danger?' I was desperate to know the extent of his message. Everything pointed to Annika as the murderer. Didn't it? But if so, why would she be in danger?

With Cloud beginning to fuss over Leila, I figured my time to get answers was limited.

'Poison!' Becker shouted as Cloud leaped forward and began shaking her mother again.

'Wake up, Mum. Wake up.'

I looked back and forth between Sayed and Ameerah, who appeared to be as confused as I was. Well, at least Becker had backed up what I thought about the use of poison. I jumped up to give Cloud a hand as she continued to shake Leila. While Cloud coaxed her mother to wake, I continued to push Becker. 'What should we look for, Becker? What?'

Leila began to stir, as Becker got one more message out. 'Triss-san,' he said. It was mumbled, yet I was reasonably sure I had understood him: Tristan.

'Leave her alone, now,' Cloud raised her voice as she addressed me. Her cheeks were red, her brow creased.

I knelt with Cloud in front of Leila. I could feel Cloud's dark mood spreading, causing the air around us to fester. 'Are you okay?' I asked Leila.

'A-okay,' came her reply. I lifted my head to the dark sky and smiled, relieved. A noisy breath escaped Leila as she asked, 'Was it a success?'

'We got something,' I told her. 'I'm certain Becker told us that Annika is in danger. And it may be that we are, too … though it doesn't make sense. Then he said Tristan. I'm sure he did. Thing is—'

'Tristan?' Cloud spoke over me again. 'I certainly didn't hear that.'

I turned to Ameerah and Sayed. 'Did you hear the name Tristan?'

'I … I'm not sure. I'm sorry.' Ameerah's face scrunched up as though she'd let me down.

'I thought I heard it. But I can't be sure,' said Sayed.

'If he did say Tristan, what does he mean by it?' I asked. 'Well, let's look into it. That's all we can do.'

CHAPTER FORTY-ONE

The following morning, my first stop was Deepwell Police Station. I was going to take another shot at getting some action. After all, this wasn't some cute mystery novel where ordinary citizens get about solving crime. It wasn't my job to catch killers and I had developed suspicions as to *why* my brother was dragging his feet …

At the station, Constable Derek Jessup met me at the front counter.

'Where's Lionel?'

'He's due in soon. Want him to call you?'

I had planned my points the night before; I knew this remained a long shot and wanted to make the best of it. How did you explain that you knew a death wasn't natural because you spoke with the dead guy himself? Then I realised that Becker hadn't really confirmed that, had he?

'No worries. I'll catch him later,' I said and went to sit on the bench outside for a moment.

What had Becker said exactly? He had asked for help and said the word danger. He mentioned Annika and Tristan. But he never really said more than their names. Oh, and poison. He had said poison. Now I thought about it, the cops still weren't going to care. Argh. I still felt compelled to run it by the station, though.

I knew in my gut that Becker was trying to solve the puzzle of how he died. More critical now was that Becker was trying to warn us that someone was in danger. That was a here-and-now problem that needed to be dealt with.

I got up and marched back inside. The cops may not care about my hunches, and maybe I'll be laughed out of the station. But all I need is for one officer to harbour a smidge of doubt, then they might visit Annika. I would leave out all the supernatural stuff, of course.

A few minutes later, Derek was staring at me, stunned mullet style.

I took a deep breath. 'Yes, Derek. A hunch.' I knew my voice had risen a bit too high, but I couldn't help it. 'I know what you're thinking, but …'

'Look, I know you've been through a lot. I can understand—'

'Because of what happened to me? Okay, clearly I did *not* know what you were thinking. Because of the Troy thing? For God's sake, Derek. I'm telling you someone is in danger.' I paused a beat, then added in a squeak, 'I just don't know who.'

'I'm not saying this to be harsh,' Derek told me. 'But try and see things from my side, mate. You sound—'

'Crazed?'

'No. But, I mean, there's no solid proof or anything …' Derek looked pained. He didn't want to upset or disrespect me. 'Maybe if you just wait for Lionel to get in, hey? Come on now. Come and sit down. Have a cuppa.'

'No,' I protested.

'Look, I can drop in there this morning sometime, see if the girls are doing alright. How does that sound? But I can't promise you anything. I've got no grounds to do a search, and I've got to be honest with you, I don't think I would find anything anyway.'

'Well, thanks,' I said with just a hint of sarcasm. As I left, I tried to slam the door behind me without realising it had a soft-close attachment installed.

Reflecting in the car, I realised my conversation with Derek had gone as well as I should have expected. 'You've done what you can for now,' I said aloud. Then I brushed it off and drove back to The Brew. It was time for work. I had responsibilities.

***

Keeping busy that morning had been the best thing for me. Laura and I dealt with customers, while Sayed worked behind the scenes, in the kitchen. Each one of us was perfectly capable of doing most jobs in The Brew, and Laura had been working with us for almost since the café opened, yet we had drifted subconsciously into this pattern.

Leanne popped in for her usual mid-morning coffee break, and I had to watch my tongue. I was holding all manner of news that she would find fascinating, but I made sure not to let anything slip that she might grasp as odd. If I had, she would have honed in and tried to find out more. Leanne was a hot gossip-seeking missile. Instead, I asked her how her kids' team was faring. The boys were old enough now that their soccer games weren't confined only to the winter season.

At one point, as I delivered a fried breakfast to a front table, Leanne mentioned that she'd seen Annika near town that morning. 'She didn't look too good,' Leanne said.

'Yeah, well her father did just pass.'

Leanne seemed to accept that—as she should. It was always more comfortable to lie when the lie contained a base of truth of course.

Lunch saw The Brew's tables max out, so not only was I kept busy, and unable to ruminate on the whole Becker deal, but we were making money, too. I was glad for that, having arrived back from the police station that morning to the news we'd barely covered our expenses the month before. 'The mortgage will get paid, but we're going to be strapped for other outgoings,' said Sayed, my posture crumpling as he spoke. I had to pump myself back up again to start attending to customers. So, yeah, full tables were a spirit-lifter.

The Brew hummed along to Kasey Chambers and Shane Nicholson's tune 'Devil's inside my head', punctuated by the whoosh of the cappuccino machine and the beep of the EFTPOS machine. Not for the first time, I felt grateful for The Brew. Despite our precarious financial position, the constancy of owning and running our business had been positive for me. The Brew was ours—mine and Sayed's—and our time and effort building it, and even the struggles, gave me satisfaction. But the world of ghosts, ethereal planes, a world where wolves were people, and people were wolves, was just there in the periphery. In what seemed like a parallel universe, the supernatural world was pressing in on my other life. How to harmonise the two?

It was about two o'clock when a small flash of light caught my eye. I looked through the front window to see dark brown, slicked hair and the glimmer of gold jewellery; Annika was walking past.

'Cover for me a minute,' I said to Laura as I rushed outside. I wanted to gauge Annika's reaction when I raised Tristan's name, and on the street seemed like an excellent place to do it. I certainly wouldn't risk going inside her house again.

'Annika!'

'I do not want to talk to you.'

I caught up so I wouldn't have to say it too loud. 'I know about everything.'

Sure, I didn't. But Annika didn't know that. All she did was sneer at me.

'The poison?' I added, with an eyebrow arched. That produced a look of utter horror on Annika's face. I was on to something. 'I know it was you,' I said, laying a further trap.

'No. No.' Her hands tried to push my words away.

'What I don't know is …' I paused, pondering the implications too late. Would I be placing Tristan in danger by mentioning him to Annika? It was impossible to know. Right or wrong, I pushed on. 'What does Tristan have to do with all this?'

'Jesus Christ, Dora. Shut up,' Annika said, looking left, right, then left again. Her face looked pale, her forehead frowning. 'Fuck! Isn't it enough that you nearly got yourself killed all those years ago? Now you want me dead too.'

I stepped back a pace, shocked at her sudden outburst. I'd expected a reaction—just not that one. 'What danger are *you* in?' I asked her.

Whatever was going on behind the scenes had everyone connected to this drama running scared.

'Maybe I can help,' I continued. 'I know something's going on. I'm not letting up on this.'

Annika's head drooped as she looked at the footpath, stretching her scalp to its limits. I could see that she was biting her lip. 'How did you know?' she asked, looking around to be sure no one was approaching.

'About the poison? Look, I spoke to your Dad, okay?'

To say Annika was shocked would be an understatement. For a moment, I thought she might stumble. I reached for her arm, and she let me stabilise her. 'Come over here,' I told her, guiding her closer to the edge of the footpath where, if we kept our voices down, we wouldn't be heard.

'You spoke to him?' Her voice was deeply disbelieving.

'Through Leila Cowles. I know you wanted Leila to help you. Well, I persuaded her to. Your father's upset, Annika. He wants me to help. He told me about the poison, and he mentioned Tristan.'

'I didn't know.' Annika began crying. 'I didn't. Not until it was too late.'

'Tristan did this? Tristan poisoned your father?'

'Yes.' Annika was bawling now. 'I didn't know until after Dad had eaten the food. His face ... I've never seen such a colour. Then Tristan ...' She looked at me, her eyes steeped in heartbreak, and whispered, 'He wouldn't let me call the ambulance. I tried to. But he said that if I did, he'd tell them that I did it. He said he had my prints on something and they'd believe him because I'd just stood by while Dad died.'

'Oh, Annika,' I said, rubbing her shoulder. That's why she'd been so messed up. Not only did she know her father had been murdered, but she was being threatened by her own husband.

'I couldn't say anything afterwards. To the police, or to anyone. I didn't know what to do. You understand, right?'

'You have to do something, though. You can't leave it like this. Tristan's a murderer, Annika. Holy crap. Your Dad's worried for your safety. That's why he can't settle.'

'He needs to be, too. You've stirred it all up. Tristan will come for me too. I need to talk to Dad.'

'We need to get down to the police station right now is what we need to do.'

'Please. Please,' Annika said, wiping her face gently with her hand. 'I have to talk to Dad. Then I'll go to the police. I promise you.'

I felt around inside the pocket of my waiter's apron for a serviette and handed it to her. She smiled sadly at me and used it to dab under her eyes and then her nose.

'Fine. Let's go to Leila's.' I led Annika through the alley to the back of The Brew. From there, I left my apron in the kitchen and told Sayed what I was up to. Though I had now switched my suspicions from Annika to Tristan, Sayed wasn't too sure. He made sure that Annika saw him. That way, she'd be an idiot to try anything—like murdering me in the car on the way there.

As we buckled up, I said 'You realise the full extent of the danger you're in by not going straight to the station, right?'

Annika nodded.

I shook my head and added under my breath, 'Not to mention me, now.'

CHAPTER FORTY-TWO

Vantage Rd was quiet because Annika and I had left at two-thirty, before the afternoon school rush began. Not that it ever got really busy on Deepwell's roads. Light bounced off the vegetation. Occasionally, the sun—coming from the west for much of the journey—would catch my eyes in the rear-view mirror, stealing away my sight momentarily.

Leila was ready for us, but didn't look happy to see Annika. Like Sayed, Leila didn't have the information I had, and so still believed Annika to be the likely murderer. She listened to my explanations well enough but remained unconvinced. Despite that, I thought Leila greeted Annika with calm professionalism, and she agreed to help her speak to Becker.

'Thank you so much,' Annika was saying before we'd even got through the door. 'You have no idea what this means to me. To be able to speak to Dad just one more time.'

'Where's Cloud?' I asked.

'Not coming.' The answer was short and sharp. Okay, I thought. Mother and daughter are obviously still mid-tiff. Could we handle this on our own, though? 'We don't need her. Not now. No point,' Leila continued as though reading my mind—I must ask her about that sometime.

'You think it's enough to have me here?'

'Yup. But don't get a big head.' Leila smiled a little after she said that; she had just cracked a joke.

I certainly felt more secure performing the ceremony inside rather than in the bush or the graveyard. Candles were already in place, and we were going to use chairs at a round table. The covering was white cotton, the edge of which was embroidered with delicate kangaroo paw flowers. A stubby vase held flowers in the centre of the table as though we were sitting down for a ladies' breakfast. Annika bent down and lifted the edge of the tablecloth to check underneath. Returning to a sitting position, she said, 'Well, that's what people do in the movies, isn't it? Check for wires and stuff.' She smiled even though her face was full of sadness.

'Believe me, you do not need to check for wires,' I told her. 'This is the real deal. Steel yourself.'

Leila pointed at Annika. 'You follow my lead. And Dora's.' Then, turning to me, she added, 'You focus when I say so. Listen. When Becker comes, talk. Help Annika to ask the questions. Help her get the answers she needs.'

'Yes, okay,' I said. 'I will.' Annika nodded meekly. That was new.

This was the first time I'd worked with Leila without Cloud for back-up. Since Leila didn't seem concerned, I decided that I wasn't going to be either. I'm ready, I told myself. Then I said it out loud. 'I'm ready.' I really meant it.

The process was quick. Becker was close already; I had known it the moment we arrived at Leila's Hunter Street abode. I could feel his energy thumping—the pressure. He needed to talk to his daughter just as much as she wanted to speak to him. I wondered what that meant, and I would soon find out.

'Danger,' Becker started loudly, causing me to startle. I looked around the table. Becker had not waited to inhabit Leila's body this time. It was evident that Leila had heard him too, but not Annika. She still sat looking expectant and hopeful.

'You don't hear that?' I asked Annika. I wanted to encourage her to try. She squinted at me.

'Tristan,' Becker boomed. I reacted and Annika remained unmoved but interested in my facial expression.

'I know, Becker. But *what* about Tristan?'

Annika's face opened right up, her mouth dropping; her eyes looked as though they may fall out onto the table. She pulled herself together and focussed on me. Then she looked to the air above the table and cried, 'I'm so sorry, Dad,' with the tears bursting through.

'It's okay,' he said. 'You need to put him away. That's how you'll be safe. That's how I can rest.' I repeated each word to Annika, assuming she still wasn't hearing it.

'I'm scared,' she said, her eyes red. 'Tristy's going to put the blame on me. That's what he said. I think he will, too. He can. I was there.' Her face dropped, so she was looking into her lap. I felt terrible for her, but it was also hard to move forward now that I knew she called her husband *Tristy*. I had to remind myself that it was not the time.

'Becker,' I said firmly to get his attention. I needed concrete answers now. 'What poison did Tristan use?'

'Don't know. It was in the curry.'

'I know,' said Annika sadly. 'It was those purple flowers. He told me afterwards. It was too late by then.' So, it was confirmed.

'Annika, did you take a wolfsbane stalk from Leila's garden?'

'No,' she said. 'I swear it. It wasn't me.'

'The stalk that was missing,' I said. 'It must have been him. Tristan.' I felt a surge of anger towards Leila. Most people would go to the cops if a poisonous plant was stolen from their front yard. What about public safety? But this wasn't the time. I had to put my frustrations aside for the moment. 'So, Tristan took the wolfsbane? But how did he know about it?'

Annika started bawling again, salty drops falling to the tablecloth and soaking in. 'Dad, I'm so sorry. It's my fault. I told Tristan that I'd seen it here.' Turning to Leila, she explained, 'I told him I didn't think you should have it here, because it was poisonous, and it was dangerous to keep it where a child could touch it, put it in their mouth, be poisoned. He would never even have known if I'd kept my big mouth shut!' She dropped her head into her hands and continued to cry.

'That's not important now,' Becker said gruffly. 'Get a hold of yourself, girl.'

Momentarily glad that Annika couldn't hear her father's ghost speaking to her, I summarised the message, softening it a bit. 'You've got to focus, Annika. Your Dad says he needs you.' Creative license is a glorious thing.

Becker sure sounded like, well, Becker. 'You've got a job to do,' he boomed.

'Righto,' I said, although I wasn't sure who that was directed at. 'You'd better watch the way you speak to people if you want their help, Mr Becker.' I added 'wanker' under my breath. 'Look, how do we help you?'

Annika's eyes were like saucers, making me question whether she'd ever seen someone stand up to her father before. 'Yes, how, Dad?' she asked. 'If I go to the police now, what would I say?'

I found this interesting because we had agreed before coming out to Leila's that the station *was* the next step. Had Annika meant it, or had she been lying to get her way? Or was she simply in the process of changing her mind?

Still, I could understand her point. Even though she did so under threat from Tristan, Annika had placed herself in a sticky position by withholding information. My own conversation with Derek Jessup that morning stung as it returned to my mind. The police weren't going to help us without concrete evidence that a crime had been committed. What if they were swayed into thinking that Annika was the murderer, rather than Tristan?

'Annika, I know you didn't mean for this to happen,' Becker continued. 'But, with Dora, you have to help finish it. Go and talk to Lionel. Today.' I repeated Becker's words to Annika and marvelled that he had, indeed, lightened his tone towards us. The man can learn.

Annika glanced at me and then looked up into the air above the table. Her face was anguished, some black mascara blotches forming under her eyes.

I jumped in, since Annika wasn't saying anything. 'Becker, can you give us anything that might help us?'

'Scissors. Gloves. Tristan had them when he was handling the plant.' Becker's voice was starting to sound like a bad connection.

'Do you think he'd keep those? And what if they have Annika's prints, like Tristan threatened?' I asked.

'Scissors and gloves,' Becker repeated, his voice scratching over the supernatural airwaves. Then Leila, who had remained quiet throughout most of the session, having appeared to be in some sort of hyper-focus or trance, began to stir. 'Scissors and gloves,' she slurred.

The candles snuffed suddenly, just like a paranormal horror film, and Becker was gone. I no longer felt the atmospheric pressure, and I knew he was no longer there.

'He's gone,' I told Annika, who was looking depressed. 'But that went well. He's given us a clue. Scissors and gloves. Come on!'

CHAPTER FORTY-THREE

An odd smell clung in the air at Deepwell Police Station. I pursed my lips. It was always the same—musty paper and upholstery, old sweat, and even older computers.

Jessup wasn't exactly happy to see me again but worse, Lionel was fuming. Let him fume. I was pretty much over my brother by then.

Annika was ushered in to speak to Jessup and Lionel while I waited. They didn't close the door, though, so I could hear most of what was said. I was glad in that instance, but shouldn't officers think about privacy? Useless.

Annika told them everything, from how Tristan found out about the wolfsbane, to her horror at realising her father had been poisoned. For the first time, I heard in excruciating detail how she had tried to save her father. That is, she made attempts to, which Tristan had prevented.

With the way the words flowed from Annika's lips, I started to worry she might keep going and tell the part where she went to Leila's and spoke to her father's ghost. Of course, it would be old hat to Lionel. But Jessup? I don't think it would sit very well with him—a conservative guy from a farming family who thought tarot cards and good energy were 'bullshit, mate'.

Just at the right moment, Annika pulled up. Good girl, I thought.

My confidence in Annika's story at that point was pretty much rock solid. I figured that if she *had* played a part in Becker's murder, then by this point, Becker himself would have known it, or at least have had his suspicions. It would have come out around the table at Leila's earlier.

Lionel and Jessup's tunes changed quickly on hearing Annika's story. Finally, the investigation into Becker's murder was gaining traction. Deepwell wasn't crime-ridden, which was a good thing, but that meant there were usually only two constables on duty at any given time. Pretty soon Lionel came bursting out of the interview room and straight for the office to call in Senior Detective Jones from the Noosa Station. Even from where I sat, watching my brother through a window, I recognised Lionel's 'let's get this done' air. He used to get that same energy on his way to his rugby league games as a teen.

It wasn't long afterwards that Cloud arrived. She seemed rather twitchy, and it soon became apparent why.

'So, you spoke to Leila?' I asked. It was nice that she was worried about her mother. Still, Leila's job was letting ghosts camp inside her, so perhaps she could handle herself better than her daughter was giving her credit for. 'Look.' I turned towards her. 'The police are taking Annika's statement right now. It was Tristan. They're going to arrest him, so your Mum will be out of danger very soon.' Cloud looked confused; I had obviously missed something. 'Wait. Why are you here?'

'Leanne. She saw your car outside the station. How does this involve my Mum?'

Gossip travels fast in Deepwell, especially once Leanne gets involved.

'Annika and I were out there an hour ago. There have—'

'You took that murderer out to my mother's place? What the fuck, Dora?'

Ouch. 'As I was saying, Cloud, there have been developments. It wasn't Annika. Just wait, and you'll hear the whole story.'

'Of course it was Annika. If you don't think that, then it's because she's tricked you into believing it was someone else. No doubt she'll try and set up anyone she can.'

'I honestly don't think—'

I didn't get a chance to finish because Cloud turned and barrelled for the door, sandals flip-flopping. She tried to slam the door behind her, just like I had.

'It's soft-close, bitch,' I muttered under my breath.

I made a note for the future that, despite Leila's profession, I should be careful what I involved her in. Clearly, Cloud was a lot more protective of her mother than I'd anticipated. I'd only seen brief snippets of Cloud's other side, and I didn't care to tangle with it further.

More important than personal entanglement was that Cloud still thought Annika was the murderer. Could Annika have fooled Leila and me? And now the police? Indeed, she would have had good reason to try: to avoid a murder charge herself. I could imagine her doing it, too. She had been a sneak from way back. Despite all the bullying Annika was involved in during high school, she managed to escape most punishment by presenting a holier-than-thou exterior. Was she trying the same tactic as an adult?

I thought back to the séance that afternoon. Becker said Tristan was the murderer and told us what evidence to look for. Was it possible …? Surely not … I hoped. Could Becker be helping Annika get out of this by framing Tristan? With such a confusing array of semi-facts I felt like my head might explode. I couldn't just sit around anymore. I jumped up, told the receptionist I was leaving, and headed for the door.

As soon as I got in the car, I called Candy. 'Candy, are you there by yourself? Oops. Sorry. This is Dora Hermansen.'

'Hi, Dora.' She sounded confused.

'Is Tristan home?'

'No. He'll be home so-'

'Look, your sister's down at Deepwell Station, making a statement against him over your father's death. I would get down there right now if I were you. And if you see Tristan, act normal and get away from him safely.' Once I'd told her that, I could tell she was going to hotfoot it.

Hanging up the phone, I saw Lionel race out of the station and towards my car.

He threw himself into the passenger seat. 'Go on then,' I said dryly. 'Tell me I've stuffed everything up.'

'I'm sorry,' he said.

'What?' I looked at him as though he might be ill.

'You *were* right, but I haven't got time for that now.'

'Okay, but I definitely want to circle back to that "you were right" part later.'

'Annika's story checks out. It's just …'

I waited a few seconds. 'You're not giving me much to go on, bro.'

'Cloud said something weird …'

'I have to be honest, a lot of what she says, and does, is weird. I like Cloud and all—'

'No. Cloud called me just before,' Lionel butted in. 'She had this story about her Mum and Annika. I'm worried Leila is involved, Dor. I think Leila might have done it, after all.'

'Leila?' I shook my head dramatically. 'Cloud rang you and told you that her own mother murdered Becker?'

'Well, her and Annika.'

'That *is* pretty weird because I would say, not ten minutes ago, Cloud was standing next to me in your station and telling me not to believe Annika's story, telling me that it was Annika who committed the murder. But she never mentioned Leila.' Lionel looked at me, disbelievingly. 'I'm not joking. Cloud must have called you right afterwards. But why with a different story?'

My mind reeled at coming full circle back to Leila. It sounded like Cloud was playing a strange game and I wanted to know why.

I let my head drop back onto the headrest. 'You know what? She probably just didn't want to talk openly with me. I've got to say, Cloud and I seem to have gotten off to a pretty bad start.'

'I don't know, Dor. Jesus Christ, we're chasing our tails here!' My brother sounded desperate. This situation wasn't just work for him. He'd fallen for Cloud and, though I couldn't imagine her being involved in the murder—what motive would she have, anyway?—she was sticking her nose into it, causing further confusion and conflict.

It was impossible to put the pieces of the puzzle together in any way that made sense.

'Argh,' I grumbled. 'I need to get out of here. It's been a long day.'

A screeching sound caught my attention. I saw Candy pulling up sharply into one of the parking spots. 'I called her,' I explained to Lionel. 'Didn't want to leave her at home alone with Tristan, and I thought she should know Annika was here.'

Then, before Lionel could say a thing, another car pulled in. Candy was already heading inside as Tristan got out of his sports car. He sure rushed into the station—like his arse was on fire, and the station had the only water supply.

'You came outside at the right time, eh?' said Lionel, exiting the car. He was right. There was no way I would want to face Tristan right now. It wasn't going to be easy for Annika. Hopefully now she had been honest with the police, they would protect her.

Lionel's phone rang as he headed towards the front of the station. 'Wait there,' he yelled back at me.

I sat in the car for about five minutes—doors locked, mind whirling, a sick feeling building in my stomach. It was never easy when you didn't know what to believe. Finally, Lionel came running back to the car.

'Leila's house,' he ordered, jumping into the passenger seat. I gave him my best questioning look. 'I've got some questions to ask her. The detective's on her way and she's going to interview Tristan. They're keeping Annika there, too. For the moment. That means we have a window.'

'A safety window?'

He snorted lightly. 'Yeah, you could say that. We'll be fine.'

'But now we're back to not knowing who killed Becker, can I offer you some advice?'

'Sure.'

'Just don't eat or drink anything Leila offers.'

'Not bad advice.'

CHAPTER FORTY-FOUR

When I started down Leila's front path, the first thing I noticed was that there was a brand-new plant in her flower bed. The entire wolfsbane plant had been removed and in its place were multicoloured snapdragons.

The smell of frying eggs wafted from Leila's front door. It was approaching dinnertime after all, and Lionel and I had explicitly chosen not to give her a heads up that we were coming. Leila's eyes questioned as she stepped out onto the verandah. She stood, strong and silent, in the light from an unshaded bulb. Moths flapped and flicked against it; I had always felt sorry for insects when they did that.

'Leila, we're not here officially,' Lionel began. 'But I would like to ask you a few questions. Do you know Tristan Cotter?'

'Annika's husband? No,' Leila answered.

Emboldened by the primal anger caused by my confusion of not knowing who to believe, I asked her, 'What have you been fighting about with Cloud lately?'

'None of your business,' she said.

'I've seen you. There was the night of the séance out at the plant. Oh my God, even that terrible night at my apartment. You were off with her. I could see it.'

'No need for you to worry. I'll take care of it.'

'We are worried, though,' Lionel jumped in. 'You need to come clean, or you'll find this chat turns official pretty quickly. I'll drag you down to the station if I need to.'

'Fine,' she said. 'Let me get the kettle.' Leila started shuffling towards the kitchen as the kettle whistled.

'Let her,' I told Lionel quietly. 'She can have a tea. Just none for us.' I gave Lionel a grimace behind Leila's back as we followed her to the kitchen door.

'You got rid of the wolfsbane,' I said.

'Yes. It's nothing suspicious, I can assure you. I was worried about it, that's all.'

'Look, Leila, I've had the shittiest week. I need answers, now. Just tell me why you and Cloud have been fighting.'

Leila looked like she was on the verge of tears when she glanced over at me. I'd never seen a sad or broken side to her before. 'You sure you don't want one?' she asked, pointing to the cup.

'Yes,' Lionel and I said in unison.

Sitting on the couch, I felt as though Leila had resigned herself to spilling whatever secrets she'd been holding close. 'I never knew anything before. It was that night at your apartment.'

'The night Sayed was possessed? What exactly happened that night?' I asked Leila.

'You yelled at Cloud. I remember now,' Lionel added.

'Cloud had always been such a help to me. But that night she was off. She didn't even seem to be trying. We were fighting for the life of a man. Your man.' Leila gave me a slight nod. 'I felt like she was dragging her feet, and I can't have that. I need people I can count on. Power. Precision. It's so important.' Leila looked at the floor and sighed. 'I had no idea about the secrets, everything she'd been hiding. Honestly. You think you know that girl, but you don't really know anything.' She addressed the last part to Lionel who sat on the edge of the couch looking more concerned by the minute.

'Keep talking,' Lionel urged her gruffly.

'I kept getting scrappy messages from whatever spirit was harassing you, Dora. Like little slices of memories or something.

That doesn't usually happen, but with the two of them working together—the demon and Troy—things got a bit mixed up that night.'

'That's a bloody understatement,' blurted Lionel. Even amongst the seriousness of what we were discussing, I found some amusement in his comment.

'What did you see, Leila?' I asked.

'It was Troy ...' Leila said, then stopped. Just the sound of his name caused an uncomfortable shuffle in my stomach; some things would always remain difficult.

On continuing, Leila's face changed as though she'd placed a slice of lime in her mouth. 'Troy, with Cloud,' she spat.

'What was he doing with Cloud? Was he hurting her?' Lionel sat to attention now.

'They were together. You know, hugging and ... they were a couple. I knew then that Troy had been in a relationship with my daughter.'

'They what?' I blurted. My heart palpated, and I felt clammy suddenly. It wasn't that I cared who Troy had been with, but I did feel concern for the safety of any woman involved with him. Besides that, there was the shock of finding out there was such a strange connection.

Half an hour previously I'd been upset by not knowing the truth; now I was upset by hearing this doozy. I saw Lionel was having trouble dealing with the sudden history change, too. We both had to drink a cup of cement and harden the fuck up, that's all. This was no time to buckle.

Leila went on to tell us that Cloud and Troy had been a couple before Troy and I met. And that possibly their relationship had continued into my relationship with Troy. The shocks just kept coming.

'So, to get this straight, you're saying you didn't know that Troy and Cloud had ...' Lionel made a clearing sound with his throat. 'Before that night?'

'I knew nothing.'

'Why would she keep that a secret from you?' I asked her.

'You'll have to ask her that. But that's why she wouldn't help, I guessed. There was still something between them.'

'Between Troy and Cloud?' I threw myself back on the couch, catching flies.

'It was shocking to think she would enable this malevolent force just because of her past relationship with that idiot.' Leila's hands shook as she spoke. 'I didn't know what to do. You obviously remember. I didn't want her involved once I'd realised. I couldn't have her energy ruining everything. Not when so much was at stake.'

'Thank you,' I said sincerely.

Leila gave a slight dip of her head in acknowledgement. 'Once I had the spirits captured, I made sure Cloud didn't know where I buried them. I didn't know the full story behind her and Troy, but I knew I couldn't trust her, my own daughter. She'd always been such a support. She's my only child.' Leila was quickly deflating.

'Did you find out the rest?'

'I did.'

'Well, the truth is coming out one way or another.' Lionel wasn't messing around. I could tell he had taken offence to the news of Troy and Cloud. He got up and started pacing.

'The truth? I questioned her. You won't like it.'

'I already don't like it,' Lionel said.

'Cloud was angry at you—' Leila's finger pointed straight at me.

'Angry at Dora?' Lionel jumped in.

'Let her talk,' I told Lionel.

'Over Troy's murder.'

'She must have still had feelings for him, because she felt bitter. She felt you were responsible for Troy going to prison. Then, when he died, well ...'

'Aren't we forgetting something?' Lionel interjected angrily. 'I've been in a relationship with her for a couple of months. We were happy. We were! I thought we were. Cloud never mentioned Troy. She said ...' he trailed off, obviously deciding to keep whatever it was private. 'She never said a thing about Dora.'

'I hadn't realised how duplicitous she could be either. She said she was sick of playing it safe while people like Dora walked all over good people.'

'Holy shit,' I spat.

Lionel yelled, 'Bullshit! That's bullshit. You're coming to the station with me, Leila Cowles. Maybe there we'll get some truth.'

Leila could have refused. I wasn't a lawyer, but I was pretty sure that Lionel couldn't enforce a trip to the station given he wasn't arresting her. But she dipped her head in agreement and stood up to grab her handbag.

The thing was, Lionel wasn't thinking straight.

'I know you're pretty shaken up. Me too. But you can't drag Leila into the cop shop. You're making a mistake. All sorts of stuff could come out that we don't want to see the light. The possession? The séance? You need to get a grip. Rethink.'

Lionel listened, his breathing shallow. He sounded like a horse stuck in a pen: huffing, trying to decide on his next move.

He turned to Leila. 'You tell me right now. Did Cloud target me because of Dora?'

'I don't know. Honestly.'

'Let's just go,' I suggested. There didn't seem any benefit pursuing it further.

'But what happens now?' Lionel asked.

Suddenly, Leila came to life; she looked worried. 'I'm trying to get Cloud under control, but I can't guarantee she won't do anything else.'

'What do you mean?' I turned to Leila. 'What has she done so far?'

Cloud had refused to help during the possession at The Brew that night. But was there something else?

'With the spirits …' Leila looked down at the floor.

'Leila, what did Cloud do?' I repeated.

'I had to hide it. You have to understand that.' I turned my head and squinted my eyes. I wasn't going to let up. 'The malevolent spirit. She raised it herself so Troy could try and lock onto it, harness the power. But you have to understand that she was never a bad girl. Troy would have put her up to it. I'm certain.'

I was gobsmacked. 'My husband nearly died. You can't just let her get away with this. Lionel?'

'It's a bit tricky when every wrong she's done is in the spirit world. The police aren't going to be interested in that, just like you said.'

'So, what do we do?' I asked.

'Well …' Lionel thought as he spoke, desperately trying to come up with a successful idea. 'Leila, you keep trying to, ahem, help her see what's right. But don't tell her that you've spilled your guts. Meanwhile, if she goes after someone again, who would it be? Dora? Or maybe Sayed again?'

'It could be you, Lionel. You're my brother.'

'I can take care of myself. But you and Sayed need to be careful. I might come over tonight and stay. But right now, I think I need to get back to the station and find out what the hell is going on with this murder investigation.'

We headed for the car but not before I stopped and asked Leila, 'What did you do with the wolfsbane?'

'Burned it,' she said gravely. 'In the fireplace out the back. I feel terrible about what happened. Really. I don't want anyone else to misuse it.'

***

'She was a surfer chick.' I could hear Troy's voice as clear as though he was standing right in front of me. It was back when we lived in

Rosella Estate. 'She had the blonde hair, tanned skin. So hot, but slightly hippy, too. Into some weird shit.' He had been telling me about his ex. Troy and I were only in the early stages of our relationship, but already living together—huge mistake.

Troy had put his hands up and waved them, almost like jazz hands, but slower. 'Woowoo stuff, you know?' he'd said. 'Reading tea leaves and bullshit like that.'

Troy had never mentioned the name Cloud, though. Cece. That's what he called her. I always thought it was short for Cecelia. It now it seemed much more likely to be CC: Cloud Cowles. I felt sick.

Even when Troy and I had been together for about six months, he would still talk about her. Though I wasn't prone to jealousy, I did think at the time that it wasn't an accident he kept bringing this woman up, keeping her memory alive. It always seemed to be about how good looking she was, or how smart she was. Not anything negative. And his words had that casual drawl to them.

Was she the one who got away, I had wondered. Later, though, as I got to know what he was really like, I assumed he was using the anecdotes to play with my emotions. If she *was* the one who got away, she was the lucky one, I decided eventually.

'Why did you and Cece split up?' I had asked Troy once. My limbs had been stiff as I awaited the answer—afraid of not knowing as much as I was afraid of knowing the truth. I struggled to recall his answer. What had he said all those years ago? Didn't he tell me she'd moved away and that it wasn't his choice?

Lying in bed next to Sayed, with an anxious insomnia overtaking me, I had to wonder: had they split up at all?

CHAPTER FORTY-FIVE

Sayed and I were just fine, even though Lionel never made it to our place to stay over. When I woke, I received a call from him to say that Annika's official interview had been filed, and that the Noosa Heads Police Station was sending a detective to look into it all. Annika had put Tristan right in the hot seat. Lionel sounded triumphant when he told me, 'We searched the Becker house, and guess what? We found them. The gloves and scissors. Just like Annika told us. Just like you told us.'

'You mean just like Becker told us. Finally, you listened to me,' I toyed with him.

Then came the apology. 'Okay, you were right about Becker's murder. Still, you know that we have to work based on evidence. I've got rules I hav—'

'Stop. I was fucking with you. The main thing is that Tristan's behind bars, right? So Annika's safe. We're all safe.'

'He is. Doubt he'll make bail given he threatened and co-erced Annika.'

'Have you spoken to Cloud?' There was a barely perceptible noise—a sigh. 'Can I give you some advice, brother of mine? Be careful. It may be supernatural stuff she's into, but I don't think she's stable.'

'I hear you, but I've got to go. Meeting. Love you.'

So, Becker's advice had been spot-on, and in the end it was Annika's story and courage that enabled us to get the police to take notice. Had Annika covered for Tristan, he might still be walking around Deepwell free as a bird. Those of us who'd been stirring things up to uncover the culprit would have remained in fear.

Since the shock of Leila's admission that Cloud carried a supernatural vendetta against me, Sayed and I had decided on extra precautions. For starters, after finishing work that afternoon, we would leave together. The problem was that the 'supernatural' part of a supernatural vendetta wasn't so easy to guard against. You could lock your front door and put in a new security system. But how did you prevent a crazy surfer girl from helping a demon set up in your apartment? Or, inside your husband? Not so simple.

***

'You have to admit, it's disconcerting. Dealing with fuzzy, controversial, unbelievable, crazy shit. You've got no back-up. You don't have the normal channels other people have to get help. You can't triple zero that shit.'

I sighed. 'Yes, Jules. I know. But I'm trying to stay solution-focussed here. Do you want me to be *more* worried?'

'Gotcha.' She used her fingers to zip her lips.

'Goof,' I shot back at her.

We were hanging in the kitchen of The Brew and I was trying my hardest to fill her in on everything that had happened.

'Table six needs clearing,' Laura said on the way past, one plate in each hand and another in the crook of her arm.

'Got it,' I said. As the boss, I knew that Laura would only order me to get out and help if it was vital. Not that I generally shirked my duties. I worked just as hard as Laura. Still, there had to be a few perks to being the boss, right? Two minutes later and I was back in the kitchen only to find Jules preparing to leave.

'I'll see you over the weekend then, yes?' she asked.

I nodded as I pulled out my phone which was buzzing in my pocket. Jules mouthed that she was leaving through the front way to see Sayed, as I answered the call.

'Hello? Dora Hermansen speaking.' I hadn't recognised the phone number, so I'd put on my business voice.

'This is Detective Jones. I'm calling regarding the Becker case.' Case? I liked the sound of that. 'We'd like you to come in and make a statement.'

'Sure. I can do that. When?'

'Now, if you're free.'

'That should be fine. I'll be about fifteen minutes, though.'

I ended the call and told Sayed, 'I should be back before the lunch rush starts. I mean, there's only so much I can tell them.'

'Be careful. It'd be really easy to give too much away,' Sayed said quietly, as though he were offering some risqué gossip.

I laughed. 'You make it sound like I'm guilty and have to cover something up.'

'You know what I mean.'

'I guess I *am* guilty of being into weird stuff that people don't believe in.'

We laughed.

'I'm so relieved this is coming to an end,' Sayed added.

'You and me both.' I kissed him and called out to Laura, 'Back soon, guys.'

As I shut the metal screen on the back door of The Brew, I wondered if I should have pushed the appointment back to later in the afternoon when things were quieter. Still, I felt sure of being back before it got really busy. Also, I was looking forward to having this done and dusted. A little like a dental check-up, there was probably no need to worry, but you would never look forward to it.

I zipped across the courtyard. The sun was already belting down, and I wanted to get into the car and turn up the air as quickly as I could. Halfway across, I noticed the pile of wood that had been sitting there forever—another job we had put off until 'one day'. The heap had grown in size since we'd purchased the property. Any time labourers had offcuts that we thought might be useful 'one day', we told them to add to the pile.

I was distracted because a few pieces looked out of place. I guessed that our Jenga pile had grown unstable enough to topple at some point, and a couple of pieces were now lying near the path. There was no time to restack the whole pile with the pressing engagement down at the station, yet the thought that someone may trip stopped me.

'Damn it!' I reached down and starting to push the larger pieces of timber back towards the pile.

Within seconds, sweat began to dribble down my chest. Not wanting to ruin my white shirt—better to look presentable at the police station, I thought—I quickly undid the buttons and hung it over the wall. Fortunately, I had a singlet on underneath to soak up the beads of sweat that continued to form as I crouched down and manoeuvred the first of the larger timber pieces back towards the pile.

'Ouch!' A splinter worked its way under my skin. I was feeling more and more annoyed. I tried to draw it out, running my fingernail along the length of it gently. The most important, and most challenging, part is making sure you don't break off the end, leaving the rest of the splintered wood underneath your skin.

One moment I was focussing on my stinging finger, the next I was in shadow and found myself stumbling backward.

Shocked, and feeling a pressure on my head, I looked up to see Cloud leaning over me, a block of wood in her hand.

I brought my arms around in front of my face with no time to scream.

Cloud raised the two by four and began to bring it down on me again.

'Argh,' I managed as my arms met the timber with a sickening thud.

Once again, Cloud brought the wood down, a crack accompanying the excruciating pain I felt.

Someone would hear. They would hear me soon from The Brew or from Leanne's salon. They'd be here to help me at any moment, I told myself. In the meantime, I had to do something. I kicked out at Cloud from my position on the ground. She stumbled backwards but quickly regained her composure and moved into place again.

As Cloud raised her arm for what must have been the fourth time, I saw that her knuckles were white with the pressure of holding the woodblock so tightly. Her face radiated anger, and I realised I would have to do something, or she was going to kill me.

The wood made a swooshing noise as it came down towards me. This time I rolled myself a little to the side. At the same time, I kicked out again with my right leg, hoping to destabilise her and buy myself some time.

My leg hit nothing but air.

Cloud was already raising her weapon again, so I waited until she began to bring it down and I rolled again. This time when I kicked my leg with all the force I could muster, I got her fair in the shin.

There was a groan as Cloud doubled down and grabbed her leg, her hair falling like a curtain as she did. Then she limped backwards giving me the chance to get myself off the ground.

I made a run for The Brew's door. 'Sayed!' I screamed before feeling a thud in my back and falling flat. Cloud had thrown the woodblock at me. As I got up, I saw that she had positioned herself between me and the door to The Brew. I had no choice but to step back, further away from help.

As I backed towards the carport wall, I found myself near the woodpile again. This is how it was going to be, I thought. I grabbed a piece of hardwood.

There were a few seconds of stand-off during which I yelled to Sayed and Laura. It was the air-conditioning—that bloody aircon. They couldn't hear me over it and, of course, when the aircon's going, all the doors and windows are closed tight. I was on my own.

I swung the wood in front of Cloud, missing her by inches. She swung at me and would have got me if I hadn't jumped back a little. She was wielding a longer piece than me. I wondered if I could steal a moment to upgrade. But it seemed I wasn't going to have a chance. On my next swing, she used her block to stop me, and quickly returned the attack.

I fell back.

Stirring as though waking from a long sleep, my mouth felt wet and gluggy. Salty iron was what I tasted. My body was warm, and moist too.

Cloud stood over me, her eyes bulging and strands of blonde hair sticking to her sweaty chest and arms. She dropped and put her forearm across my neck. I couldn't breathe.

Like a horror movie, my worst fear was being realised. Cloud was strangling me right there in the courtyard—just like Troy had tried to do, but this time there were people I loved just metres away, unknowing.

My hands grappled, reaching, grabbing. Yet I wasn't able to gain any traction. I couldn't reach Cloud's eyes nor any sensitive part that could help me. I moved my hands to the ground beside me. They worked quickly, my fingers scanning for any item that might save me, but there was nothing. I kept reaching further and further as I began to lose consciousness.

Then, something hard. My fingertips scraped it on the left: the brick wall. We never did get the loose bricks towards the bottom fixed—another thing on the 'one day' list. With what felt like my last energy, I scraped at the wall, not even noticing my fingernails breaking, one even turning back on itself. I kept scratching until a piece of the brick, long since separated from the cement, pulled out. I grasped it, folding my hand tightly and bringing it up over me towards Cloud with as much force as I muster.

The brick smacked into the side of Cloud's face. There was a cracking sound. As she fell towards the ground on her right side, I also rolled to my right. When Cloud didn't move, I too stayed still. It gave me time to take in air—to fill my lungs as best I could with life-saving oxygen.

When I tried to call out for help, all I managed was coughing and gasping.

I dragged myself into a sitting position. My singlet was wet with blood.

Cloud still wasn't moving. Placing my fingers on her neck, I felt a light pulse. I raised myself into a standing position and began staggering towards the back door of The Brew.

Holding onto the wire in the security door, I hammered it over and over.

CHAPTER FORTY-SIX

I couldn't hear the usual hospital noises—trays clanging, medical equipment beeping, and doctors and nurses speaking—over the noise of the Hermansens. My immediate family surrounded my bed, as well as Jules and Sayed of course, and Wren had even phoned to talk to me.

Leanne had already been in for a quick visit. 'Just to make sure you're going to be alright,' she'd said, then started bawling. 'You sure you don't need anything? Oh my God, it kills me to know that I didn't hear you out there.' She'd brought me a large bag of Maltesers. I had no idea why, but I wasn't going to argue.

'We'll be wrapping you in cotton wool in future,' Dad had said when he first arrived, trying to keep the situation light. But his face screamed 'not coping'; his eyes were all crinkly, and his mouth pursed as he tried to be resilient.

Jules had made herself comfortable on the bed beside me, taking care not to lean on me. I was covered in bruises. For the second time in less than two weeks, I had been given serious pain-killers to help me through.

'You know that none of this is your fault. Right?' Dad asked.

'Of course,' I told him.

I thought back to a couple of hours before when the police had come in to question me. The detective hadn't been interrogating me—at least I didn't think so—but the police had that way of speaking that's unlike any other. There was a seriousness to it. It wasn't like any conversation you might have elsewhere.

But it hadn't been a formal interview; I was too off-my-face on pain medication for that.

'We got prints from the scissors,' Jones had told me.

'Thank God,' I said quietly. Proof.

'Tristan's prints weren't on them.'

'What? No. No,' I said, as though I could change the outcome if I disagreed vehemently enough. 'So he's not in custody?'

'We're still holding him, but we'll have to let him go soon.' I let out a worried sigh and sank further into the hospital bed. 'The prints belonged to Cloud Cowles. Dora, do you know if Cloud and Tristan knew each other?'

I felt as though I'd been pushed backwards. Roughly. Again.

'I don't. I mean, I don't know if they knew each other or not.' I was extremely confused by the new information and what it could mean. My head was spinning, but also my mind was working slower than it usually did. Despite that, I was racking my brain, searching for a connection between Tristan and Cloud. Finally, I said, 'I know about her relationship with—.'

'Yes, Cloud used to spend time with your ex, Troy Sloper,' Detective Jones cut in.

'Right. I only found that out recently. Troy and Cloud went out. Before me. How did Deepwell keep that a secret?' I asked rhetorically.

'You'd be surprised what people manage to hide, Eudora.' Was that directed at me? I couldn't be sure. 'Cloud really came at you,' Detective Jones continued. 'I want you to know that at this stage, we are not looking at you. There won't be charges brought against you concerning this morning.'

'Charges?' It never occurred to me that was a possibility. 'It was self-defence. Like you just said, Cloud came at me. With a lump of wood that she smashed into my head.' I had gone from confused to 'I'm not going to take this lying down' within two seconds flat.

'Yes, that's what I'm saying.' Detective Jones used her hands to settle me back down. But honestly, she had an odd way of putting things.

'Just a few more minutes, then let her rest,' a nurse interjected on his way past and down the hall.

Detective Jones continued. 'Well, I think we're almost done here ...'

I reached out and touched the top of the detective's arm. 'Is she going to be okay? Cloud, I mean.'

'I'm sorry, Dora, but Cloud Cowles passed away not long after arriving at the hospital.'

'No,' I said, trying to change history with my words. 'No.'

Then I sat silently. I had no idea what else to say. I had only wanted to stop Cloud from attacking me. I had never intended to kill her—my own brother's girlfriend, Leila's daughter.

'This certainly is a right mess. But you should know that it was the fall that killed her,' said Jones, trying to improve the situation.

'Right,' I said, utterly hollow. Never mind that it was me who hit Cloud with a brick that caused that fall.

'I'd better let you rest now. I can come back if there's anything else you think of.'

'Right.'

Right. But nothing *was* right.

I was crying when Sayed arrived shortly after. 'I've killed someone,' I kept repeating. 'I'm a murderer.'

'Dora, you're not a murderer. You did what you had to do.'

'I didn't even think about the possibility that I could kill her when I swung that brick. Never gave it a thought.'

'Of course you didn't. You were fighting for your life. You didn't have time to think. And let's not forget that this wasn't even the first time that woman had tried to hurt us.'

Sayed was right, of course. Cloud had colluded with my abusive ex's ghost, drummed up a demon to my house, ransacked said house, and caused the possession of my husband. She was hardly an innocent party in all this, and she had definitely been aiming to kill when she attacked me in the courtyard earlier that day.

Still, it was unnerving and upsetting to have played a part in the death of another person. I decided to cut myself some slack, though, because I had some significant healing to do: physical, emotional and, once I thought about it, spiritual. That was going to take some energy. My arms were swollen and bruised, and I'd received over fifty stitches—mostly on my head but some from defensive wounds on my arms as well. Plus, I had to rectify in my mind that I'd had not one but two people try to kill me. What did that say about me as a person?

Obviously, I wasn't going to be back serving at The Brew that week, and maybe not the next either. I didn't doubt that reality would come back to haunt me, yet in the hospital that night, with nursing staff taking care of all my physical needs, and surrounded by the people I loved the most in the world ... well, I had a feeling of security that I found deeply satisfying.

CHAPTER FORTY-SEVEN

A rushing sound came from the hall of the hospital ward. I startled momentarily before Annika charged into my room.

'Oh my God. Oh Jesus. It's true.'

I wasn't feeling quite so good as I had the previous evening.

'Hey. It's alright,' I told her. 'I'm going to be fine.'

Annika looked like she hadn't slept at all; I remembered Tristan.

'Do they still have Tristan?'

'Yes, but what if they let him out? I don't know what I'll do. He's going to know, Dora. He'll come for me.'

I could see her point. Within hours, she might be in grave danger if the police weren't able to find hard evidence against Tristan. 'You know what? The moment he's out, you and the kids head for The Brew. Go to my place. You can be safe there. Sayed will take you in.' Annika looked unsure. 'He will,' I said emphatically. 'Go home now and pack a few things to take, okay? That way, you'll be ready by the time you have to pick up the kids from school.' I remembered Annika wasn't going to be the only one in the firing line. 'Candy too,' I added.

'Really? You're so sweet, Dora.'

'Have the cops spoken to you since last night?'

'No. I'm on my way there now.'

'Well, I need to ask you something, and I reckon they are going to ask you too. Did Tristan know Cloud?'

'No. Why?'

269

'The police didn't tell you, then?'

Annika screwed up her face as though she was expecting bad news. 'What?'

'The prints on the scissors were Cloud's, not Tristan's. So you're right to be worried. He could actually be released and back home today.'

Annika's face went white. Her mouth was open, but no words came out. She seemed lost in thought. I waited. It was difficult for me to talk anyway.

Finally, Annika woke from her thoughts. 'He was having an affair,' she said.

'Oh.'

'I was pretty sure, anyway. No proof, but you just kind of *know* in the end. I was going to do something about it but ... I'm going to sound pathetic.' She took a tissue from the box next to me and wiped away the tears threatening to spill over her bottom lids. It's incredible how deeply unfaithfulness can affect people. Annika had not long found out that her father was dead—and that her husband was involved in the murder—and still speaking of his cheating cut her on such a deep level. I reached out and touched her arm.

'I had decided to ignore it for a while longer. I thought it might stop, you know? A passing thing ...'

I nodded, even though I didn't really know. I could only imagine. And I felt terrible for Annika, really awful.

'Was it Cloud?' I asked.

'I think it was,' she said. 'I saw them in Noosa together a few months back.'

'Annika, that could explain why Cloud's prints were found. Do you think they did this thing together?'

'Maybe,' she said weakly.

'They seem an improbable couple. Then again, I only just found out about Cloud and Troy.'

'You didn't know about Cloud and Troy?' Annika's head moved back on her neck in shock; it made her look a bit like an otter.

Ignoring her, I said, 'So maybe Cloud took the wolfsbane to Tristan if her prints were on those gloves. It would have been easier for Cloud to pick a stalk than for Tristan, of course. He would run the risk of discovery by Leila. But why would Cloud want to help Tristan ...'

I was going to say 'kill Becker' but then I remembered who I was talking to and thought better of spelling it out so bluntly. Annika was understandably despondent already. I quickly said, 'Anyway, the police will find a link if it's there.'

As soon as Annika left, I phoned Sayed. I told him that Annika and her family may need to take refuge in our unused accommodation wing. He made a joke about our place becoming some kind of halfway house for those running from murderers, both alive and dead. It was kind of funny, I had to admit. He was pleased by that.

***

A week later, the sun shone brightly at the end of our front verandah, but Sayed and I were sitting in the shade on the south end. I reached for my mug and took a sip of java. It seemed like a long time since we'd done anything this normal. I felt happy and relaxed.

Sayed and Dad had picked me up from the hospital two days earlier, just in time for Christmas. The Hermansens had got together and managed to have a relaxed, if rowdy, time after the earlier December drama. Even my sister Wren was there, and she seemed as though she was getting it together. I was thrilled.

I was glad to be home. While I'd been gone, Sayed had bought us a new carpet for the lounge and installed a lock on the ceiling hatch. I couldn't blame him for that. Plus, Leila—yes, Leila—had come one day and performed a cleansing ceremony.

The atmosphere in the apartment felt much improved, and I could tell immediately that Becker had left the plane of the living. I was happy for him. All felt calm and quiet.

The police had let me know, a few days before I left the hospital, that the murder of Bruce Becker had been planned by both Cloud and Tristan. The two had been in a relationship, alright. It seems that Cloud had a history of falling for unavailable men with problems. She also had a history of sociopathic behaviours when she didn't get her way. Cloud was indeed the one who had taken the wolfsbane from Leila's garden and given it to Tristan. She even helped Tristan prepare it, since he had no idea about herbal preparations—in Becker's own kitchen, no less.

But it was Tristan who had ultimately administered the poison via Becker's lunch that day. The reason Cloud had helped Tristan in this crime was supposed, by the detectives, to be for love, while Tristan's purpose was twofold. Firstly, it would accelerate his movement up the chain at the Deepwell Water Treatment Plant and bring forward, by as much as twenty years, the reading of Becker's will, which would see Annika—and thereby Tristan himself—inherit a sizeable amount. Yeah, don't let a man's life stand in your way, I thought sarcastically.

But there was more, and I was unsurprised to hear it involved a link to Deepwell development. Apparently, Bruce Becker and another local, Matty Jenkins, were very interested in a property deal for another new housing estate. The land was on the west side of my Dad's house and it had been a wildlife reserve. Don't get me started about the council letting so many of those dense bushland parcels go. But it turned out that Tristan was also interested, which put him at loggerheads with Becker and his mate.

Overall, the police had some solid motives for the murder. Looking for pluses, I hoped the project would stall now, or at least slow down. I didn't think Matty would have enough capital to make it happen on his own, and he would need time to find another investor.

I was happy to have played a part in bringing Tristan and Cloud's crime to the attention of the police. I forgave Lionel for his slow uptake, but I had given him a sisterly talking to. I reminded him that he was there for the people. As such, perhaps he shouldn't be so dismissive when someone—even his own sister—comes to him with information.

Annika had known Tristan was sleeping around on her but did not want to deal with it head-on. That was her choice, of course. But I was pleased to hear there was no evidence that Annika had known, or even suspected, that Tristan had been planning a murder.

The upside to all the pain and confusion was that those responsible for the murder were either behind bars or dead—and dead in a quiet kind of way. Fortunately, I had not seen any signs of Cloud remaining here on the human plane. So, it seemed the individuals who had been caught in the crossfire—Annika, Candy, Sayed, Leila and me—were now safe.

'Leila helped out a lot while you were in the hospital,' Sayed told me. 'It was more than just the cleansing. She was anxious for you.'

'I guess she feels guilty after what Cloud did.'

'It was more than that.' I looked at my husband, trying to gauge his intent.

'It must be hard for her,' I softened. 'How is she coping?'

'Well, she's a strong woman. Leila cares about right and wrong. She's experiencing the pain of the loss, but I think she also wants to move forward. I think you may have a friend and confidant in Leila.'

'Really? Even after I killed her daughter.'

'I don't think you should focus on that. Leila's a lot more sensible than to hold that against you, especially when you were the victim.'

'Thank God.'

'I invited her to the thing at Jules' on Saturday. Hope that's okay?'

Well, if things were as Sayed described them—and he was a person I felt I could count on—it was better to jump right back on the horse.

Chapter Forty-Eight

We were an odd little group, milling in the mottled light that shone through the trees surrounding Jules' mud shack. I could smell the scent of eucalypts waft through the forest, and somewhere nearby lemon myrtle—one of my favourite smells in the world.

As the person who had known and loved Cleo the longest, I had kicked off filling her grave with the rich brown dirt. It was a symbolic gesture before Sayed took over, shovelling slowly until the hole was full. Then we created a small mound on top on which I placed a plaque I'd had engraved in Noosa: *Cleo Hermansen-Bousaid. Beloved friend to her people and to Doggie Brasco.*

Earlier, I'd been waiting for everyone to arrive while holding Cleo in my arms. Though wrapped in a blanket, the cold from her frozen body was seeping through onto my arms.

Lionel was still hurting from the sucker punch of finding the woman he loved wasn't what he had thought, not to mention her death ... and at the hands of his sister? Don't even go there. His emotional life had completely turned around in the space of a few days. Still, the reality was that Cloud was never what Lionel believed she was; he had never fully known her.

'Trust you to have a funeral for a cat, Dor. Jeez, mate,' said Lionel. I knew he was joking, but I still felt the need to defend myself.

'It's not a funeral. I told you that. It's a ceremony for Cleo's burial. And she deserves that.'

'All the dead deserve it,' Leila added thoughtfully. I smiled at her and wondered if she was thinking about her daughter. I agreed with Leila. I believed that, for those who loved them, even people like Cloud and Troy needed a funeral. It was necessary for those left behind to wrap things up and say goodbye. Sayed had told me he thought Cloud's internment would be in a few weeks. Though I wouldn't attend, we had decided he should go.

Leila made it clear that it was the malevolent force occupying the apartment that had killed Cleo—whether that meant Troy, the demon, or more likely a combination of the two, I neither knew nor cared. But I would never be able to write this off as an accident.

It was a beautiful ceremony, and Jules' land was a fitting place for Cleo's body to go back to the earth. A place for her to rest, the beautiful soul that she was. If ever a cat did deserve a funeral, it was Cleo.

Later, we sat on Jules' verandah. Getting this little group together as a form of clearing the air was an important part of the mourning. We were all either sensitives, or involved with sensitives—in other words, some of the group had been drawn into the recent dramas because of who they knew.

Jules brought around homemade lemonade, which I figured someone else must have made. She gave glasses to the boys who were chatting on one end of the verandah: Lionel, my Dad Peter, Sayed, and even John the Baker had come. On the other side, Sayed's sister Ameerah, Leila, and I sat together. Even Laura, and her girlfriend Sammy, had turned up, as we had closed The Brew a couple of hours early that afternoon.

I should have felt awkward sitting there with the mother of the woman I had killed just a week earlier, and I'd be dishonest if I said I was completely comfortable. But Leila and I both knew the reality of our situation. We were big girls, wearing our big girl pants. I was beginning to understand and appreciate Leila on a level that I never thought I would. She was a strong woman and a good person.

'Leila, I want to thank you,' I said with a controlled smile.
'No need.'

'There is, though. I couldn't have done this on my own. I wouldn't have known how. I would have been overpowered at the apartment that night. Sayed could have died. It was you who saved us.'

Leila shrugged gently and looked down. 'I should have called Cloud out earlier. But I thought I could handle it.'

'Wouldn't it be great if we all made the most sensible choices all the time?' I offered—a rope for Leila to grab hold of. 'Actually, I owe you. Not so much an apology, but ... I didn't want to help them. The ghosts left behind. I was always just, afraid, you know? And I saw all of that as another thing I had to get away from. After Troy and the PTSD. A nightmare to escape.'

Leila was slowly nodding. 'I understand that.'

'But I want to help you now. Help you to help the dead. Though I guess what I'm really asking is if you will still help me to learn. When you're up to it, I mean,' I added quickly.

Leila sat still. I could see her broad chest rising and falling underneath her maroon cheesecloth blouse. Then she laughed a little, a sad sounding chuckle.

'I can teach you and work with you. Yes.'

'Great.' I smiled at her. 'I want to hone my skills. I don't want to be that same person who hides and ignores the dead. Not when I'm part of the one per cent.' I had recently learned that sensitives made up an estimated one per cent of the population. 'So, it's a deal.'

'Deal,' said Leila. I thought about touching my hand to hers at that moment, but Leila wasn't a touchy-feely person, so I let it go.

'Speaking of deals,' Jules interrupted. 'Sammy just told me something disappointing. You know the project Tristan was willing to kill for? Annika's taking it over. She's teaming up with Matty Jenkins. Wants to see it through to fruition for her father.'

'I thought I might have time to make more fuss over the plans,' I said, pouting.

Then I remembered Becker's t-shirt at the funeral: Deepwell Tyre and Mechanics. That was Matty Jenkins' business.

CHAPTER FORTY-NINE

Three months later. From the *Noosa News*:

Not all welcome local "Ghost Busters."

LOCAL women Eudora Hermansen and Leila Cowles opened a business in Deepwell last week to help people who find themselves bothered by spirits.

Cowles has worked as a tarot reader and psychic since the 1970s, while Hermansen only recently got into the business.

'We know it's a controversial subject and many people will say a great many things about us. But for those who need it, we provide a service,' said Cowles yesterday.

Not all Deepwell locals are happy about the new business. Shopkeeper John Deeker says, 'I think it's all bunk.'

Others, who wish to remain anonymous, are opposed on religious grounds stating that 'dealing with things of this nature is best left to clergy', and that 'these women are playing with fire.'

For all the many non-believers, there seem to be just as many supporters. A Queensland police officer, who asked not to be named, is one. He says he's seen the work these women do for himself and that 'it's strange, but necessary.'

Both women have dramatic pasts. Cowles' daughter, Cloud, was involved in the murder of local business icon, Bruce Becker. She died late last year during the attempted murder of Eudora Hermansen. Hermansen herself is already a domestic assault survivor. Troy Sloper, who was convicted of her attempted murder, was recently murdered himself while serving his sentence.

***

Sayed, Laura, and I were all vying to see the article that had come out in that day's local rag.

'They had to add that last paragraph in, didn't they?' Laura said.

'Makes us sound a bit … unstable, doesn't it?'

Sayed grabbed my shoulders. 'It was bound to happen. But don't worry. It certainly stirs up the story.'

'What about the mention of a "Queensland police officer"?' Like everyone in town won't suspect it's Lionel. He's going to find it hard to make detective if he goes around talking about ghosts to the media'

'Yes, he's really putting his neck out. Still, he's a big boy. He can make his own decisions.'

'I can't believe you're really doing this.' Laura looked excited. 'It's so fucking cool.'

'Until we go broke.'

'No way. There have been more people coming, even from Brissie, *because* of this whole ghost thing,' said Laura. 'Yesterday that big group that arrived in the minibus had come specifically because of the last article. People love it. I reckon you should have done this ages ago.'

It was early days. The *Sunshine Coast Daily* had already run a similar story the week before, and Laura was right. For better or worse, we'd seen an increase in customers from outside of Deepwell since then. The odd story was creating a spooky buzz for The Brew, making us something people wanted to get in on. I started to wonder if The Strange Brew might be a better name for our little café.

'I think we could become an attraction,' Laura told me.

I thought about it. Perhaps Laura was right. It had been two months since the beginnings of our story began leaking out into the community, and we had experienced a minor upsurge in business. We certainly hadn't lost any. Of course, not everyone was happy about the openness. Leila and I had received some threatening phone calls from other sensitives who didn't want to have the truth known about them. We'd never meant for this go public, but once the story got out, we weren't able to contain it. So, we started a business.

'What do you think, hubster? Are we ready to be a spooky attraction?'

Sayed laughed. 'It's not how I imagined business growing, but hey, we'll take what we can get.'

He reached around, gave me a hug and planted a noisy kiss on my cheek. Feeling his arms around me, I felt like we could get through anything. I gave him a quick kiss, then started for the kitchen to prepare for opening.

'Crazy bitches!' We heard the yelling and turned towards the front windows to see a ute driving past, hoons hanging from the windows. 'Here's some blood for yous!' The voices receded as the ute passed, but not before the balloons hit our glass windows. Two bounced off, but one burst, leaving a red gooey liquid dripping down the glass.

Though we had a bit of cleaning up to do, we laughed at the fact that only one in three of the balloons had burst.

'Morons,' said Sayed shaking his head good-naturedly.

'Makes a change from you getting yelled at to go home,' I said. 'I hope it settles down.'

'I think it will. Don't worry, Dor. You'll be old news soon. I'll go and rinse down the front,' said Laura.

'Leave the front and I'll get onto it while you make a start on prep. Thanks, though. You're a godsend, you know that?' Laura smiled at me.

'Well,' I announced as I unlocked the front door and turned the sign to open. 'Here we go.'

The End

Thank you so much for reading The Strange Brew!

If you have enjoyed this story, the kindest things you can do for me are to tell people about The Strange Brew and leave reviews where you buy your books..

Acknowledgements

Special thanks to my mum for being the first reader of The Strange Brew and for her encouragement.

To my editor, Georgina: I chose well. You helped me bring my vision to life.

Thanks also to The Queensland Writers Centre for selecting me for their 2020 Printable program. I gained a lot from that process.

I've drawn from several interesting traditions in The Strange Brew to which I owe thanks. They are the Hoodoo conjurors of the United States' Deep South, European witchcraft traditions, and the Islamic idea of Jinn (Djinn). Ultimately, however, this is a fictional work meant to entertain rather than to be definitive, instructive or historical.

Finally, to the readers of The Strange Brew, you're the best! Thank you, thank you, thank you!

About the Author

M. N. Cox writes paranormal and mystery stories with shades of low fantasy, cosy mystery, and even horror. She's interested in small towns, psychology, and exploring monsters in safety.

The mother of three grown kids, when not writing she is found painting, reading, and listening to records and the local birds.

A Queensland native, M. N. Cox lives and writes happily and quietly tucked away in the Noosa Hinterland.

You can connect to her online via social media or through www.thelonghotspell.com.